WIN BIG

WYNN HOCKEY

KELLY JAMIESON

CONTENT NOTES

Content notes for this book and all my books are available on my website at
https://www.kellyjamieson.com/content-notes

THE WYNN DYNASTY

Bob Wynn, owner of the California Condors. Originally married to Grace Rogers (deceased), parents to Mark and Matthew with Grace. Parents to Everly, Asher, Harrison, and Noah with Chelsea Wynn. Grandfather to Jean Paul (JP), Théo, Jackson, and Riley.

Chelsea Wynn (formerly Clark), married to Bob Wynn, mother of Everly, Asher, Harrison, and Noah.

Matthew Wynn, owner of the Long Beach Golden Eagles. Son of Bob Wynn. Married to Aline Gagnon. Father of Théo and Jean Paul (JP).

Mark Wynn, coach of the Long Beach Golden Eagles. Son of Bob Wynn. Divorced from Victoria (Tori) Kendall. Father of Jackson and Riley.

Théo Wynn, general manager of the California Condors. Son of Matthew Wynn and Aline Gagnon. Grandson of Bob Wynn (with Grace).

Jean Paul (JP) Wynn, son of Matthew Wynn and Aline Gagnon. Grandson of Bob Wynn (with Grace). Plays for the Long Beach Golden Eagles.

Jackson Wynn, son of Mark Wynn and Victoria (Tori)

Kendall. Grandson of Bob Wynn (with Grace). Plays for the Chicago Aces.

Riley Wynn, daughter of Mark Wynn and Victoria (Tori) Kendall. Granddaughter of Bob Wynn (with Grace). Goalie coach for the San Diego Hawks, affiliate team of the Long Beach Golden Eagles.

Everly Wynn, daughter of Bob and Chelsea Wynn. Executive director of the Condors Foundation.

Asher Wynn, son of Bob and Chelsea Wynn. Sports reporter for *Playmaker* (hockey blog).

Harrison Wynn, son of Bob and Chelsea Wynn. Plays for the Pasadena Condors, affiliate team of the California Condors.

Noah Wynn, son of Bob and Chelsea Wynn. Plays for the San Diego Hawks.

1

———

EVERLY

They say that everything happens for a reason.

But sometimes that reason is you're drunk and make bad decisions.

In my own defense, it was New Year's Eve. Who doesn't get drunk and make bad decisions on New Year's Eve? Right?

Not me. I never make bad decisions. Well, not anymore. Not since I was sixteen years old and broke my parents' hearts, destroyed their trust in me, and nearly wrecked a bunch of lives. Since then, it has been my life's goal to never disappoint them again. That means never screwing up, working hard, being perfect. Easy peasy.

I'm lying in Wyatt Bell's bed.

This is totally contrary to my life's mission, on so many levels.

At least I'm alone, thank fuck.

Wyatt Bell. Six feet two inches, two hundred twenty

pounds of sex on skates. Plays defense for the California Condors.

I know we made out for a while with our clothes on. It was hot as hell and I was happily oblivious to all the reasons we shouldn't be doing that—chiefly, the fact that I hate him—as my lady parts combusted in a feverish explosion of lust. Wow.

I nearly have to wave a hand in front of my face as scorching heat rises to my cheeks.

A hockey player. On the team my dad owns.

God! How *stupid* could I be?

Anyway, my clothes are still on—a body con, short black dress, bra, and panties. Not like I had a lot to remove, but there's comfort in the fact that I'm still clothed. And alone.

Where is he?

A headache drums at my temples and I lift my hands to rub there, closing my eyes. My mouth tastes like I licked the inside of a dumpster, and my stomach is . . . iffy. I think I have a hangover.

I'm not sure because it's been that long since I had one. I don't get drunk enough to be hungover.

I'm annoyed at myself.

I crack open my eyes. Daylight brightens the edges of the window around the blinds. I have no idea what time it is, but obviously the sun is up. I lift my head, which makes it pound more, and peer at the bedside table. No clock.

I go backward in my mind . . . pretty sure I brought my purse . . . which has my phone in it . . . it has to be here somewhere.

And where is Wyatt?

Welp. Best find out.

I throw back the covers and swing my legs over the side of the bed. A sick wave washes over me, but it doesn't last long. I think I'll live.

I eye the room. The open door appears to be an en suite bathroom. Excellent.

Feet bare, I pad across the big bedroom to the bathroom. I barely note the gorgeous stone tiles, a massive shower with multiple heads, and the big granite vanity as I take care of business. As I wash my hands, I observe my reflection. Hair standing on end, mascara smudged beneath my eyes, and . . . is that . . . *whisker burn* on my jaw? Dear God. I close my eyes.

Then I draw in a deep breath and tiptoe across the bedroom to the other door. I've never been here before and even though this condo is in the same building as my nephew's, where I've been many times, it's a completely different layout. But I find my way to the kitchen/living area, which I now vaguely remember from last night.

The place is empty.

This is good. Great. I spy my purse on the coffee table and make a beeline for it. I can grab it and get the hell out of here before I have to face Wyatt.

"Morning."

I jump, my feet literally leaving the floor, and whirl around at the deep, gritty voice.

Oh sweet Jesus, he looks just as good the morning after. His dark gold hair is kind of long on top and right now it's tousled all over. Dark gold beard stubble shadows his jaw. His eyes are hazel, and I know from seeing him close up they're more green than brown, with gold flecks in them. I nearly whimper. "Morning," I choke out.

"Want some breakfast?" He stretches and the T-shirt he's wearing rises and reveals skin between the hem and the top of the sweatpants, which are sitting so indecently low on his hips they should be illegal. Not to mention the, uh, enticing bulge at his groin, which is clearly recognizable. I swallow as I avert my gaze. "Or coffee?"

"No! I'm good. I need to go. Uh . . ."

"Yeah?" He heads to the kitchen and the Keurig on the counter, popping in a K-Cup.

"Where did you sleep?"

He turns and flashes a wicked smile. "You don't remember?"

I trudge toward him, straightening my dress. "I don't remember much. Ugh."

He purses his lips and studies me. "You feel okay?"

I drop my purse on the counter and lean my elbows there. "If by 'okay' you mean feeling like my brain is bleeding out my eyes, my stomach is full of battery acid, and I'm about to die in five minutes, then yes, I feel okay."

He bites down on the smile that tugs at his lips. "That good, huh."

"Okay, I'm exaggerating."

"Here." He opens a cupboard and produces a small white bottle. He shakes out a gel cap and hands it to me, reaching next for a glass, which he fills with water from the fridge dispenser.

"Thank you." I toss the pill into my mouth and swallow it. I guzzle that delicious cold water down until the glass is empty. "God, that's good water."

His lips twitch again. "Sure you don't want coffee? Some toast might help with the battery acid."

I sink onto a stool and rest my head in my hands. I want to leave, but I also want to feel better. "Okay."

"I slept in the spare room." He busies himself at the Keurig again, then the toaster.

"Oh."

"After you passed out, I figured I'd let you sleep it off alone."

I gasp in outrage. "I did not pass out!"

He gives me a look, chin down, lips pursed. "Uh-huh. Anyway, don't worry, I didn't take advantage of your state of inebriation."

"*You* weren't inebriated?"

"Yeah, I was. I admit it." He grins. "Not as much as you, judging from your condition this morning."

"Ugh. I haven't been hungover since I was a teenager. I really don't like it."

"No one does. By your age, you should have learned how to pace yourself."

I frown.

He slides a mug of coffee across the counter. "Do you need milk and sugar?"

"A little milk?"

"Sure." He opens the fridge and pulls out a carton.

I splash a tiny bit into the dark brew and stir it with the spoon he provides, then pick up the cup and sip it.

"What do you want on your toast? I have butter, peanut butter, or . . . well, that's it."

"Just butter." I don't usually eat bread, but I need something in my stomach. "Thanks."

While I eat mine, he makes himself toast, spreading his thickly with peanut butter.

I don't know what else to say to him. Last night we had plenty to say to each other . . . we argued about politics, hockey, and climate change, which he didn't even take seriously! There's something about him, a cocky confidence, that makes me want to poke holes in that self-assurance, disagree with everything that comes out of his mouth, and prove him wrong.

One of the first times we met, we got into an argument about men being "showers" or "growers." Wyatt was trying to tell me there was no such thing and I concluded I needed to do some research on that, which seemed to piss him off.

I enjoy pissing him off.

Judging from the dick print in those soft sweats, he's a "shower."

I normally try to avoid conflict, but there's something about sparring with him that makes my blood sizzle and energy flow through me.

As for kissing him . . . whoa. If I thought my blood sizzled just from talking to him, making out with him had me shorting out and melting down.

"So, looks like JP and Taylor are a thing."

"Yep." I smile, my chest softening. My friend Taylor looked so happy last night, after the guy she loves showed up to apologize for being a dick to her, and did it in style. She and I were supposed to share a room at Théo and Lacey's place, who hosted the New Year's Eve party, so we didn't have to drive home, but after JP arrived and he and Taylor made up, how could I not let them have the room?

Which is how I ended up at Wyatt's place, in need of somewhere to park my drunken ass for the night. And how we somehow ended up rolling around on his bed, desperately kissing and groping each other.

It was hot.

I gulp some coffee.

"I'm happy for them," I say, not letting on how my heart swelled with tenderness watching the scene last night. "They're good for each other."

"Can she keep him out of the penalty box?"

I lift an eyebrow.

JP is my nephew, and don't think that makes me old. My dad remarried and had me when he was forty-eight, right around the time the kids from his first marriage, my half brothers Mark and Matthew, were having kids. I'm twenty-seven, only a year older than JP. JP is also a hockey player, like Wyatt. JP plays for the Long Beach Golden Eagles—the enemy. Awkward, due to the fact that Matthew owns the Eagles, Mark coaches for them, another nephew and my brother play for their farm team, and my niece is the goalie coach for the farm team.

Yep, we're a hockey family.

"Well, I don't think it's up to her," I say, lifting my chin. "But she's good for helping him manage his emotions, so that may be a benefit."

Wyatt shrugs and starts peeling an orange. "If you say so."

My family's a bit messed up for a bunch of reasons, and I'm not very happy with the fact that my half brothers are currently suing my dad for allegedly stealing money from them. I'm not happy with the fact that Matthew bought the Long Beach Golden Eagles as a way to get back at my dad for allegedly stealing their money. And I'm not happy with the fact that Matthew stole Mark from us. Mark was the Condors' coach until Matthew hired him. (I say "us" because even though I don't actually work for the Condors, I do run the Condors Foundation.)

I can criticize my family, but if anyone else does, I'm coming for them. "You're just pissed because he punched you in the face at Théo's wedding."

My family's messed up, remember?

"I was trying to help, for Chrissakes," he says, rubbing his jaw as if it still hurts five months later. "He didn't need to do that." He holds up the peeled orange to me, offering it.

I reach for it. "Thanks." I break it apart. "I don't think he meant to hit you," I add begrudgingly. There was a bit of a brawl on the dance floor and Wyatt had intervened. I wasn't a fan of Wyatt's even then, but he didn't deserve to get whacked in the face.

"Yeah, I know, he told me that." He shakes his head. "Your family is something else."

My defenses go on alert again. Can't really dispute that statement, though, much as I enjoy arguing with Wyatt.

"It's been entertaining since Théo moved in here," he adds.

"Glad you find my family entertaining." Théo is my nephew; JP's brother. Théo is also Wyatt's boss. Oh my God.

He laughs. "I'm not dissing your family, hot stuff."

My eyes fly open. "Hot stuff?"

He leans on the counter, opposite me. "Oh yeah. I always suspected you were hot stuff under that snooty, arrogant front."

My jaw slackens. I blink. I open my mouth but nothing comes out. Finally, I manage to screech, "Snooty? Arrogant?"

He lifts one big shoulder. "You're Princess Wynn, right?"

My eyeballs are no longer in danger of bleeding, they're in danger of popping out and bouncing across the counter. I jump off the stool. "Princess Wynn? Are you fucking kidding me?"

The corners of his mouth lift. "See? Hot stuff. After last night macking down on my bed, I have no doubts about that."

"Aaaargh!" My fingers curl into my palms. "You are . . . *you're* arrogant, too!"

"Good comeback." He finishes peeling another orange. "I'm disappointed, hot stuff."

Heat rises inside me, and now I splay my fingers out at my sides. "You're just a party-loving, woman-chasing . . . jock."

Oh my God. My entire family is jocks. As if that's the best insult I can come up with.

I blame the hangover.

He laughs softly. "Hmm. We disagree. What a surprise, princess. How about we settle this like adults . . . in the bedroom." He cocks an eyebrow, smirking.

I suck in a fast breath and my cheeks flame. "Oh my God. Princess . . ." Heat boils inside me. "You . . . you have no idea." I don't finish that thought, just grab my purse and stalk away from him toward the door. Luckily my shoes are there—black stiletto heels I wore to the party last night.

"Thanks for the breakfast," I call over my shoulder

through clenched teeth. I may hate him, but I was raised to be polite.

"You're welcome."

I jump, because he's followed me to the door.

"And for the Advil," I grudgingly say. "And . . . a place to sleep."

"Next time . . . we'll do more than sleep." He leans in closer, lips curved in a sexy smile.

God. I haven't brushed my teeth. I probably smell like a winery and look even worse. He is not going to kiss me. Much as I might like that . . . because he looks amazing, and I know he tastes amazing and feels even better . . . "Yeah, that's gonna happen . . . *never*."

He chuckles again.

I make my escape. Yes, I am a living clichéd walk of shame, in my short, tight party dress and heels, making my way to my car parked a couple of blocks away on Pacific Avenue. I have absolutely nothing to be ashamed of, it's just an expression. Except I am a tad mortified that I succumbed to Wyatt Bell's sexy appeal last night and let him feel my boobs and kiss me until I couldn't breathe.

Arrogant. Snooty. Oh my God. My teeth grind together as a stalk down the street.

Princess Wynn. He has no idea.

2

———

WYATT

"I WANT TO SEE A SHARK!"

I scoop up Owen as he runs to greet me. "Yeah?"

"Yeah!"

Owen's mom, Heather, smiles. We're standing in the foyer of her small Santa Monica bungalow.

"I want to see an octopus. Do you know how many legs an octopus has?"

"Ummm . . . eight!"

"That's right. You're smart, my man." I set him down on the floor. "Are you ready to go?"

"I'm all ready!" He hops around.

"Thanks for this," Heather says. "He's been so excited about it."

"Me too." I grin. "Sharks are pretty exciting." I'm taking Owen to the aquarium at Santa Monica Pier for the afternoon. We'll probably do some other stuff too. "What are you going to do?"

Heather makes an excited face. "Maybe have a bath? Read a book. Clean the kitchen."

I laugh. "That sounds exciting too."

"Did you go out to celebrate the New Year last night?"

"Yeah. I went next door to Théo and Lacey's place. They had a little party."

Then I took a hot chick back to my place, made out with her until she passed out, and spent the rest of the night alone in my own guest room. Not how I'd pictured the evening ending.

Taking her back to my place, yes; sleeping alone, no. Damn.

"Nice and close," Heather says. "I didn't even make it till midnight."

She's not complaining, just matter-of-fact about being a single mom to a five-year-old boy.

"Okay, my man, let's roll." I set my hand on top of Owen's head and we head out.

I buckle him into the booster seat in the back of my Land Rover SUV and make the short drive to the Pier. I find parking and we enter the aquarium. As always, Owen is full of energy and bouncing around.

I love the kid.

We see octopi and sharks (small ones). Owen loves the touch tanks, where he can feel starfish and sea urchins. The seahorses are really cool too, and Own stands and stares in fascination at moray eels undulating around rocks.

And we learn about the Heal the Bay project.

This reminds me of Everly Wynn last night, arguing so earnestly about the importance of climate change and cleaning up the ocean. I really got her going, but of course I believe in keeping our oceans and watersheds clean. She's just so damn cute. And smart. And hot.

Forget about her. After last night she's never going to talk to me again, probably. She was obviously embarrassed about conking out. Not to mention feeling sick as a dog. I didn't really think she drank that much. Not that I was watching.

Okay, I was.

I admit it, I can't stop watching her.

Could there be anyone worse for me to hook up with than the daughter of the owner of the team I play for? I don't think so.

And yet . . .

I'm all about living in the moment. I don't worry about shit that may or may not happen. We're only here once and I'm gonna enjoy it.

And right now I need to focus on enjoying this time with Owen.

After the aquarium we walk up to the Pier and stroll around. Of course Owen wants to go in the arcade, and I blow a bunch of money on games for him. I take him on the carousel, and then we get hot dogs and lemonade and sit at a picnic table near the railing, the salty ocean breeze whipping around us.

"I want a dog," he announces as we eat. "Mommy says no."

"Huh. What kind of dog?"

"A big one."

I nod. I'm staying out of this one. I'd give the kid anything he wants for the rest of his life, but I get that Heather's in charge.

"Also, I want a brother."

Whoa. I give my head a shake. "Hmm. Did you tell your mom that?"

"Yes." He pouts. "She said no to that too. She's no fun."

"Hey, your mom is lots of fun. She took you to Disneyland, right?"

"Yes." He frowns. "But you came too."

"It was your mom's idea. Also, moms aren't supposed to be fun. Well, not all the time. She has a job to do—making sure you grow up to be a good man."

He blows out a breath. "I am a good man."

"Yeah, you are." I have to smile. "Okay, dude, let's go home."

We start walking back to the parking lot, but Owen stops at a kiosk selling a bunch of touristy junk. I expect him to want some kind of toy, but he pauses next to a rack of gaudy jewelry. He looks up at me hopefully. "Can I buy Mommy a necklace?"

I clear my throat. "Sure. Which one do you think she'd like?"

"This one." He pulls out a purple beaded necklace with a palm tree dangling from it.

"Nice."

We take it to the counter to pay for it then continue on our way, me slowing my strides along the wooden planks to match his small steps, him clutching the paper-wrapped jewelry. He hops down the stairs to the beach level, where we parked, and as we stroll along the paved path, my attention is snagged by a runner coming toward us. A woman, slender and fit, dressed in tight little shorts and a long-sleeved tee, a baseball cap on her head and sunglasses shielding her face. I admire the shape of her—long legs, sweet curves. I like women.

I'm smiling as she nears us, because hey, I'm a friendly guy, and then something about her ticks over in my brain. Something familiar . . . that shape . . . that mouth.

Everly Wynn.

Her steps slow as she recognizes me, but I can't see her eyes. She sets her hands on her hips and walks the last few paces toward us. I stop, my smile broadening. "Hey. Feeling better, I see."

I can tell she rolls her eyes. "Yeah, I'm feeling better. I thought maybe a run would get rid of the toxins in my system."

I chuckle. "Good plan." I gotta give her credit for pushing herself.

I sense her attention on Owen, and he's looking at her curiously.

"This is Owen," I tell Everly. "Owen, this is my friend Everly Wynn."

"Hi," he says.

"Hi, Owen." I feel the curiosity crackling around Everly. She takes off her sunglasses and perches them on her hat. "Nice to meet you."

"We went to the 'quarium," he says. "And I touched a starfish."

"Cool." She lifts her gaze to mine. I know she has questions, but she merely says, "Well, nice to see you both. I better keep running. I'm on my way home."

"You live close to here?"

"Eh, not too far."

I nod. "Guess you don't want a ride."

She laughs. "That would defeat the purpose of going for a run."

"True enough." I'm reluctant to end the conversation, but I have to get Owen home too, or Heather will start freaking out. "Nice to see you too."

Lame.

She waves and set off again. I watch her from behind this time, enjoying the view of a firm, rounded ass.

Owen tugs on my hand. "Wyatt. Let's go."

"Yep, yep." With a shake of my head, I grab him, pick him up, and start running, which makes him giggle.

When we get home, he dashes inside to give his mom her present.

"It's beautiful!" Her eyes meet mine and she gives the briefest of winks. "Thank you!"

It's tacky but I can tell she's touched. "It was Owen's idea."

She hugs him.

"Mommy, did you know starfish aren't really fish?"

"Um. I guess I didn't."

"Why do they call them fish, then?" Owen's little forehead creases.

"Maybe because they live in water."

"Yeah."

"Thanks for taking him." Heather looks up at me again. "Are you sure you don't want to stay for dinner?"

I almost agree, because I have no plans for tonight and I pretty much hate hanging out at home alone. But I say, "Yeah, I have stuff to do at home. Game tomorrow."

She nods, understanding, and I give Owen a goodbye hug and head out.

Sure, I have stuff to do. Watch TV. Play video games. Can't really use cleaning or laundry as an excuse, since I have someone come in once a week to do that. Linda is a goddess.

The sun is low over the ocean as I drive back to my condo in Marina del Rey. January first. Lots of people make resolutions to start the new year—things they want to change. Things they want to do better at. I don't do that. Anything I want to change is in the past and that's impossible. And like I said, I try not to think of the future. Right now is what matters. And since going home doesn't appeal to me and everyone else is probably nursing hangovers and writing down their resolutions, I drive to a bar near my place.

Sure enough, Abby is working behind the bar tonight and she greets me with a big smile. "Hey! Happy New Year!"

I slide onto a stool. "Happy New Year to you too. How'd you get stuck working today?"

"I had last night off." She wrinkles her nose. "For once I got to go out and celebrate."

"Good for you."

She pulls a draft beer for me and slides the glass across the smooth wooden bar without even asking what I want.

"Thanks." I lift the glass in a toast. "Cheers."

Happy New Year. What a joke. I'm not happy. But that's okay, because I don't deserve to be happy. I just fake it, because nobody wants a sad sack wet blanket hanging around. So I'm the life of the party, always laughing, cracking jokes, flirting with women.

And that's what I do now.

WE'VE JUST FINISHED OUR GAME DAY SKATE AND A COUPLE of short special teams meetings. I'm looking forward to lunch, laid out for us in the players' lounge by the team. They change things up but there are always healthy options. Today I go for a piece of grilled salmon, along with some brown rice and asparagus. All the veggies on a game day are green; you won't find carrots or corn on the buffet table. I sit with my buddies Jimmy Bertelski, the captain of the team; Arvid Bergström (we call him Bergie); and Derek Jablonski (Jabber).

We talk about New Year's parties. Jimmy, Jabber, and Bergie all went to some swanky party at a fancy L.A. hotel with lots of hot women hitting on them all night. My party at Théo's seems tame in comparison, but they give me shit about it.

"Not all of us get invited to party with the GM," Jimmy says.

"Yeah, be careful what you say around him," Bergie adds with a smirk.

They're yanking my chain; I live next door to Théo and we're sort of friends, but he's definitely not talking shop to me and telling me who he plans to trade or who's not getting a contract renewal. I ignore them and eat my meal. I for sure don't tell them about taking a five-year-old to the aquarium yesterday. Not many people here know about Owen, and that's fine with me.

I've just finished my meal when Everly Wynn strides into the lounge.

Whoa.

Sometimes I see her around the arena; the office of the Condors Foundation is there too. But she doesn't usually come down here.

She scans the room and her gaze falls on me. She crosses the room with purposeful steps and stops near our table. "Hey. Can I talk to you for a few minutes?"

The other guys eye us curiously, but this isn't really that out of the regular. I'm the one who feels like it is, though, because of our smokin' hot make-out sesh the other night. Maybe she wants more of that. Maybe she wants to finish what we started.

She looks all business, though, in a gray-and-white tweedy dress that fits her curves, and high-heeled gray shoes. She's always perfect—hair, makeup, clothes. Posture, even.

She wasn't perfect yesterday morning when she woke up in my bed. Heh.

I toss down my paper napkin and rise from my chair. "Sure." I follow her out of the lounge and into the corridor. "What's up?"

She walks around a corner, where we're mostly alone except for assistant coach Stanislov Petrov crossing the hall to the equipment room. "Why aren't you coming to the Birds' Banquet on the eighteenth?"

I frown. This is what she wants to talk about? "I can't."

"Why not?" She holds my gaze with authority. "It's expected that all the Condors will be there."

"I can't make it. I have a conflict."

Her eyes narrow. "You're popular with the fans. Especially the female fans. You need to be there."

I sigh and rub the back of my neck. "Look, I would if I could."

"What's the conflict?"

I study her and my own eyes narrow at her demand. "That is none of your business."

She jerks back, eyes flickering. Her lips tighten.

She may be the boss of the Foundation, but she's not the boss of me.

Christ, I sound like Owen.

Some of the guys come out of the dressing room, yakking.

Everly looks around, then opens the door to a media room, which is empty right now. She flicks on the lights and waves me in.

My muscles tense and my blood heats. I step into the room and close the door behind me. We're alone in a silent box with chairs set up in rows and a dais at the far end. I move closer to her, and she steps back into the wall. "Who put you in charge of the team?" I ask quietly.

Her eyes flash. "I'm not in charge of the team. I'm in charge of the banquet. The team commits to working with the Foundation to raise money for the community, and one player isn't above everyone else."

I grit my teeth. "That's not what this is."

"I know you're relatively new here."

I tip my head in acknowledgment. Last season, I had quietly requested a trade to one of the California teams, and I'm grateful that the management of the Red Wings made it work right at the trade deadline. So, yeah, I wasn't around last year when they did this big banquet, an annual event that apparently raises a shit ton of money for the Foundation.

"I've got nothing against community service; I know the expectations of the team and I do my part. But I can't do this."

She meets my eyes. We're not touching, but we're close enough that I can see all her long eyelashes fanned out above her crystal blue eyes, the shiny pink gloss on her lips, and the pulse fluttering in her throat.

I remember kissing her throat . . . sliding my tongue over it, sucking gently on the thin skin there. I remember her moaning, her fingers in my hair . . . My dick thickens and my skin heats.

The air around us changes, pulsating. My heart picks up speed.

Our eyes are locked together.

"Can I tell you what takes place at the banquet?" she asks, her voice husky.

"I know." My own voice is low and raspy too. I bend my head closer to her.

Heat shimmers between us. I study her mouth, so shiny and pretty.

"It's not that bad," she says. "You don't even have to stay long. Just make an appearance."

I close my eyes and let out a breath. "What time does it start?"

"Six. That's the cocktail reception. The dinner starts at seven."

I open my eyes. "I can't be there at six." I'm thinking. "Let me see what I can do."

She nods slowly, her lips parted, showing a hint of teeth. I breathe in her scent . . . some kind of expensive spicy, sexy perfume. I inhaled the hell out of it the other night in my bed and now I want to bury my face in the side of her neck and breathe her in.

Her father is Bob Wynn. Owner of the team. The king of hockey. *Jesus.*

I take a step back. "I'll let you know."

"Thank you. I appreciate that. And more importantly, all the kids who are helped by our contributions will appreciate it."

I yank open the door and step out. It swings shut behind me, which is a good thing, because Bergie and Jimmy are just passing by, walking down the corridor. They eyeball me.

"What the hell were you doing in there?" Jimmy asks.

"Nothing." I join them in a brisk pace, praying that Everly doesn't fling open the door and shoot out of there. "Going home for naps?"

"Yeah."

Luckily Everly's a smart cookie. We round the bend and head to the exit before she does that.

"See you later." In the parking garage, I reach my vehicle first and hold my fob at the door to unlock it. "Later, dudes." Jimmy waves and he and Bergie continue to their own cars.

Shit. I sit with my hands curved around the steering wheel for a moment. January eighteenth is Owen's birthday. It's a Friday night, and I offered to take Owen and nine of his closest friends to Monkey Biz, a big indoor playground. It's already booked for six o'clock. There's no way I can bail; Heather can't handle ten five- and six-year-olds on her own. And I can't let down Owen. Besides, I want to be there.

When I get home, I pick up the phone to call Heather. She's at work; she's a business analyst at a big healthcare company. Luckily, she's at her desk and she answers.

After some chitchat, I tell her, "I've got a bit of a scheduling conflict the day of Owen's birthday party."

After a beat of silence, she says, "That's okay. Don't worry about it."

"No, I'm not canceling. I'm just wondering if we could possibly make it earlier that day. Like maybe five?" That'll still make me late for the banquet and I'll be driving like a freak through L.A. traffic to get from the playground to the arena, but it could work.

"I work till four," she says. "That's why we made it six, so I have time to pick him up from daycare." She pauses. "Maybe I could get off a little early."

"I can call Monkey Biz," I offer. "To see if we can move it."

"What if they can't?"

I rub the back of my neck, wandering to the window that looks toward the ocean. "Well, I'll figure something else out."

"What's the conflict? Hot date?"

I snort. "Nah. Big fundraiser the team does every year. I thought I could miss it, but apparently not."

"Oh. Well, I guess that's something you need to do. Business. Really, don't worry about us."

"I'm not worried," I say quietly. "I want to be there. For Owen."

"Of course." Her tone is subdued. "Okay, I'll see if I

can work through lunch and leave an hour early, and you check about rescheduling."

I feel like shit. Heather doesn't want to burden me, I know she doesn't, but I could feel her dismay just talking to her on the phone.

I try to help her and Owen as much as I can, but sometimes I worry maybe I help a little too much. Not that Heather takes advantage of it; but I know she's coming to rely on me.

Which freaks me out. But then I feel glad that I'm freaked out, because I deserve it.

But it's okay. I can do this. I want to be someone who can be relied on. I'm just terrified that I'll never be that guy. I've already let her and Owen down in the worst way possible. Why would I think I can ever make that up to them?

3

EVERLY

"Okay, why are we all here?"

I look around my dining table at my various relatives—nephews JP and Théo; my three brothers—Asher and Harrison, who are twins, and Noah; and my niece, Riley, who just asked that question.

We're all close in age. Riley, at twenty-three, is the youngest. Théo is the oldest, at twenty-eight. The only one we're missing from this younger generation is Jackson, who lives and plays hockey in Chicago.

I've convened the meeting at my place after extensive planning, since we all have crazy schedules. "Apparently Harrison and JP think we need to do something about this, uh, dispute between my dad and Mark and Matthew."

"And by 'dispute,' you mean lawsuit," Asher mutters. Asher, like me, doesn't play hockey—but he writes about it, as a sports reporter.

"Yeah, that."

I don't know why Harrison thinks I can solve this, but

he somehow convinced me to get everyone together to talk about it. I'm good at organizing, so I managed to find a day and time everyone could make it. I'm not going to solve this problem, but I'm pretty good at facilitating, so maybe with all of us on one room, we can come up with some ideas.

"What do we know about it?" JP asks, looking around the table.

"Mark and Matthew think Dad stole money from them," Harrison says. "That's bullshit."

"I don't think they'd sue him if it was bullshit," JP says with an edge.

I pat the air with my hands in a "calm down" gesture. "Let's not get defensive. That's part of the problem here. Everyone's taking sides and we don't know the whole story."

JP relaxes. "True enough. Sorry."

I smile at him. He can be hotheaded, but he's relaxed a lot lately. Might have something to do with Taylor.

I look to Théo. When it comes to problem solving, he's the man. "What do you think, Théo?"

He shifts in his chair and peers down at his hands. "I don't know much about the lawsuit."

"Much?" I lean forward. "Or anything?"

He meets my eyes. "I heard Grandpa and Chelsea talking one day. She was . . . not very happy with him. It kind of sounded like . . . he did take some money."

My stomach tightens. But to be honest, I've overheard some things too, over the last couple of years. And I have my own fears about what's going on.

Théo and I are probably in the best position of anyone here to find out the truth. He works with Dad every day and, well, Dad's my dad. Also, my mom knows something about this.

"Have you noticed how much time your mom is spending at the office lately?" Théo asks me.

I swallow. "Yes. I have." My spine tingles.

"Do you know what that's about?"

This time I avoid his eyes. "No."

He grunts.

Nobody else says anything. I look to my brothers, first Asher and Harrison. "You guys need to talk to Dad."

Harrison purses his lips. Asher makes an unhappy face.

"Come on!" I press my hands to the table. "Harrison, you're the one who started this! I can't fix it all myself."

Yes, I'm the oldest sibling, and yes, I tend to take charge. Some may have called me bossy. I feel like that's a gendered term—boys don't get called bossy. It's totally unfair. Nonetheless, I *have* worked on replacing orders with requests. As the head of the Foundation, I'm not bossy . . . I'm *the boss*. And I've learned there are actually better ways to get results than by ordering people around and demanding results. I've learned the differences between a boss and a leader, and I want to inspire people, not piss them off. I want to coach them to be better, not criticize them (okay, most of the time). I'm not afraid to admit I don't know everything and to involve my team to get results. Yet here I am with my family, falling back into old patterns.

I turn to Riley, who hasn't said much. "What do you think about all this, Riley?"

She and I are both fiercely loyal to our families, so she's been on Mark's side while I've been defending Mom and

Dad for years. It's caused friction between us. Not that we see each other that much.

"I think Grandpa took money from Dad and Uncle Matthew. I've always believed it." She lifts her chin. "But I don't know why. I do believe there's some kind of explanation for it. And . . ." She hesitates. "I used to think Chelsea was involved, but now I'm not so sure."

"Same," JP says immediately.

Wow. My throat tightens up briefly. Théo, JP, Riley, and her brother, Jackson, have always hated my mom. That's been really hard, and has made me keep my distance from them throughout my life. Ha-ha—well, we've always been *physically* distant; my brothers and I grew up here in California, Mark moved all over but spent a bunch of time in Winnipeg, and Matthew lived in Quebec. But I've always known that Mark and Matthew were suspicious of my mom, thinking she married Dad for his money, which of course rubbed off on their children. Then when this issue of theft arose, they were quick to blame Mom. Are they finally getting it, that my mom's a good person, and that Mom and Dad love each other?

I've never once doubted that.

"Thanks," I say quietly, sliding glances to my brothers.

"I agree too," Théo adds.

"Does anyone know anything about this money? Does Dad think it's his?" I look around.

Théo's jaw tightens. "The money is Dad and Uncle Mark's inheritance from our grandma."

I sit back in my chair. "Are you sure about that?" I don't want to believe Dad would take money from his own sons.

Dad's first wife was from a wealthy family in Toronto. I've never really had much to do with them. Grace died a few years before I was born; Dad remarried pretty quickly, and her family was livid about that.

Grace helped Dad buy into the Condors, making him part owner at that time. Other than that, I don't know details about how much money she had or who she left it to when she died. It was never something Dad talked about.

"Yeah." Théo's voice is rough.

Heaviness fills my chest. I nod. I don't want to believe this, but I also don't want to be defensive or in denial. If Dad did something heinous, I have to deal with it.

"Maybe we should involve Chelsea in this discussion," Théo adds.

"I already thought of that," I admit. "I guess that should be me. Harrison and Asher will talk to Dad and see what they can find out. JP and Théo, you talk to your dad. And what about Mark?" I direct my attention to JP. "He's your coach. What do you think?"

JP grimaces. "Him being my coach has nothing to do with this."

"I know, I know! I just meant, you might have opportunity."

"If I get an 'opportunity' to have a conversation alone with Uncle Mark, it's in his office with the privacy door shut because I fucked up."

I smile and everyone else laughs.

"I'll see," he says reluctantly.

"I'll talk to him," Riley says. "For God's sake, he's my dad."

I smile. "Thank you." I jot down notes on the pad of paper in front of me. "Okay, let's set a time line for follow-up."

Everyone groans, but Théo grins and rubs his hands together. "I was hoping you'd say that."

We figure out an approximate date when we'll reconvene and present everything we've learned about the issue.

"Excellent. Now, who wants a drink?"

All hands go in the air.

So, this is weird, all of us being together like this. It's also weird without Taylor and Lacey here, who I've gotten pretty close to. In fact, they've come to be my closest friends, which is nice, since my best friend, Jess, took a business transfer to Houston last year.

Lacey is married to Théo. Lacey and Taylor were neighbors and became friends when she and Théo moved here, which is how I got to know Taylor. And now Taylor and JP are a couple.

I need to talk to my girls, since I haven't told them what happened with Wyatt the night of the New Year's Eve party, which I tried to put behind me until I had to confront him at the arena the other day about not coming to the banquet. I thought I could do it, but I got all quivery inside and he got all dominant and annoyed at me, which made my knees go weak. I like being in charge, but damn, sometimes it's super hot when a man takes control. Though I should hate that.

It confuses me.

"When does Lacey work this week?" I ask Théo, sitting back down now that everyone has a drink.

"Hmm." He rubs his chin. "She's off Wednesday, I think."

"Oh good! We can do happy hour drinks."

"Uh-oh." But he grins.

"Taylor too," I tell JP.

"That's fine," he says. "We're on a road trip. Winnipeg, Detroit, Minneapolis. We leave tomorrow."

I nod. "Perfect."

Lacey and Taylor aren't part of the Wynn family, other than by marriage (Lacey), so they're a little more objective about some of the stuff that goes on. They both already know about the "family meeting" I held.

It's a crappy day—dark, overcast, and drizzling—so we're sitting inside at Indigo Iris in Venice Beach, where the atmosphere is warm and cozy with lots of old brick and wood, and brass lamps.

I'm eyeing Taylor's crab salad sandwich on a brioche bun with envy. In my carb avoidance, I ordered a salad. It's great—Greek chicken salad, with lots of feta and olives, yum—but sadly there's no bread. Lacey's vegetable curry also looks delicious. I fork up a chunk of marinated grilled chicken. "So, do you want to hear about the family meeting?"

"Yes," Lacey says. "But not yet."

I raise my eyebrows.

"First we want to hear about New Year's Eve and you

spending the night with Wyatt." Taylor leans closer to the table. "Spill."

"Ahahaha. I didn't 'spend the night' with him."

"Yes you did. You texted us the next morning when you got home."

"Yeah, but . . ." I pause. "Okay, we made out."

They both straighten and give me piercing looks.

"That was it." One corner of my mouth pulls down. "Apparently I passed out in the middle of it."

Lacey winces. "Ooooh."

I sigh. "Yeah. Drank a little too much bubbly."

"Huh." Taylor's eyebrows pinch together. "How did he react to that?"

"He went and slept in another room."

"And the next morning?" she prompts. "Was he pissed?"

"No." I think back. "He was sort of . . . amused."

Taylor smiles like a cat who just chowed down on a small yellow bird.

I frown. "What? What's that look for?"

"You can tell a lot about a man from how he reacts to being, uh, cock blocked."

"This is true!" Lacey speaks up. "I know Wyatt comes across as kind of . . ."

"Slutty?" I raise my eyebrows."

"I don't like that word." Lacey taps her chin. "But I know what you're saying."

"Anyway, it shows he's not a dick to women," Taylor says. "Not that I thought he was. He's always been nice to me."

"He's always been a jerk to *me*," I mutter.

"You do kind of push his buttons," Lacey says.

"I do not! He pushes *my* buttons! He's always arguing with me."

Lacey and Taylor exchange glances. "Tell us more about the making out," she suggests gently.

"God. It was hot. And I was really into it, against my better judgment—"

Lacey cracks up. "Better judgment? Are you kidding me? You're even businesslike in bed?"

My chin jerks down. "Hey."

She tilts her head, eyeing me. "Um . . . that struck a nerve."

"Are you a dominatrix?" Taylor's eyes bug out.

My head swivels to lay a stare on her. "No." I pause. "The opposite." I make a face.

"Oh! Now we're getting somewhere." Lacey waves her fork. "Why do you look like that? It's okay to submit to a man in bed, Ev. You're in charge of so much in your everyday life—running the Foundation, trying to fix your family—it's understandable that you like to give up control when it comes to sex."

I cover my eyes with one hand. "We don't really need to talk about this. We never got to the point of having sex."

"But you wanted to."

"Yes. I mean, my body wanted to. And . . . I guess due to the alcohol, my mind gave up telling me it was a bad idea."

"Yeeeaaah," Taylor drawls out with a grimace. "Your dad owns the team Wyatt plays for."

"Right? Terrible idea. Also, I actually don't like him. He's an ass. Life's a big joke for him. All fun, no work. You know what they say."

"Um, what?" Lacey eyes me.

"All play and no work makes Jack a mere toy."

Taylor taps her bottom lip. "Hmm. I don't think that's how the saying goes."

"Okay fine. All work and no play makes Jill the boss."

Taylor and Lacey both laugh.

"Does he have a son?" I blurt out.

Their laughter stops. They frown.

"A . . . son?" Lacey asks. "Like, a child?"

"Son. S. O. N."

"Um . . . I don't know." Taylor slides a look toward Lacey.

"Me either." Lacey purses her lips. "Why do you ask that?"

"I saw him . . . New Year's Day. At the pier. He was with a little boy. They looked really close."

"Huh." Lacey's forehead wrinkles. "I've never heard him talk about a son. Obviously, he's not married, I know that. But you'd think if he had a son and shared custody, he'd have him with him sometimes, or talk about him."

"True." I nod. "Or he keeps him secret."

"But why?"

I shrug. "Because he wants to bang chicks and party all the time. Having a kid is a mood killer."

Both my friends stare at me.

"Don't you like kids?" Lacey's eyes widen.

"I love kids, sure. I'm just saying, he doesn't act like a dad. He acts like a big kid."

"Well, maybe it was someone else's child," Taylor offers.

"I guess. Never mind. It doesn't matter."

"There's no make-up make-out session?" Lacey smirks.

"No." Then I remember the heat in the media room the other day when I had to talk to him about the banquet. "There almost was." I relate that incident as well.

Taylor nods. "It'll happen. Sooner or later."

"No, it won't. I'm not going to let it. I was drunk. That's why I let that happen. He's not the kind of guy I'm in to. I don't have time for a relationship right now anyway, and definitely not with him."

"You had time for Dan Diaz." Taylor gives me an innocent look.

"Yeah. That wasn't going anywhere, though. Dan's a great guy, but he's not over his wife." She passed away less than a year ago. "I don't want to be somebody's rebound. So we just went out a few times. As friends. Although, I do like older men. They're more mature and stable. *Not* like Wyatt. He's actually younger than me."

"Okay." Taylor shrugs. "Now tell us about the family meeting."

I'm surprised they're letting me off the hook about Wyatt that easy. I'd sort of like to argue more about it. Oh well. "It was . . . productive. I guess. We all talked about what we know of the issue and then I assigned everyone tasks with due dates."

Lacey grins. "Théo must have loved that."

I laugh. "He did seem to like the structure."

I tell them what we know—it's not secret, especially from these two, who are now part of the family. Sort of. JP and Taylor's relationship is pretty new, but I feel good about them together.

"I could try talking to Aline," Lacey offers, referring to her mother-in-law. "We're pretty close."

I tip my head to one side. "That would be great. If you don't mind."

"I don't mind at all. Aline's a sweetheart and I'd bet my left boob she knows a lot about this whole situation."

My own relationship with Aline is cordial. She's on the "other side," but I have to admit, I do like her.

"Why your left one?" Taylor asks, lips twitching.

"I don't like my left one as much as my right one." Lacey grins. "Don't tell me both your boobs are exactly the same?"

"Okay, no," Taylor admits.

"What are we even talking about here?" I ask, trying not to laugh. "How did the conversation turn to mismatched boobs?"

"That always happens around Lacey." Taylor shoots our friend a smirk.

"True. Anyway, yes, thank you for talking to Aline, if you can." I sigh and drop my gaze to my plate. "It's hard, thinking that my dad might have stolen their money."

"Well." Taylor pauses. "I know he's your dad and you love him and look up to him, but it's not a reflection on you."

"I know. I just don't get it. My dad has lots of flaws, but he's not a thief. At least, I never thought he was."

"Wait until you find out the truth," Lacey says softly, reaching out to touch my arm. "All the facts. That's what Théo would advise."

"Yes, he would." I smile. "Okay, you guys, who wants to come to the Ariana Grande concert with me? Tickets go on sale next week."

"I love Ariana Grande! I want to go!" Taylor claps her hands.

"Me too!"

So all three of us plan how we're going to get tickets to the concert and also plan to get together at Lacey's place this weekend, since JP will be away on a road trip.

4

WYATT

I LIKE TO SCORE.

Off the ice, and on the ice.

But I'm a defenseman. That doesn't mean I don't score *any* goals, however. The year I left Detroit, I had fifteen goals, not bad for a D-man. But I'm known more for my hard-hitting play. I once saw an article online about the top twenty hardest hitters in the NHL, and I was listed at number twelve.

My physical play often sets the tone for a game. I like to throw the body around and I'm fearless when it comes to blocking shots. At six-two, two hundred twenty pounds, I never back down. But I keep it simple and I never take crazy runs at guys.

This means I'm often hurting.

Tonight is no exception. We played against Colorado and in the opening minute of the game I took Sokolov hard into the boards. The crowd went nuts and it energized the team. I'd like to think it helped us win, three–two.

As the loud beat of "Free Heart" by Jordyn Banks pumps through the dressing room after the game (she's one of our fans and this has become our victory song, even though she's married to a player for a rival team), a jubilant satisfaction settles in me. It feels good to win.

My left shoulder and hip are throbbing, along with my leg where I took a puck, but that's okay because we won.

"You're fucking crazy, Bellsy." Jimmy shakes his head at me as he takes off his shin pads. "Blocking that Miller shot."

"I know." I grin.

"But thanks."

Late in the game, the Avs got a three-on-two rush against us, and if they'd tied it up, it could be a whole different atmosphere in here right now. I got a pat on the shoulder from Coach for that.

The best place to take a shot is in the shin pad or the pants, or maybe the outside of the skate where there's more protection. But you can't always control that, and tonight the puck hit me right below the shin pad and just to the side of the tongue of my skate. My leg went numb right away, so I kept playing. It didn't seem bad. Now it's hurting like a motherfucker. Teddy, our head trainer, drags me, hobbling, into the training room. Fuck, putting weight on my leg kills.

Teddy examines first my shoulder and hip, then my lower leg. It's swelling up and red, but he pokes, and moves my foot around, and he's sure nothing's broken. He slaps an ice pack on it and I lay on an exam table for a few minutes, staring at the ceiling, my left leg bent, my right straight out with the ice pack on it.

I don't mind the pain. I mean, I'm not a masochist. I

don't think I am anyway. I don't *enjoy* it. But I do kind of relish it . . . like I deserve it.

I let my mind wander while I lay there and as often happens lately, it goes to Everly Wynn.

Standing with her in the media room last week, staring at her mouth, breathing in her scent, that spicy, sexy scent I remember so well from my bed New Year's Eve . . . damn. She was pissed that I was trying to get out of the banquet. It's not that I don't want to participate (although dressing in a tux and serving food to rich fans isn't high on my list of fav activities), but I can't tell her what my conflict is.

I don't talk about Heather and Owen to my friends. I can't.

But I wished I could tell Everly, so she'd understand and not think I'm an asshole.

Why the hell do I care what she thinks about me? I've only ever *tried* to be an asshole around her. I don't give a shit what anyone thinks of me.

I wanted to put my hands on her. I wanted to press her back against the wall and kiss the breath out of her. Like we did that night. Kissing her was . . . I don't even know the words. Intense. Heart-stopping. Breath stealing. Soul burning.

There's something about her that makes me crazy.

Dave Martin, our coach, walks by. "How you doing, Wyatt?"

"Good." I lift my head and give him a thumbs-up.

"We've talked about blocking shots."

"Yeah."

"That was a good one. But we don't want you hurt."

"Me either." I grin. "I'm okay."

He nods and continues on.

I like playing for Coach. Last year, when I started playing with the Condors, Joe Daneck was our coach. Nice guy, but out of his depth trying to build a team with the mishmash of players we had. No wonder they kept losing. Then Théo took over managing the team and promoted Dave from assistant coach to head coach, and things are way better. I'm developing an intense loyalty to the guy, as are the other players. He's smart and knowledgeable, tough and fair. He's passionate about the game and that rubs off on the rest of us.

My leg feels better with the ice on it. Maybe I can go home now. I don't mind a little pain, but I don't want to be injured either. I need to be playing. The thought of sitting around doing nothing for weeks or longer scares the shit out of me. I take a deep breath and push that thought aside.

Thinking of Everly Wynn is stupid, but at least it doesn't give me a panic attack.

"How are you doing?" Teddy returns after giving some attention to our young new star, Rintala, whose hand got slashed in the third. Luckily, nothing's broken.

"Good. Can I go now?"

He lifts the ice pack. "Okay. Keep icing it. You know the drill. We'll look at it again tomorrow."

Tomorrow's an optional skate. Guess I'll be here, but we'll see about the skating.

I go shower and change. The room's pretty much cleared out now. Saturday night, lots of guys are heading out on the town. When I check my phone, I have a couple of texts from Jabber and Bergie telling me what club they're at.

I just want to go home. Take some Advil, prop my leg up, and maybe drink a beer.

I cruise home along Pacific Avenue, through Venice Beach, which is lively at this hour on a Saturday night, and into Marina del Rey, then turn off the dark side street to my place to park in the tiny garage that barely fits my SUV. I enter up the stairs into a mudroom, where I hang my keys, then the kitchen of my unit. I'd already loosened my tie and unbuttoned the top two buttons of my shirt on the drive home. I head straight to the fridge and grab a cold beer, then limp over to my balcony.

The ocean's vast and obscure, the sky above it streaky navy and purple clouds, a lifeguard tower pale against the dark gold sand.

Voices carry on the cool night breeze, female voices laughing, low chatter, then I distinctly hear the word "pegging."

"Whoa. Whoa." I speak loudly enough for them to hear me on the terrace below. My main floor balcony isn't at the same level as Théo's terrace. "I can't be overhearing shit like that."

I peer over the railing to see three female faces tipped up to look at me. Lacey, Taylor, and Everly.

Lacey grins. "Nope, you sure can't."

"You better take that inside," I warn them. "I don't want to know what you and Théo do. He's my boss."

She laughs.

"What are you doing outside anyway?" I ask. "It's cold."

"Um. We just stepped out for a minute. We'll go in. Come on down and join us, if you want."

"Okay. I need to change, though. Just got home."

I shouldn't go down there. Everly is there.

Who am I kidding? *She's* why I want to go down there.

I strip off my suit as I hobble into the bedroom. I grab a pair of worn jeans draped over the chair in the corner and step into them, and pull a clean, long-sleeved tee from a drawer. Then I pick up my beer, shove my feet into a pair of leather flip-flops, and head next door.

The women are back in the living room, glasses of wine in hand, visibly tipsy.

"Girls' night?" I ask, taking a seat in an armchair.

"Yes." Lacey's cross-legged on the couch. "JP's on a road trip, and Théo was at the game tonight, so we got together. Are you limping?"

"Yeah." I shrug. "Took a puck to the ankle. I'm okay."

"Good game," Taylor adds. "We had to switch back and forth between the Condors and the Eagles."

"Did the Eagles win?" I lift my beer to my lips, trying not to look at Everly.

"Yes! Four–nothing. JP got a goal and an assist."

"If he fought, he had a Gordie Howe hat trick."

"No fighting." She shakes her head.

"Thank God," Everly says.

I grin, now looking at her. Christ. She's so fucking beautiful. She may be drinking wine and dressed casually in ankle-length jeans and a loose sweater, but she still looks perfectly put together, her dark hair all shiny with long bangs in a sexy swoop across her eyes, her lips a pale pink. "Are we going to debate fighting in hockey again?"

"Let's not go there," she says with a wry smile. "I think we covered that one."

"Well, we're sure as hell not going to discuss pegging."

I watch in amusement as all three women turn red and don't meet my eyes.

"Was it blocking that shot near the end of the game when you got hurt?" Lacey asks.

"Yeah. It hurts, but I'll be okay." I grimace. "Thought it was going higher."

"That's crazy," Taylor says. "Why do you do that?"

"To stop the other team from scoring," Everly answers. She eyes me. "But it is crazy."

I shrug. "Just doing my job."

"Have you talked to Théo about that?"

"Uh, no." I don't talk business with Théo when I see him, if I can help it. It's a little weird living in the same building as the man who controls your career. "He doesn't come down to the dressing room much, and usually not to discuss blocking shots."

"Well." She smiles. "He'd tell you that teams that block the most shots don't win the most games. He has numbers and everything."

"Of course he does." Lacey smiles.

"He also has numbers about how many shots from the point actually go in the net, which leads to the question: is blocking a point shot actually worth it?"

I stare at her. Jesus.

"Also, just because a defenseman blocks a lot of shots doesn't make him a good D-man."

"Ouch." I rub my chin. "Shot received."

"I wasn't talking about you specifically," she adds.

"Really." I lift an eyebrow.

"Some players have to block a lot of shots because they keep getting caught in their own end."

"True." I'm trying not to get defensive, even though she's pushing buttons.

If she were a guy, I'd tell her to fuck off. But I can't do that, and it strikes me at that moment how weird it is to be having this discussion with a woman. Not that women can't know hockey—hey, I'm not that sexist! But you gotta admit, Everly is at an elite level.

As a Wynn, she probably came out of the womb spouting plus-minus stats.

"You could just get out of the way," she says. "That wouldn't make you less of a man."

Heat slides through my veins and my fingers tighten around my beer. "I don't do it to prove my manhood," I grate out.

"Sure." She smiles gently.

Christ. I want to turn her over my lap and spank that cute little ass and then flip her over and kiss that smart mouth until she's moaning, not goading me. I feel a tug of desire in my groin.

Théo arrives home at that moment, providing a distraction as Lacey gets up to greet him with a heated kiss. "Hey, babe." He grabs her ass and squeezes, right in front of all of us.

I bow my head to hide my smile

"Nice win," she says to him, as if he played.

"Yeah." His gaze lands on me over his wife's shoulder. "Hey, Wyatt. Good game tonight."

"Thanks."

"The way you knocked the puck off Price's stick in that breakaway was stellar."

My chest puffs a little. "Thank you."

Théo releases Lacey and disappears, returning a moment later with a beer. He takes off his suit jacket and slings it over the back of a chair and sits.

"We were talking about the shot he blocked," Everly tells Théo.

"Yeah, another good move."

"Tell us your honest opinion about blocking shots," Everly says with a smirk.

Théo smiles wryly and glances at me. As the general manager of the team, he keeps his opinions about a lot of things to himself. He needs to because the league is so political. "Well." He takes a gulp of his beer. "I can tell you that unblocked shot-attempts from the right or left points have a two percent shooting percentage. For shots from the point near the middle of the ice, it's three percent."

Everly nods while Lacey and Taylor look at Théo as if he were speaking Klingon. Man, this woman really does it for me.

"Yeah," I drawl. "When you look at shooting percentages and the risk of screening the goalie, you have to consider if it's worth it to step in front of a point shot."

Everly swivels her gaze back to me. "I just said that!"

I shrug. "You weren't wrong."

She looks like she wants to jump up off the couch and come punch me. "You were just arguing in favor of blocking shots!"

I grin and lift my beer at her. "I wasn't arguing. You were the one who was making blocking shots about manhood. It's not about feelings. It's about facts."

She glares at me. Because I'm right.

"I don't block *every* point shot," I continue. "I make the best decision I can in a split second."

"Is saving a goal worth losing one of our best defensive players, possibly for months, due to injury?" Théo waves his beer.

"Is it?" Everly challenges.

"It depends." Théo smirks again.

Everly sighs.

"In the dying minutes of a must-win playoff game, I'll block that shot every time," I say.

Théo nods.

"But in a different game, if I decide not to, it's not because I'm a coward." I meet her eyes. Our gazes lock and hold, and damn, heat slides down my spine. "And you don't believe that either."

Her lips twitch and she tosses her hair back. "Maybe not."

Damn. Adrenaline surges through my veins, excitement fizzing inside me.

I catch the glances being exchanged among the others. What the hell is that about?

"I need more wine!" Lacey bounces up from the couch.

"Me too." Taylor rises as well.

"I'm okay," Everly says.

But when Théo follows the other two women to the kitchen, Everly and I are alone. We eye each other.

"Did you figure things out for the banquet?" she asks.

"I'm working on it." I've already rescheduled the party. I'll be at the banquet, but I'll be late. I'll let her know that . . . at some point. "So, princess, where're you sleeping tonight?"

Her elegant eyebrows arch. "Princess?"

"Princess Wynn?"

Her lips thin. "Oh right. Look, I'm no princess."

"Your dad's the king of hockey. That makes you a princess."

"Right." She rolls her eyes. "And I'm sleeping here."

"My bed's available if you need it."

"I don't think I'll get dumped for a man this time, since JP's in Detroit."

She was supposed to share a bed with Taylor that night, but Taylor and JP ended up there so she was bedless. Which is where I came in. "So you're sleeping with Taylor."

"You make it sound dirty."

"Nope. Sounds fun to me."

"Oh my God."

I laugh. "What's wrong with a threesome?"

"There'd be nothing wrong with it, if it was two men."

Whoa. "I'm not into dudes, but I'll try anything once."

She bursts out laughing. "Geez, I thought that would turn you off."

Once again our eyes meet and hold. The air thickens around us. "Is that what you were trying to do?"

Before she can answer, Théo appears, followed by Lacey and Taylor with full wineglasses.

"I brought the bottle," Lacey says, setting it in front of Everly. "Because I knew you'd need a refill in about two minutes."

Everly laughs and reaches for it. "Why not? I'm not driving anywhere."

"My place is definitely walking distance," I say with a wink. "Just keep it in mind."

5

EVERLY

No, I didn't spend the night at Wyatt's place again, tempting as it was. I was a good girl, like I always try to be, and kept to my side of the bed I shared with Taylor.

But I was thinking about him.

I've been thinking about him a lot in the week since then. Now it's the night before the Birds Banquet and I'm not just thinking about Wyatt, I'm thinking about a million things. This is the biggest fundraiser of the year for the Foundation.

What if no one comes tomorrow night? What if we've done all this work for nothing?

What if people do come, but the food is awful? What if one of the chefs doesn't show up? What if there's a fire and we have to evacuate the arena?

I know these things are ridiculous. Of course I know it. I just can't stop thinking them.

It's how I roll.

What if I slept with Wyatt and he told the whole team I'm an über slut and everyone hates me and mocks me?

What if I get to the banquet and I go completely tongue-tied and have no idea what to say to anyone? I picture myself hiding in the ladies' room all evening because I'm too terrified to interact with people.

My breathing is getting faster. My heart rate accelerates.

I slip my earbuds in and turn on my brain music, as I call it. I lay down on my yoga mat in my bedroom and close my eyes, focusing on breathing all the way into my belly.

As a kid, I always worried. I used to think about my homework when I lay in bed in case I forgot something. If Dad was out late, I worried that something happened to him. I worried that our house would catch fire. I always wanted to know what was going to happen next, tomorrow, tonight, this afternoon.

It wasn't really a problem until I was a teenager. Until I made the worst decision of my life. Until Mom and Dad had to get involved with aspects of my life I never wanted them to. After that, I had a hard time living with how I'd failed them.

Then my crazy catastrophizing started to interfere with my life. I nearly missed an exam in college because I couldn't make myself leave the house. I missed parties. I couldn't pick up the phone to make a doctor's appointment, even though I knew I needed to. My first panic attack landed me in the hospital. It was embarrassing, but also a relief to know what was wrong, and it pushed me to get help.

I think about the guests who are coming tomorrow night, mentally matching names to faces, trying to remember facts about the people I know so I can make small talk with them. I review my lists in my head. I've already double- and triple-checked things, but maybe I've forgotten some detail . . .

And I breathe. In . . . out . . . in . . . out.

It's going to be fine. Details don't matter. If there's a flower arrangement missing from a table, nobody will care. If things don't go perfectly, it's not the end of the world. The only one who expects perfection is me.

It'll be fine.

I think about Wyatt. I think about the feel of his mouth on mine, the taste of him. I think about his hands on my body. I remember how he feels under my hands, smooth skin over firm muscle, the big, hard bones of his shoulders, the insistent bulge at his groin that made my inner muscles squeeze and ache. The way I rubbed against him where I needed to be touched and it felt so good.

I'M STILL THINKING ABOUT WYATT THE NEXT NIGHT, BUT now it's because he's not here, dammit.

I'm in the Santa Monica Coliseum, in the thick of the Birds' Banquet. All kinds of celebrities are here—pop singer Jordyn Banks, although her husband, Chase Hartman, who plays for the Chicago Aces, isn't with her; several Hollywood actors; the Lakers even have a whole table. My parents are here, schmoozing with the Gretzkys, and Dan Diaz is here. He's not really my date, but we're sitting together for dinner. I had to be here early to oversee the setup and preparations.

I'm okay. I'm okay. Everything is going fine.

You'd think I'd be used to things like this, and I am, but I can't help the butterflies and sweaty palms and fluttery heartbeats I've been enduring since yesterday. I only slept about two hours last night because my mind wouldn't shut off, still thinking through every detail of the event in case I'd forgotten something. The harder I tried not to think about it, the more I thought about it.

Deep breaths. In . . . two . . . three . . . four . . . five. Out . . . two . . . three . . . four . . . five.

I do this a few times. Does it help? I'm not sure.

I survey ice level of the arena.

Twenty of the top chefs in Los Angeles are here, donating their time to cook amazing dishes for the guests, and the Condors players are here, dressed in tuxes and white aprons to serve the dinner. Right now, they're mingling with guests for cocktail hour. Some of them seem to enjoy it, others are more awkward, looking like they'd rather be in goal with no equipment, facing Ovechkin on a breakaway. But at least they're *here*. Unlike Wyatt Bell.

I grit my teeth as I smile at the coach of the team, Dave Martin, and his wife, Mia.

"So nice to see you again," I say. "How are your kids?" They have two teenage girls, if I remember correctly.

Mia smiles. "Growing up so fast! They're in high school now. Both have boyfriends." She grimaces.

I laugh. "That's fun, though."

We chat a bit, and then Matt and Honey Heller

approach us. I greet them with hugs. "Hi! So great to see you!"

We have all kinds of connections. Matt used to play for the Condors; Honey's dad, Steve Holbrook, and my dad were both owners of the team for a while, until Dad bought him out; Mom and Dad are friends with Steve and Sela Holbrook; and Honey used to work for the Foundation years ago. She still does some volunteer work for us, to help with fundraising.

"Hi!" Honey greets me with a hug. "You look amazing! I love your dress."

"Thank you. You too."

I greet Matt as well. He now owns a high-performance gym that a lot of pro athletes in L.A. go to during the off-season. He's still very fit, with a boyish smile. "Hi, Everly. Good to see you."

"How are the boys?" I ask them.

They have three boys, now teenagers, all playing hockey. They're going to be another dynasty, like my family.

"Busy." Honey rolls her eyes. "All I do is drive them around. We've been talking to the folks at Boston College. Erik's going there next year.

"Ah." I nod. "I'm sure he was in high demand by a bunch of colleges."

Honey's pride is evident, although her words are modest. "Yes, but we try to keep his feet on the ground. Or the ice. Ha."

I grin. "Are your parents here?"

"Yes! They're actually right there with your mom and dad."

I glance over and Mom beams a smile at me as they

move toward us. "You've done an amazing job, sweetie," Mom says to me. "This is beautiful!"

"You'd never know we're in the arena," Dad adds, looking around.

"I didn't do the work," I tell them. "I have a great team."

It was a huge endeavor, to cover the ice and transform the arena into an intimate, glamourous setting for a dinner, not to mention set up the stations for the chefs who are cooking here tonight. Various businesses have sponsored tables, which are each decorated with a theme. They're all unique and all stunning, from tall flower arrangements and gleaming glass and silver, to a replica Stanley Cup table in all silver, to a Roaring Twenties theme.

A photographer stops in front of us, and Mom, Dad, and I smile for a few pictures. I've done this a million times, so I'm experienced at it, but I'll never like having my picture taken. Then the photographer moves on, and we step apart. I watch Condors' defenseman Derek Jablonski precariously balance a tray full of martinis as he makes his way toward us. I smile as I accept a drink. "Good job," I tell him.

"This is harder than it looks," he says. "I'm sweating like a hooker in church."

A laugh bursts from my lips. "Oh no."

He grins. "I can handle it."

"Where's your buddy Wyatt?"

"He said he'd be here. He said he'd be a bit late, though."

I swallow my sigh. "Yes, he did." Dinner hasn't even started, so I guess I can't be too upset.

I have a few other things to attend to, so my martini and I head toward one of the cooking stations where they were having some electrical problems. Fortunately, this has been solved. I thank the chef for being here and apologize for the delays, and he's gracious about it, thankfully. Some of these chefs are total divas.

At a few minutes past seven, our emcee for the evening, comedian Rick Radman, gets up to announce dinner is starting and request everyone take their seat. He makes a few other housekeeping announcements and a few of jokes that get people laughing. I move to the table I'm sitting at with Dan, a couple of city councilors and their wives, and the assistant GM of the team, Scott Jermy, and his wife. We tried to spread around people who work for the team, like Mom and Dad; Dave; Barry, director of hockey operations; and assistant coach Stanislav Petrov, so various guests sit with people from the organization.

Still no sign of Wyatt.

I roll my eyes. We'll manage fine without him. I don't know why I'm so irritated by him not showing up.

Our table is being served by goalie Arvid Bergström and Nick Romano. As they're serving a starter—veal tartare crostino—I slide into my chair next to Dan. I flip my napkin onto my lap and smile at him. "How are you doing?"

"Great. Amazing event. As usual." He leans over and kisses my cheek.

I pick up one of the appetizers and take a bite. Delicious, although I am far from hungry. My stomach is tight with nerves. What I really need is more wine.

That's when I see Wyatt. He's scowling at us, standing there looking gorgeous in his tux.

I blow out a short breath. "Excuse me for a minute."

Dan gives me an exasperated look, like he wants me to sit and enjoy the food. I push my chair back and stalk over to Wyatt. "Thanks for coming," I say with a sarcastic edge to my voice.

"I got here as fast as I could." He sets his jaw.

"You're working with Jimmy and Derek," I tell him, pointing to the table the two men are serving. "Go see Amy, she has an apron for you and she'll get you set up."

He's annoyed. I don't know why. Maybe he doesn't like being told what to do by a woman. Too bad. I don't have time for that shit.

I head back to my seat. "Sorry, Dan. One of the players just arrived, late."

"No worries. There's always something, isn't there?"

"So true." I shake my head.

I try not to follow Wyatt with my eyes as he crosses the room. It's a struggle, though, because I want to watch him. He's flashing that bad boy grin around as he ties on an apron, listening to Amy with his head bent and nodding. Seems it's just me he's ornery with. Then he picks up a tray of food.

I smile and manage small talk as we eat amazing food. I do have to excuse myself again, when Amy comes by with another small problem I need to attend to. I take care of things and return to my seat for dessert.

After dinner, Rick Radman entertains with a witty stand-up routine and then we mingle and enter the silent auctions. There are amazing items being auctioned off, thanks to generous donors, including a luxury spa getaway, diamond jewelry, and hot air balloon rides.

I do my duty. I've been schmoozing with people my whole life, since Mom and Dad love to entertain and frequently had all kinds of people over for dinner parties. I could hold a conversation with hockey players, coaches, businessmen, and movie stars by the time I was twelve. Which is pretty much what I'm doing now as I move from group to group.

Now that dinner is over, the players have ditched their aprons and are mingling as well, posing for pictures with fans and signing autographs. Wyatt appears to be popular with the guests. This isn't a surprise to me; since he arrived here last season, he'd quickly become a fan favorite. The ladies love him for his good looks, ripped physique, and wicked smile; the men love him for his bro charm. And everyone loves him for his hockey skills—his willingness to play hard, make hits, and sacrifice himself for the team. And the odd time he lets go a blistering shot from the point that hits the back of the net.

Right now he's surrounded by women, beautiful women all hanging on his every word, edging closer and closer. He appears to be enjoying himself, making them laugh and flip their hair back.

He looks up and catches me watching him, and one corner of his mouth lifts into a smirk.

Jerk.

Heat washes through me in a sudden memory of rolling around on his bed, his tongue down my throat and his hands all over me. Oh God.

My knees wobble and I determinedly turn away from him to smile at Dan.

The prizes are being drawn with much excitement. My

feet are killing me in four-inch heels so I find a seat in a shadowy corner and check my phone as if I have important organizing stuff to do.

Someone sits next to me. I glance up and see Wyatt. My belly somersaults and my heart misses a beat.

"I apologize for being late," he says formally, which is weird for him. "I got here as quickly as I could. Traffic was nuts."

I nod, keeping my expression cool. "It's fine. Thank you for making the effort."

"I wasn't trying to be an asshole," he says. "I really thought no one would miss me if I didn't make it."

"Judging from all the women crowded around you the last little while, that seems remarkably wide of the mark."

His lips twitch. "Aw. You were jealous."

I roll my eyes. "I most certainly was not."

Then I feel it. Or hear it. The faint buzzing in my ears. I close my eyes. Maybe it's just because of the noise in here —music, Rick Radman blasting over the microphone the names of the silent auction winners, laughter, chatter . . . that's all it is.

"What's wrong?"

I open my eyes to see Wyatt focused on me with a notch between his eyebrows.

"Nothing." I force a smile. "Just tired. It's been a long day. Actually, it's been a long few months getting ready for this."

"I'm sure it takes a lot of work."

"Yes. It's our biggest fundraiser."

One corner of his mouth flicks up. "So I've heard."

I pull in a slow breath, filling my belly in the way I've learned, and let it out in the same measured way.

"Do you need something?" He frowns. "Do you want me to get your, uh, date?"

"No." I know he means Dan, and he's not really my date, but I'm too distracted to explain it.

"Do you need to go home?"

"Can't." I breathe again. "Too much to do."

That's a lie. They don't need me here to oversee the teardown. The arena staff are experienced at stuff like this, turning the playing surface from a hockey rink to a basketball court, or a concert venue, in a matter of hours.

In reality, leaving sounds great to me. As the ringing in my ears intensifies, a telltale dizziness makes my head spin briefly. *Shit.* I don't just want to leave. I *have* to leave.

"I'm not feeling well." I rise abruptly, clutching my phone. "I need to go home."

He blinks at my terse words and stands too. "Are you driving?"

"No. I arranged a car service. I need to call them."

"I'll drive you home." He cups a hand around my elbow, barely touching me, and yet it feels steadying.

"No." I don't want to be with him when I'm like this. "That's okay."

"Don't be stubborn, princess." His voice is low and calm. "Do you have a coat somewhere?"

"My office." My head whirls again, this time putting me off balance. My steps falter.

"Did you drink too much?" His tone is mildly amused as he leads me off the ice surface, down the tunnel to the elevator that goes to the offices of the Condors and the Condors Foundation.

"No! I mean, I did have a few drinks, but that was over the whole evening. I'm not drunk."

"If you say so."

He doesn't believe me. But that's okay. I'd rather he think I'm drunk. Of course, he might get the idea I have a slight alcohol problem since I seem to be wasted every time I see him. Ugh.

I lean against the elevator wall, trying to appear normal even though the buzzing in my ears is louder, I'm dizzy, and it's starting to make my stomach turn over. Christ.

We don't say much as I use my security card to unlock the offices and collect my coat. I have my little evening bag with me, over my shoulder. The offices are silent, the halls empty, unlike the brisk atmosphere that usually fills them during the day.

Wyatt takes my coat and helps me into it like a perfect gentleman, even lifting the ends of my hair out from the collar. "Thank you," I manage.

We take the elevator, this time to the underground parking where the players have spots. He leads me to his SUV and helps me in.

I close my eyes and try to relax into the seat as he starts the engine and drives out of the parking garage. I focus on breathing, but I know that won't do any good. I'm just going to have to wait this out.

"I need your address," Wyatt says as he turns onto Wilshire.

I give it to him. "It's not far. Keep going until 17th Street, then left."

He nods. "It seemed like the evening went well."

"Yes."

He gets that I really don't want to talk right now. My heartbeat is erratic, skipping all over the place and racing. It's impacting my breathing, so I try to pay attention to that, in . . . out . . . in . . . out.

He cruises through dark streets, Ed Sheeran playing quietly on his sound system, but I mostly keep my eyes closed. Fuck! I hate this so much.

6

WYATT

She's fucking hammered.

I don't know why I find this surprising.

It's also a little concerning. I mean, New Year's Eve, sure, lots of people get wasted, but at a charity event that she's responsible for? That doesn't seem like Everly at all. What I know of her anyway.

She's so . . . together. Confident and in control. An overachiever. The kind of woman who makes everyone feel like a loser. Okay, maybe that's just me.

Nah, she doesn't make me feel like a loser. She irritates me and she can be a little intimidating, but she also energizes me. Like . . . a breakaway. The perfect shot through the five hole. Scoring against the best goalie in the league. Like a . . . a challenge.

I know she works hard at her job and everyone respects her. The Foundation does a lot of good in the community. She doesn't seem like someone who'd have an alcohol problem. She seems like she enjoys being in control way too much to give in to booze. I know addiction doesn't work like that, but that's how I feel.

I glance over at her, leaning back in the passenger seat of my SUV, eyes closed, breathing slowly. Jesus, I hope she's not going to puke. I don't do well with vomit. One time I was babysitting Owen, he threw up and we both ended up sick.

I find her place and park on the street under a palm tree. The two-story, Spanish-style building has a tiled roof, pale stucco, and arched windows, and is surrounded by lush landscaping. When the vehicle stops, her eyes flutter open. "We're here?"

"Yep. Come on, princess." I unbuckle my seatbelt, jump out, and round the vehicle to help her.

"You don't need to come in with me," she protests, but holy shit, she nearly falls over when she gets out of the SUV. It could be those sexy-as-fuck shoes with the skinny heels. Or it could be the booze.

I hold her up and lead her to the sidewalk. "I'm not leaving you alone like this."

"I'm fine." Her voice sounds like she's ninety years old.

But I'm not letting go. "Which unit is yours?"

"Unit E."

The building has townhouse-style units with their own entrances. We walk down a sidewalk through shadowy trees and shrubs. She unlocks the door to hers and I follow her inside. It's a long, narrow apartment, with only an open-concept kitchen/dining/living room on this level, but a staircase just to the left of the door leads up to the second level.

"Okay, I'm home." She slaps a light switch on the wall

and a modern chandelier above us illuminates the foyer. "Thanks for the ride."

She's pale and sweaty despite the strained smile she attempts.

"I'm not leaving." I close and lock the door behind us. "Where's your bedroom?"

"That's a little personal . . ." Then she sighs. "I don't even have it in me to make a joke. Upstairs."

I bend my knees and pick her up. She squeaks and grabs on to my shoulders. "Jeez, Wyatt, you don't need to carry me."

"You seem a little unsteady." I take the stairs. She's not a heavy woman, but let's be honest, carrying a hundred and twenty pounds up the stairs takes a bit of muscle. I'm a hockey player, not a bodybuilder, and the stairs are all the same honey-toned hardwood as the main floor, meaning, it would be easy to slip. Don't want that.

There are two bedrooms up here and she waves to the one on the left. I enter a spacious room with a big bed in the middle of it, pale in the darkness and piled with pillows. I cross more hardwood and deposit her gently onto the mattress.

She sinks back into a fluffy duvet and a mound of pillows with a soft sigh, eyes closing again. After sucking in a deep breath and letting it out, she says, "Okay. I'm good now."

"Good to hear." I reach down and curl my fingers around one slender ankle. Her leg jerks away, but I keep hold of it. "Let's get these sexy shoes off you."

"You like my shoes?" she murmurs.

"Oh, hell yeah." I had a hard time focusing on serving dinner watching her walk around in those shoes. There's not much to them, to be honest. One little strap across her toes and one around her ankle. I work at the tiny buckles and set the shoes on the rug at my feet.

She wiggles her toes. "That feels good."

I try not to drool over her legs, which are stellar. "Here." I sit on the bed near her feet and lift one onto my lap.

Again, she tries to pull away. "What are you doing?"

"Giving you a foot massage. Your feet must be sore from walking around in high heels all night."

"Mmm. A little. You don't have to do that . . ."

"I know." I press my thumbs into her arch and she moans. Her foot feels delicate, small-boned and soft-skinned, her toenails painted a soft pink. I work my way down to her heel, then back up to her toes, my fingers digging in and massaging.

"Oh my God. That's amazing."

"You're welcome."

I'd like to run my hands up her calf, but I resist the temptation, and after a few minutes on that foot, I switch to the other. She lies there, eyes closed, sighing soft appreciative sounds that make my dick stir. Once again, I'm not going to take advantage of her drunkenness to get into her panties. Much as I'd like to.

What would it be like? She's so fucking sexy, so smart-mouthed, so bossy . . . does she like to be in charge in bed too? Because I sure as hell do. That could be . . . interesting.

Fuck. I can't think stuff like that.

I smooth my hand over her instep, both her legs resting

on my thighs, daringly stroking up to mid-shin then back down. "How are you feeling? Need anything?"

She sighs. "I'm sorry."

"What are you sorry for?"

"For being like this. I feel so shitty and I hate it."

Probably lecturing her isn't going to go over well. "I'll get you some water."

"Bathroom's right there." She waves a languid hand.

I flip on the light and enter the bathroom. This is a great place—gorgeous stone floor and wall tiles, a huge glassed-in shower with a bench. I run water into a drinking glass sitting on the vanity and carry it back into the bedroom. "Here you go."

"Thanks." She pushes up onto one elbow and guzzles down the water.

I sit again near her feet.

"You really don't need to stay. I'll be fine. This happens all the time."

"It does, huh." I bite the inside of my lip.

She scrunches up her face as if she regrets saying that. "I just need to sleep it off."

"Right." I eye her. She still doesn't look well. "You know, I think I'm gonna crash in your other bedroom." I assume there's a bed there.

I know she's not doing well when she doesn't even argue.

"You should get out of that dress." It's beautiful—sheer layers of pale pink with beads and sequins on the bodice. It looks expensive and probably not something she wants to sleep in.

"I don't care."

"You will tomorrow. Sit." I tug gently on her hands and lethargically she lets me pull her up. I reach behind her for the zipper and lower it. The narrow straps fall down her arms and the dress loosens, giving me a view of her strapless bra and cleavage. Damn. That is some sweet cleavage.

I help her the rest of the way out of the garment, revealing a lacy beige thong. I swallow hard as I take the dress and carefully lay it over the back of a nearby chair. "There you go. Get under the covers and go to sleep."

Without a word, she crawls under the duvet and practically disappears, just the top of her dark hair showing. I shake my head and walk out, leaving the door half-open.

I poke my head into the other bedroom. Yep, a functional guest room, perfectly decorated.

There's even another bathroom, this one smaller but just as nice. I make use of it, then strip to my boxers and climb into the bed. With my hands stacked behind my head, I stare up at the ceiling in the darkness.

This isn't how I envisioned the evening ending up.

I was in a crusty mood when I got to the banquet, having left Owen's party early, driven through insane traffic to the arena, where I changed into a goddamn tux in the dressing room. Then I saw Everly practically cheek to cheek with Dan Diaz, the mayor of Santa Monica. And I remembered that they'd been seeing each other. And it pissed me off.

He's a good-looking dude, considering he's old enough to be her father. Tanned skin, dark hair, decent build. Wears his tux well.

Whatever. It doesn't matter to me who she's seeing.

Does it matter that she gets trashed every time she drinks?

I'm not being judgmental. I like to get trashed too, every chance I get. I like to party and have fun, because life is fucking short. We're here for a good time, not a long time. That's my motto.

I *don't* get trashed every chance I get, though, because I take my career seriously, even if I take nothing else seriously. And I'm surprised Everly's not like that.

Don't judge, asshole.

And while I'm lecturing myself, might as well admit it *does* matter to me who Everly is seeing. Because I'm so damn attracted to her it hurts.

Another man's girlfriend. The boss's daughter. What a cliché. I snort out a laugh. And she's a gorgeous, bossy little lush. What more do I need to convince me to stay far, far away from her?

Why does that feel so impossible?

I don't do complicated. I do easy and fun, live and let live.

I roll over and bury my face into the pillow to try to sleep.

I WAKE UP DISORIENTED, NOT SURE WHERE I AM. I'M NOT hungover; I only had one drink last night. Oh yeah. I'm at Everly's, because she got wasted and needed to be driven home.

I sit bolt upright. Is she okay?

Throwing back the covers, I swing my legs over the side of the bed and jump out. I don't bother putting anything on over my boxers as I quietly pad out of the room to the door of Everly's bedroom. I peek in and see . . . an empty bed.

Perfectly made. All those pillows piled decoratively.

In the daylight, I see how elegant and feminine the room is, walls a pale . . . what? Blue? Greenish-grayish-blue. White trim around windows and doors. White bed and cushions in shades of white and pale blue and green. White furniture and an armchair upholstered in a blue, green, and beige fabric. Thick beige carpet on the hardwood floor.

The bathroom door is open, the light off, so she's not in there.

I turn around just as she says "Good morning" from behind me. My feet nearly leave the floor.

"Morning," I choke out.

Her gaze slides down my chest and abs, then shoots back up to my face. Her cheeks get rosy.

I try not to smile.

"Looking for me?" she asks.

"Checking on you. Wasn't sure how you'd feel today."

"I'm fine." She waves a breezy hand.

And she looks fine. Okay, better than fine. Her shiny dark hair is perfect, her skin glowing, eyes bright. She's washed off last night's makeup and is now dressed in a pair of cropped leggings and a hooded sweatshirt.

"Good." I study her, perplexed. Wish *I* could get over a hangover that fast.

"I came up to see if you're awake. I wasn't sure if you have a practice today."

"Nope. Coach gave us the day off because of the banquet last night."

"Oh, that's good. Do you want breakfast?"

I lazily rub my abs, flexing them as her gaze follows my hand there, enjoying the way her lips part. "I am kinda hungry."

"Okay. Have a shower if you want. Help yourself to anything in the bathroom you need. I'll get the bacon and eggs started."

I watch her turn and jog back downstairs, her ass sweet in those snug pants.

I tip my head back and close my eyes. Jesus, give me strength. I need to resist.

The cold shower helps only a little. Then I get dressed. All I have is my tux, so I put on the pants and shirt, leaving it untucked. I carry the rest downstairs with me and deposit it on the back of a comfy-looking couch as I pass by, heading to the kitchen, where Everly is.

I take in the main floor as I stroll. On the left is a white fireplace with the couch and chairs arranged around it. On my right are white French doors that open onto a little patio. The walls down here are the same color as the bedroom, with more white trim and lots of light. It's uncluttered and has a serene feel. Even the music playing from invisible speakers is chill.

The kitchen is a good size with pale whitewashed wooden cupboards and stainless appliances. Everly opens the oven and pulls out a pan.

"I smell bacon."

She looks up. "Yep. How do you like your eggs? And do you want toast?"

"What kind of bread?"

Her lips twitch. "Multigrain. With flax."

"Okay, then, yeah. And I like my eggs sunny-side up." I move closer. "Can I help?"

"Help yourself to coffee, if you like." She points at the coffeemaker on the pale marble counter. "Mugs are right above it."

I pour myself a cup.

"There's juice in the fridge if you'd like that too," she says. "And can you set the table? Cutlery's in the top drawer to your right."

I purse my lips on a smile. I offered to help, so I guess I deserve to be told what to do. I add some milk from the fridge to my coffee and sip it, then follow orders. Without being told, I man the toaster as she watches the eggs and we're soon sitting at a round table, also whitewashed wood, eating breakfast together.

"I apologize again for last night," she says in a matter-of-fact tone. "I really would have been fine, but thanks for bringing me home."

"You didn't seem fine." I raise an eyebrow as I lift a slice of toast to my mouth.

She waves her fork. "It was nothing. So. Day off today. I'm sure you have plans."

Yeah, I get the message. Eat and get out. "I do, but not until later." To make up for leaving Owen's party early, I promised to take him to the public skating at our practice facility, which is open two to four o'clock today.

I watch her cut her eggs up, slicing around the well-done yolk in a neat circle to separate it from the white.

Then she spreads the yolk onto a piece of toast. "What are you doing?"

She looks up. "This is how I eat my eggs. Well, usually I don't eat bread, but I felt like toast today."

"It's great bread."

"Thanks. I get it at a little market near here. I keep it in the freezer for times like this."

"Times when you have male guests for breakfast?"

She gives me a bland look. "Yes."

"Does Dan like this bread?" His name comes out of my mouth like I'm spitting out a cherry pit.

She blinks. "Dan?"

"Dan Diaz. Your boyfriend."

She snorts. "He's not my boyfriend."

"You were at the dinner with him last night."

"We were sitting together. Yes, we've dated, but he's not my boyfriend."

A small cyclone is happening in my midsection. "Huh." I pick up a piece of bacon and chomp on it. "He's too old for you."

"I like older men."

I narrow my eyes. I already know I'm a year younger than her.

"They're more mature," she continues smoothly. "Settled."

"Huh." This appears to be the extent of my vocabulary right now. "Sounds boring."

She lifts her chin. "I know you're a . . . social butterfly."

I choke on my bacon. "Butterfly?"

"It's an expression. Better than 'fuck boy' "

"Jesus. I have a social life. I like to have fun."

"So I've heard."

"Better than sitting in an office in front of a computer all day and night. And then going on a date with an old man who probably can't get it up."

Yeah. That went too far.

She rolls her eyes. "Please. Older men are better in a lot of ways, including sexual experience."

I grit my teeth, thinking about her in bed with Dan Diaz, and force a smile. "You already alluded to my sexual experience. You have no idea what I'm like in bed."

"And I never will."

"Oooh. Burn." I make a joke, but that comment actually does sting. I lean forward at the table. "I bet I can make you come faster than any old dude."

She picks up her coffee mug and leans back in her chair. "Yeah? Why don't you have a girlfriend, then? If you're sleeping with all those women, why don't they want to keep you around?"

"Princess, it's not them, believe me." I'm not bragging; it's true. Lots of women are disappointed when I don't want to see them again, but I make it clear I'm not looking for a wife or girlfriend. Like I said, life is short. I'm all about enjoying it while I can. "I like variety."

"Sure."

"You don't believe me?" My eyebrows fly up.

She meets my eyes, and the air in the kitchen goes electric. My skin tingles everywhere and heat pools in my groin.

"I think you have a high opinion of yourself."

"It's deserved." I sound like a jerk. Whatever.

The air crackles around us and heat weighs down on

me. All I can think of is proving her wrong—carrying her back upstairs to that pretty, pristine bedroom and messing it up. Messing *her* up. Pretty, perfect Everly.

Her lips part, and her fingers tighten on the mug. Her eyes are bright, pupils dilated.

She wants it too.

7

EVERLY

It's true.

I like older men. For the reasons I just said. I like maturity. I like someone like me, who's responsible and accomplished and . . . Christ, I'm a big phony.

I act responsible and accomplished. I act mature and strong and organized. I try to be perfect.

Inside I'm a mess. A complete and utter disaster.

The last person I want to know that is Wyatt.

And he's the last person I'd ever want to be involved with. He's messy. He's all laughter and fun and flirty and unreliable. He wasn't even going to come to the banquet! Life's just a game for him, and he plays a game for a living, so that says a lot about him.

And yet . . . dammit, I'm drawn to him so powerfully it's hard to resist. He makes me smile. He pisses me off . . . but even *that* makes me smile. He's just so . . . so . . . *Wyatt.*

He has an aura; a golden, glowing aura. He effortlessly attracts people. I'm no exception.

75

Right now, my thighs are squeezed tightly together against the persistent ache low inside me, and my nipples are hard little points.

My fingers tighten around my nearly empty coffee mug. "Cocky," I murmur, then gulp down the rest of my brew. "I need more coffee. Want some?" I stand abruptly.

"I'm good, thanks."

I bet he is.

I nearly groan as I hustle across the kitchen to refill my mug. I take advantage of the moment with my back to him to close my eyes and inhale deeply.

"These eggs are perfect," he comments. "Sunny-side up can be hard to pull off. Sometimes the white is too runny. And you didn't break the yolks."

"Thanks." I fill my mug. "It's not that hard, though."

I'm pretty sure he mutters, "Oh yes it is."

Well, good. We're in the same damn boat here, floating around in an ocean of sexual frustration.

I lift my chin and return to the table.

I finish off my egg whites, which are crispy and brown. I know it's weird, but that's how I like them. I pick up my last piece of bacon.

"Perfect bacon too." Wyatt says. "Just the right level of crispy. You're pretty much perfect at everything, aren't you?"

I stare at him. If he only knew. Then I shake my hair back. "Yes."

He laughs. "What are your plans today?"

I sigh. "I'm going shopping with my mother."

"Why do you sound so put upon by that? I thought all women like shopping."

"I love shopping." I hesitate. He's not one of the family; in fact, he works for the family, sort of. I shouldn't talk to him about private family stuff. But the feud isn't exactly secret. It's been well covered in the media. "It's a pretext for getting her alone to talk to her about why my half brothers are suing my dad."

"Oh." He makes a face. "You don't know why?"

I shake my head, chewing my bacon. "None of us know, and the whole family feud is pissing us off."

"Huh." He tips his head to one side. "Let me guess— you're the leader of this investigation?"

"How did you know?" I roll my eyes. "But I was put in charge—I didn't start it."

He grins. "Okay."

"I'm sure my mom knows more than she lets on." I nibble my bottom lip and then I confess something I don't mean to. "I'm kind of worried about Dad."

His gaze sharpens. "How so?"

I shake my head. "Never mind. I shouldn't have said that."

"To me," he adds.

"Well, yeah."

"I get it. But I'm pretty good at keeping secrets. And I'm a good listener."

"You could take advantage of my father's weaknesses. What happens when it comes time to negotiate your next contract?"

"Your father doesn't negotiate contracts," he points out evenly. "And you know that. Théo's in charge now, and he's not about to let anyone take advantage. He's probably the smartest guy I know."

I purse my lips.

"After all, he traded Patrick for me."

I smile reluctantly. "True."

Wyatt glances over at the coffeemaker. "Okay, now I need a refill." He rises and pads across the room with athletic grace. He's wearing his black dress pants and the white shirt, open at the neck, cuffs rolled up on strong forearms, the tails out. The shirt is fitted to his impressive body, emphasizing his broad shoulders and chest, narrow waist and flat abs.

Which I saw shirtless not that long ago. Impressive is right.

He returns and lounges back in his chair with his mug, his empty plate pushed aside with knife and fork sitting at exactly four o'clock, as my mother taught me to do when I finish eating.

"What's your family like?" I ask impulsively.

I already know he's from New Brunswick, in Canada. I know he was drafted by Detroit and got traded to the Condors last year. I know he plays defense; I know his hockey stats; and I know the things the hockey blogs say about him, including the ones that post about "hockey heartthrobs" and "players who are hot as puck."

He smiles. "My family's great. Mom, Dad, little sister."

"How little?"

"She's twenty-four."

"That's not that little."

"I guess not, but she'll always be my little sister."

"I bet you were an annoying big brother."

"Nah. She worships me."

I laugh. "Is she an athlete too?"

"She's athletic, but not a professional athlete. She's actually a fantastic tennis player."

"Really. Do you play tennis?"

"Of course. She had to have someone to beat up on the court."

Knowing him, he's probably a great tennis player. "Where did you grow up?"

"St. John, New Brunswick. In Canada."

"I know where New Brunswick is."

"Sorry. Lots of people don't. I'm used to always adding 'Canada.'"

"I was born here, but I've visited Canada quite a bit. We used to go visit Matt in Quebec and Mark in Winnipeg. What's New Brunswick like? It's on the east coast, right?"

"Yep. It's beautiful. Right on the Bay of Fundy, which has the highest tides on earth—higher than a four-story building."

"Whoa."

"It's great for whale watching, even the right whale, which is super rare. Also humpbacks, finbacks, and minkes."

"Cool. That sounds amazing."

"There's also a lot of history and amazing architecture."

I nod, entranced with the idea of whales and high tides. "I've gone whale watching here. I loved it."

He smiles.

"So you grew up in a normal family in a maritime city of . . . how many people?"

"About seventy thousand."

"That's small."

"Yeah."

"When did you start playing hockey?"

"Jeez, I don't even remember. Probably when I could walk. Everyone skated and played hockey in the winter. When I was sixteen, I moved to Rimouski, Quebec, to play there."

I nod. "And that's where you got drafted from."

"Yep."

"Did you learn to speak French living in Quebec?"

His grin is lopsided. "I learned some, but my French is terrible."

"I loved visiting Quebec. It's so . . . old . . . and European. Matthew's wife is French, and Théo and JP grew up there."

"Yeah." He pauses. "Are we done with the detour into my family life to distract from yours?"

My lips pucker up as I try not to smile. "You're on to me."

"I wish." His eyes make contact with mine in a meaningful way and he leans forward a little. "Believe me."

I can't breathe. Once again, warmth curls through me. "You're a shameless flirt. Okay, I'm worried about my dad because . . ." Crap. I'm actually afraid to say it out loud. But it's been weighing on my mind for months now and I've never said a word about it to anyone. Not even Mom, or Asher, Harrison, and Noah. "He keeps forgetting things."

Wyatt's eyes shadow. "Yeah?"

I nod slowly, teeth sunk into my bottom lip. "It scares me."

"He's what . . . seventy-two?"

"Yes. But he's still so physically fit. He even works out! What if . . . what if he has some kind of dementia?"

Wyatt shifts his chair, actually moving it closer to me. He reaches out to cover my hand, curving his fingers around it. His hand is warm and strong. Reassuring. "I don't know much about dementia. Knowing you, you've probably googled it and studied everything about it."

I make an exasperated little sound with my tongue. "You think you know me so well."

He's right, though. I have. And it terrifies me.

Also, Wyatt Bell knowing me that well terrifies me. Because there are things I don't want anyone to know, let alone him.

"Am I right?"

"Yes."

He picks up my hand and rubs his thumb over my skin. My arm feels heavy. So do my breasts.

"Have you talked to him about it?" he asks.

"God no!"

"Why not? I mean, I know he can be intimidating, but you're his daughter."

"That makes him even more scary," I mutter. "I'm going to try to suss things out with my mom this afternoon."

"I know there's no cure for dementia. But I think there are some kinds of treatment that help slow it down. But you have to see a doctor for that."

"Maybe he has." I lift my eyes and fasten them onto Wyatt's face. His eyes are warm and steady. His mouth is beautiful. Wyatt may be the life of the party with not much beneath that, but one thing he never does is judge people. I want to tell him everything and let him be there for me.

"Maybe," he agrees. "It could be just normal aging. But if you're concerned about it, you need to talk to your parents."

Again, he's right. "I'm afraid to," I confess.

"I get it. Our parents getting older is hard."

"How old are your parents?"

"They're both fifty-five."

"Young." I sigh. "My mom's fifty-two."

He nods.

The air in the room has become heavy. And then Wyatt releases my hand, leans back, and says, "Well, the good thing about having a bad memory is that jokes are funny more than once."

I snort out a reluctant laugh.

"And he can plan his own surprise party."

"Oh my God! You're terrible."

He lifts a big shoulder. "Yep. Come on. Life is short. You gotta laugh before it's too late."

I gaze at him. He has a point. But it irritates me. Life isn't all fun and games. What made me think this guy would be there for me if I spilled my guts? "But if all you do is laugh, nothing ever gets done." I shove back my chair and grab my plate. I reach for his too, but he picks it up and follows me as I stomp over to the dishwasher.

The atmosphere has changed. He made a joke. I didn't laugh.

Now I'm annoyed at *myself,* but it's too late.

MOM AND I HAVE SHOPPED FOR A COUPLE OF HOURS AT THE Brentwood Country Mart. Despite its cute country name and appearance, it's home to a lot of high-end shops. We picked up some sweet things—Mom, a gorgeous pair of Louboutin sandals; me, my favorite Deep Blue Ocean candles, some pretty office supplies, and a new jacket. We gossiped about people who'd been at the banquet last night. Then we decided it was time for a late lunch and we headed to Pacifico, an elegant little eatery in the mall.

With our bags and purses settled beneath the table, we relax in comfy upholstered chairs and order cocktails. Mom loves a good martini and I feel like a Bellini. It's cold and delicious.

Now to bring the conversation around to Dad.

Mom's perusing her menu. "That salmon we had last night was amazing," she says. "Dad and I are going to that restaurant next week."

"Which one?"

"Bambino. The chef is Michael Bianchi."

I nod. "There was so much good food there."

"People couldn't stop talking about it." Mom smiles at me over the menu. "Another success."

"Thank you." My insides warm. Hearing words of praise from my parents always makes me happy. And relieved. Will I ever get over that?

What would happen if I failed at something? I don't even like to think about it because I've experienced their disappointment in me, and I never want to be there again.

We both order salads.

"Did Dad have a good time last night?" I pick up my Bellini.

"Yes, of course. He loves socializing with hockey people."

"Because he's the king." I smile.

"True."

"Did he remember everyone's names?"

Mom tilts her head, a little crease between her perfectly groomed eyebrows. "That's an odd question," she says slowly.

I sigh. I'm not good at subtle, I guess. "He's been forgetting people's names a lot lately. Even people who work for the team."

I can immediately tell that Mom knows exactly what I'm talking about. Her smile disappears, her eyes shadow, and her shoulders slump a tiny bit.

"He forgets other things," I continue, my voice quivering with emotion. "But he's really good at covering it up."

She nods slowly. "I've tried to get him to go to the doctor, but he refuses to admit he's having problems."

"Oh God." I squeeze my eyes shut briefly. Mom just admitted it. He's having problems. She's worried too. "He needs to go to the doctor."

"*You* want to try to convince him?" Her voice is dry. "Good luck with that. You know your father."

"Yes." I blow out a long exhalation. "Is that why you're spending so much time at the office?"

She looks up at me, her lips parted. "You've noticed that."

"Not just me. Théo too."

"Hell."

"Mom." I lean forward. "What's going on between

Mark and Matthew and Dad? I think Théo suspects you're at the office so much because you're stealing money from the team, or something."

Her jaw drops. Then she snaps it shut, her forehead pinched. "That's bullshit."

I grin. Mom projects the image of a meek little trophy wife dressed in designer clothes and shoes, always perfectly made up. But I know the real her. "I know it is."

"They've always thought that about me," she says, relaxing. She could sound bitter about it, but she doesn't. "I know it. They think I married your father for his money. And that I helped him steal money from Mark and Matthew."

I throw subtlety to the wind. "Did you?" I hold her gaze.

"No."

I nod. I believe her. "Did Dad?"

Her lips thin. "I'm not talking about this to you."

"Why not?" I straighten my spine. "It's my family too, and I hate all this stupid crap. If Dad didn't steal their money, just tell me so."

She says nothing.

"I take it that he did." My head drops forward, my stomach clenching. Fucking hell. I did not want this confirmed.

"I said I'm not talking about it." Mom's tone is firm, like it was many times I wanted something I couldn't have.

The server arrives with our salads and she immediately beams a smile at him. I ordered a fattoush salad, lots of chopped greens, cucumbers, tomatoes, chicken, and crisp, fresh pita chips. Mom's salad has chickpeas and roasted eggplant.

The server refills our water glasses and I pick up my fork, no longer hungry.

"I want to know what's going on," I mutter, stabbing a piece of chicken. "I want it over."

"It will be."

I give her a slitty-eyed look. "When? How?"

"Never mind. You don't need to worry about it."

A million thoughts are running through my mind. Mom knows about it. It seems like she's . . . trying to fix things? Curiosity burns a hole in my gut, but I know pushing her won't go well.

"Why can't you tell us? All of us. We deserve to know the truth. Have you talked to Matthew and Mark?"

"No." Her mouth is a firm line again.

"Oh my God. Mom!"

She gives me a quelling mom look that I'm well familiar with. "You left the banquet quickly last night. I saw you leaving with Wyatt Bell." She arches an eyebrow.

Oh sure, change the conversation to a subject *I* don't want to talk about. "I wasn't feeling well. He gave me a ride home."

"That's nice of him." She runs her tongue over her teeth, lips closed. "He, uh, doesn't seem like your type."

"Phhht. That's for sure." I roll my eyes, tamping down the memories of kissing him and how hot it was and what a gorgeous man he is and how he irritates me but makes me laugh. "He's nothing but a vagina hunter."

Mom chokes. "What? Oh, my word."

I grin and shrug.

Too bad my vagina's not exactly opposed to being hunted by him. In fact, my vagina is quite interested in him.

"What about Dan?" Mom probes. "You were sitting with him last night. I thought maybe you two are working things out."

"I thought you didn't like me dating him."

"Well, he's a little older than you, but you're a very mature young woman, and he seems nice."

"Okay, it was Dad who didn't want me seeing him."

She bites her lip. "You know your father worries about you."

"I know." I swallow the sigh. He has reason to. We never talk about what happened when I was a teenager, but it's always there, a hulking pachyderm in the room. "But I'm all grown up now. I make good choices."

She smiles. "I know you do."

"You changed the subject," I point out.

"Yes." Her smile is satisfied.

I let the issue of Dad and the lawsuit go for now, but I don't tell Mom that all of us are working on this, and we're going to figure it out. Because I don't like to fail.

8

EVERLY

"You're joking." I stare at Murray, the communications director of the Condors.

He smiles. "Nope. What's the problem with that?"

What can I say? Telling him I don't want to work with Wyatt Bell isn't a good enough reason. We need an ambassador for Hockey for All. The initiative is sponsored by the NHL and the players' association. Each team names an ambassador, which are to be announced February first. The ambassadors promote inclusion and diversity, and reach out to underrepresented, marginalized, or disadvantaged areas of the cities they compete in to encourage young people to play hockey, emphasizing the life skills it can teach, and how it can empower youth. We don't have a lot of time, as we need to get photographs taken and marketing materials done. I asked him weeks ago to consider who this year's ambassador should be and have been pestering him pretty much every day since.

"He'll be a great ambassador," Murray says. "Everyone

loves him. Fans love him and the guys in the room love him too."

This is true. "Fine." I sigh.

"I'll tell him to come see you after practice."

"Okay."

I'll be in my office all day with a ton of work to be done. Of course, now knowing Wyatt is going to show up at some point affects my focus, and I immerse myself in spreadsheets to distract me.

A little after noon, I'm contemplating going out to grab a sandwich, but I know as soon as I leave Wyatt will come. And a few minutes later he does stroll in, all sexy, confident swagger.

"Hey," he says, rapping his knuckles on my open door. "I'm supposed to see you."

"Did Murray tell you what it's about?"

"Yeah." He frowns and takes a few steps into my office. "I gotta say, I don't know if I'm the best one for this. I don't have a lot of spare time."

I purse my lips. "What are you so busy doing in your spare time?"

His mouth tightens. "Stuff."

"Partying. Women."

He rolls his eyes. "Yeah, that's it. Can't let a good cause interfere with my social life."

"I don't think this will interfere that much. As the ambassador for the team, you'll have to participate in some of the events throughout the month. We need to set up a time for a photo shoot. There are some dates with things already planned, but we can work other outreach efforts into your schedule."

"I think we should talk about it over lunch," he says. "I'm starving."

"Don't they feed you after practice?"

"Yeah, but I was told to get my ass up here to see you."

I can't suppress a smile. "Ah."

"You hungry?"

I want to lie, but . . . "Yeah."

"Okay, let's go."

"It has to be a quick lunch, I've got a lot to do. Apparently some charity watchdog is researching us for a report they put out every year."

"It'll be fine."

"Who knows how they'll spin things." I grab my purse and coat from the small cupboard in my office and follow him out.

We can walk to Aurora, a couple of blocks away. A chill wind tugs at my coat and the scarf wrapped around my neck, and I tug it tighter as we walk down the city street.

Wyatt doesn't say much until we get to the restaurant. The hostess greets him with a wide smile of blindingly white teeth, her long blond hair hanging in waves down her back. "For two?"

"Yes."

She checks the seating plan, and nods to a woman standing next to the lectern, pointing down. The other woman, equally gorgeous and wearing a skintight, short black dress, also flashes Wyatt a big smile and says, "Come this way."

She leads us to a window seat, which is lovely. The sun is bright and warm here inside, out of the wind. Wyatt helps me with my coat, hanging it on a nearby coatrack. I have to admit, he does have nice manners. He even holds my chair for me.

I've been here plenty of times; it's close and convenient for business lunches, and the food is good. So I don't have to take much time to look over the menu before deciding on the quiche Lorraine. Wyatt orders a croque monsieur.

"You know about this initiative," I say, once we've ordered. It's existed for a few years now.

"Sure." He leans back in his chair, shoulders wide in a navy sweater over a blue-and-white-checked shirt, long legs stretched out so far under the table they're on my side.

We discuss the goals of the program in general and then some of the specific things he'll be required to participate in.

"Your job as an ambassador is to promote diversity and inclusion initiatives. To be a leader in the locker room and a leader in the community. And, of course, a public advocate."

He nods.

"We'll be featuring you in public service announcements," I tell him. "Some print, some video that will be on TV and social media. We'll need you to use the hashtag on social media throughout the month. There are two broadcast awareness nights, and one of them is at our arena."

Wyatt surprises me with his awareness of the initiative, actually offering up a couple of good ideas.

We go over who the special ambassadors are this year, leaders from various marginalized groups. It turns out he's good friends with Baz Chadha, one of the first Punjabi players in the league.

"We played together in Rimouski," Wyatt says with a grin. "He's a year younger than me."

"Wow. The hockey world is small." I tap my fingers on the table. "I wonder if we could get you two together somehow."

"He plays for Calgary. Do we have a game against them in February?"

"Don't you know?" I shoot him an amused glance and pick up my phone. "Oh hey, yes, we do. Okay, let me see what I can work out." I pause. "If you have time, of course." I add a little sarcastic edge to my voice.

One corner of his mouth hitches up. "It's actually an honor to be asked to do this."

The low, humble tone of his words makes me look at him sharply. I suspect he's being sarcastic too. He doesn't meet my eyes for a couple of seconds and when he does I see . . . he's sincere.

"I'm glad you realize it," I say.

"I'm not a total asshole."

I make a face as if to say that's debatable.

"I'll even buy you lunch," he says, shifting the vibe from heavy to light. "Although you're probably richer than me."

I snort. "As if. I have no money."

"Uh-huh. What about that little shack you're living in?"

"Oh. Well. I had some family help with that."

"I bet."

I glare at him. "Seriously, I support myself. And I know I make about three percent of the money you do."

"That's pretty specific." He rubs his stubbled chin. "You've been checking how much I make?"

"It's common knowledge."

He nods, eyes dancing. "Sure."

"Do you have time to come back to the office and meet with Amy? She's the one in charge of this initiative."

His bottom lip pushes out. "It's not you?"

I laugh. "Sorry. I'm involved, though. We can go over the schedule she's got so far, and you can put things in your calendar."

He nods. "That would be good.

"How was your shopping trip with your mother?"

Change of subject. "It was nice. I got a new leather jacket."

His lips twitch. "Sounds hot. Is it black?"

"Why, yes, it is."

Shaking his head, he says, "I meant your discussion with her. The one you were dreading."

I sigh. "It wasn't very enlightening. The bad part was that she also knows Dad's having problems." I try to steady my voice. Just thinking about my dad maybe having Alzheimer's is enough to choke me up, never mind talking about it. "She's tried to get him to go to the doctor, but he doesn't want to. She says he's in denial."

"Or maybe he's scared too," Wyatt says softly.

"It's hard to imagine Dad being scared."

"Everyone's scared."

I bit my bottom lip. "Even you?"

"Sure." He flashes a cocky grin. "I'm scared of alligators."

I can't stop my laughter, even though I know he's being flippant when we were having a serious conversation.

I rub my temple. "Well, luckily you're in California and not Florida."

"And what about the other issue? The lawsuit? Did your mom tell all?"

I scowl. "No. She refused. She knows what's going on and basically told me not to worry my little head about it."

His eyes warm with sympathy. "But you are worried."

"Mmm. Maybe more annoyed about it. They're all acting like children, and over what? Money? Phhhht."

"Money's a big issue. Causes lots of problems in families."

"True. Maybe it's better not to have any."

"There's your privilege showing."

I wrinkle my nose. "You're right. Sorry." This man . . . he's surprisingly intuitive and thoughtful, and yet any time things get serious, he breaks the tension with a smart-ass remark. And he just called me on my privilege. I respect anyone who does that.

My chest tightens as if my bra suddenly shrank three band sizes.

I'd like to defend myself to him. I know I'm privileged, and I try to do some good with it. Bah. He doesn't need to know that.

He pays the bill with a credit card and helps me into my coat. Then we stroll back to the arena, the wind gusting in our faces this time.

"This is horrible weather!" I complain.

He laughs. "This is nothing."

"It's all relative, I guess. Are you happy you ended up here in California?"

"Oh yeah."

He says that with such heartfelt gratitude, I'm puzzled. "Most players don't like being traded."

"Change is hard," he says generically. "It was hard seeing Detroit win the Cup the year after I left."

"Oooh. Yeah. That would be hard to take."

He shrugs, not looking too bent about it. "It was a good move for me."

"To the Condors?" I shoot him a sideways, skeptical glance. "I mean, I'm a fan, obviously, but we haven't even made the playoffs for years."

"Doing better this year, though. Théo's made some great moves."

"True." This conversation leaves me feeling unsatisfied. I want to know more about him.

Crap.

We flash our security badges to Phil, the security guy on duty, and enter the arena to head up to the offices. I find Amy, and the three of us sit at the table in my office to look at schedules. Wyatt pulls out his phone and brings up a calendar. And already we have a conflict.

"I scheduled the photo shoot for Thursday this week," Amy says. "Before everyone takes off for the All Star break."

Wyatt shakes his head. "I can't do it that day."

Amy and I glance at each other.

Wyatt's jaw tightens. "Sorry, we'll have to reschedule it."

I run my tongue over my teeth. "Okay, fine. Are you staying in town for the break?"

"Uh. Yeah."

"I thought all you guys were going to Tahoe to go skiing," I comment. I've heard talk of this trip.

He makes a noise in his throat. "Not me."

"Okay, then, how's Friday?"

"That works."

"I need to check with Grant," Amy says, referring to the team photographer. "Hopefully he's available Friday. I'll get the jerseys done up with your name and number. And we have some T-shirts. I'll let you know."

"Thanks. I appreciate it."

I eye him and swallow a sigh. We continue our meeting and fortunately no other conflicts come up.

Wyatt has his jacket on and I walk him out to the reception area. He cups my elbow and murmurs in my ear, "Walk to the elevator with me."

I glance at Jennifer at the reception desk, then allow him to lead me out of the offices.

He stops at the elevator but doesn't press the button. "Thanks for having lunch with me."

"Thank you for buying lunch."

"We should do it again. Or maybe dinner."

"Are you . . . asking me out?"

His mouth lifts at the corners. "Yeah."

"I don't think that's a good idea."

"You said you're not dating the old mayor dude."

I huff out a laugh. "I'm not. That's not it. It's just . . . you play for the team."

"You work for the Foundation. There's not a conflict."

"My dad owns the team."

He grimaces. "I know." His gaze moves over my face and my insides melt a little. When he lifts a hand and strokes my hair off my face so gently, heat ripples through my belly. "But there's something here."

There is. I want to nod, but stop myself. I hold his gaze. "I'm just another vagina to you."

He chokes. "What?"

"You're a vagina hunter."

He laughs softly. "Seriously?"

"Everyone knows it. You even admit it. You like variety. You said that." I don't know why I'm pushing that, because I'm sure not looking for a relationship, and especially not with him. I could use five fingers to check off all the reasons it's a bad idea.

"Hmm. I did say that. But I'm only with one woman at a time. After New Year's Eve at my place, I haven't been able to stop thinking about you . . . about this mouth . . ." His thumb brushes over my bottom lip. Heat slides through me and every nerve ending goes electrified. "About how you taste. And how you kissed me back." His head is bent now and his mouth is so close to mine again; I can feel his breath on my cheek. I steel myself against the urge to turn my head . . . just a bit . . . and meet his mouth with mine. I'm quivering inside, aching, burning. I've been thinking the same things about him.

I swallow. Barely a breath away, we stay like that, not looking at each other. His warmth permeates my clothing, my skin. I draw in his scent . . . clean and crisp and spicy. He must have showered because he doesn't smell like gross hockey equipment.

I shouldn't do this.

For a moment, I'm transported back to when I was sixteen. There was a man then I wanted to be with . . . so badly that I didn't hesitate or question my judgment. I threw good sense into the ocean and went with my desires. It was the worst mistake of my life. I've tried so hard to never repeat that kind of blunder. I'm older and wiser now. I know better.

"Dinner," Wyatt breathes. "Thursday night."

"I thought you were busy Thursday."

"During the day. My evening is free. Come on, Everly. We can go somewhere nice and insult each other until we're both so horny we can't stand it."

I drop my head forward, laughing. "Well, when you put it that way . . ."

"Good." He brushes a kiss over my cheek. "Give me your phone number."

I recite it and he enters it into his phone. "I'll call you."

"Text me. I hate talking on the phone."

He lifts an eyebrow but doesn't question it. Again, not judging me. "Okay."

Now he pushes the elevator button and the doors slide open right away. My dad steps out.

Jesus.

I step back, trying to look casual about it. Wyatt seems unphased. "Hi, Mr. Wynn. How are you?"

Dad smiles. "Hello, Wyatt. I'm great, you?"

"Couldn't be better. Just had a meeting with your daughter."

Dad shifts his gaze to me, his expression softening. "Hi, Evvie. What are you two meeting about?"

"Hockey for All," I say. "Wyatt is our ambassador this year."

"Excellent. Good for you. I'm sure you'll represent the team well."

"I'll do my best, sir." Wyatt and Dad have changed places, Wyatt now in the elevator and Dad standing next to me. "Bye." He lifts a casual hand in a farewell gesture, his gaze lingering on my face as Dad turns around, a half smirk on his beautiful mouth.

Asshole.

I can't help but smile, shaking my head as I follow Dad down the hall.

"I like that boy," Dad says.

"Everyone likes him," I mutter.

Why wouldn't they? He's charming and fun, he has a way of making you feel interesting and worthy, and he's persuasive. Somehow he managed to convince me to say yes to dinner, when I know I shouldn't.

Seeing Dad is a reminder of exactly why.

I'm going to have to get out of this date.

9

WYATT

I spend the afternoon at a local fire station with a bunch of five- and six-year-olds.

It's a field trip for Owen's kindergarten class and I agreed to volunteer because Heather couldn't get the time off work.

The kids are all pretty revved up about seeing fire engines and firefighters, but there are enough adults to keep control of things. I'm kind of revved up myself, because hey, what guy doesn't love fire engines? It's pretty damn cool and I even get to sit in the driver's seat for a few minutes. I grip the steering wheel and grin down at Owen. "How do I look?" I ask him. "Like a real firefighter?"

He nods, eyes wide.

We gather again outside the truck. "When there's a fire, where do you think the cool, clean air is?" Firefighter Ed asks the children.

"Stop, drop, and roll!" Owen shouts.

Ed grins. "That's right, my man. Drop! Because the

cooler, cleaner air is down low by the ground. If you're ever stuck in a room during a fire and you can't escape, get down on the ground and wait for us to find you. And how can you help us find you?"

"Yell!"

"That's right! Let's all yell for help!"

"HELP!"

Then the kids are climbing inside the back of the engine, strapping themselves into the seats. This part's pretty cool too.

We end up back at school in time for the bell that ends the school day. Usually Owen goes to the daycare in the school until Heather's off work, but since I'm here, I take him. We stop for ice cream on the way home and then hang out at Heather's place until she gets there.

"How was the field trip?" she asks, dropping her bags at the front door.

Owen bounces up to her. "It was so cool! We heard the sirens and saw the hoses."

She picks him up to hug him. "That's great! I wish I could have been there." She meets my eyes, smiling. "Thank you for going."

"Not a problem." I rise off the couch. "It was fun. I like fire engines too."

She laughs. "Want to stay for dinner?"

"Ah, no thanks. I . . ." I hesitate. I don't know why. "I have a date."

Her eyelashes flutter rapidly. "Oh. That's nice."

Heather and I aren't together. We never have been, and we never will be. But sometimes I have a feeling . . . a weird sense that she wouldn't mind if we were. I've been spending so much time here, helping her out and spending time with Owen. I have to do it.

"Stay for dinner, Wyatt! Please!" Owen begs.

"Sorry, buddy, I can't. But I will another time." I ruffle his hair. "Give me a hug."

Heather sets him down and he runs to leap into my arms. I look at her over his head as I squeeze his small body. She smiles, but it's not a real smile. Shit.

"Who's the date with?" she asks casually. "Anyone I know?"

"Uh, no. I don't think so. It's just dinner." It's not just dinner. It's Everly. I've been alternating been hot fantasies, triumph at getting her to go out with me, and terror that I'll fuck it up. "I'll talk to you soon, my man, okay?" I set down Owen and head to the door.

I sense Heather's disappointment and it sticks in my gut. *Please, please don't let her be getting ideas about us.* That can't happen . . . and yet, I can't let her down again. I've already let her down so, so badly.

This inner conversation I'm having with myself puts a damper on my mood. I don't want to be like this with Everly, but shit. Sometimes I can't help the despair that swamps me, pulling me down into dark hopelessness.

At home I change from jeans into dress pants, a shirt and sweater, and slide my feet into loafers. I run a hand over my hair in front of the mirror and take a deep breath. Maybe I should cancel. I don't want to end up being a dick.

No. Everly already tried once to worm out of this, apparently having second thoughts, but I wasn't letting her get away with that. I'm definitely not giving her another chance to avoid me. Who knows if I'll have another opportunity.

I pick her up at her place, ringing the bell at the outside door of her townhouse condo. It's already dark, but the lush grounds are illuminated with glowing lights among the shrubs. She opens the door.

Just seeing her has my mood ticking up a notch on the scale of one to freakout.

I smile. "Hi."

"Hi. I'm ready." She has her purse over her shoulder and is already wearing a jacket—black leather!—over a short, leopard-print dress that shows off her killer legs.

"You look amazing." I lean in and kiss her cheek. "Mmm. Smell amazing too."

"Thank you." She locks her door and tips her head to look up at me. "You look pretty good too."

Tension I didn't know I'd been holding in my shoulders eases. "Are we actually complimenting each other?"

"It appears so." Her eyes dance.

I set my hand on the small of her back to lead her down the dusky sidewalk toward my vehicle on the street. "I don't know . . . this doesn't bode well as foreplay."

She chokes out a laugh. "Foreplay?"

"I like sparring with you. It turns me on. Maybe if we're too nice to each other, it'll be boring."

"I'll see what I can do to turn you on."

I groan. "I'm going to pretend you didn't just say that."

She laughs lightly as I open the passenger door for her.

Once I'm in the driver's seat, she asks, "Where are we going?"

"I made a reservation at Rossignol. That okay?"

"What if it's not?"

I slant a glance her way. "Okay, here we go."

She grins, her face shadowy. "Don't want to disappoint. And Rossignol is fine. Also, I'm impressed you pronounced it correctly."

"It's French." I turn onto Wilshire Boulevard.

"You said your French is terrible."

"I'm probably not saying it like Théo or JP would."

"It's supposed to be a very nice place."

"You haven't been there?"

"Nope."

"Me either." For some reason, this makes me happy. "We can pop our Rossignol cherry together."

"Oh my God."

It's about a twenty-five-minute drive, straight down Wilshire to West Hollywood. I circle the area around the restaurant a few times and can't find anywhere to park. As I'm driving down a side street, I spot a church with an empty parking lot and hang a right into it.

"Is this okay?" Everly asks.

"Sure. It's a church. It's not Sunday. It'll be fine."

We stroll down the street toward Melrose, turn left, and there's Rossignol.

"This is beautiful." Everly eyes the vine-covered exterior.

Inside, the area on our right is dark and seductive, a fire burning in a low fireplace, patrons lining the bar, where a bearded bartender is shaking up a cocktail.

The hostess seats us right away in the dining room, which is warm and elegant, with dark wood floors and furniture, and white tablecloths. A small lamp glows on each table and we're seated against a brick wall with creeping figs climbing up it.

"This is lovely," Everly says when we're settled, gazing around the room.

I smile in satisfaction. "Had to be somewhere good enough for a princess."

"I'm not sure I like that nickname."

"It's better than Vagina Hunter."

She drops her head forward, shoulders shaking. "Okay, yes."

We order wine after a short consultation with the server, who seems very knowledgeable, but make no move to look at dinner menus yet.

"So." Everly looks at me directly. "How was your day?"

"It was . . . busy."

"So I understood, since you couldn't do the photos today."

"I had some personal stuff I had to do. It's done." I adjust the cutlery on the table. "How about you?"

"Busy also."

Well, that's pretty superficial conversation. I'm aware that my reluctance to share certain parts of my life makes it difficult to be . . . close. That's okay, though, because I've never wanted to be intimate with women I date. Basically, I just want to have a good time.

But with Everly, I feel . . . guilty for not opening up. Heather and Owen are a big part of my life, but that also means opening up about a part of my life I don't want to talk about. Ever. So I don't go there.

"Your father calls you Evvie."

She blinks. "Yes."

"That's cute."

One corner of her mouth lifts. "I guess."

"I'm not going to call you that."

"Ooookay."

"If you don't like princess, I can call you . . . Cutie."

Her eyebrows rise.

"Cutie Patootie."

She rolls her lips inward.

"Poopsie. Shmoopsie-poo. Sugar lips."

Now she laughs. "How about Everly?"

"How about we stick with princess?"

"Fine."

The server arrives with our wine, pouring a taste for me. It's a smooth, plummy Merlot, and I pronounce it fine. The server fills both our glasses, tells us about specials, and asks if we have any questions.

"We haven't even looked at the menus yet," I confess.

"Take your time!"

Everly sips her wine. "Very nice."

I pick up my menu and scan it. "Jesus," I mutter. "I don't even know what half these things are."

Everly chuckles. "It's an adventure, then."

"True. And I do like an adventure." I lean forward to whisper, "Seriously, though, what is 'sprouting Romanesco'?"

She bites her lip. "I'm not sure. Want me to check?" At my nod, she pulls her cellphone out of her purse. "It's a vegetable. A green thing that looks sort of like broccoli."

"Trumpet mushrooms? Will we at least get high from them?"

"I doubt it."

"Okay, they have normal stuff too. Short ribs. Steak. Veal. But it comes with Castelfranco . . . what the fuck is that?"

She tries to stop her smile as she googles again. "It's a type of radicchio."

"Okay, I know what that is."

The menu is cracking us both up, which is good. I'd hate it if Everly was all pompous and serious about it. Eventually we order starters, which are weird salads, and then I order a steak with a bunch of fancy extras and she chooses dumplings with some vegetables and pesto.

"It's a really nice place," she assures me, once we've ordered.

"Wait until we taste the food. Sounds all fancy on the menu, but if it tastes like shit, I'm gonna be pissed."

"I'm sure it's good. This place is very popular. Whoa."

"What?"

"That's Tom Hanks and Rita Wilson over there." She gives a subtle motion of her head.

I casually turn to look. "Holy shit. It is."

"I should go say hi."

My eyes bug out. "You know them?"

"No. Kidding."

I shake my head. "I wasn't in a very good mood when I was on my way to pick you up."

"No? Bad day?" She eyes me over her wineglass as she sips.

"It was a good day. Just . . . stuff. Anyway, I feel a lot better now." I hold her gaze. She makes me laugh. Gets me out of my own head.

"I must not be annoying you enough. Want to talk about the call the refs missed in OT the other night?"

Immediately, my blood runs hot. "That was a fucking travesty!"

She smiles and sits back in her chair. "It definitely was a hand pass."

"It definitely was! I can't believe they didn't see that!"

"Did you see it on the ice?"

"I was on the bench, but the replay clearly showed it."

"See, that's the problem. We all see a million replays from different angles, in slow motion. The refs are on the ice and have a split second."

"What the hell? You're supposed to be a Condors fan!"

She laughs. "I am. Okay, I agree it was a hand pass, but you can't totally blame the refs for missing it."

"Oh, hell yeah, I can." I lean forward, lowering my voice, pretending to look around for hidden microphones. "I mean, I can say that in private, in front of you. Not for the media."

"Of course not."

We bicker back and forth as we eat our meals, which are, in fact, amazing, and not so huge that we don't have room for dessert, which we agree to share. Once again there's stuff on the menu I don't recognize. "What is vacherin?"

"Gonna have to google that one too." She pauses with her phone. "Oh, it's a kind of cheese. I'm guessing a soft cheese . . . since it's a dessert?"

It comes with meringue and ice cream, so yeah, that makes sense. "Let's try it."

She eyes me. "You sure you don't want the chocolate cake?"

"Let's be crazy."

It's crazy delicious, so creamy, with a lemon taste and the sweet meringue.

"Yum," Everly agrees.

I can't stop watching her as she slides the tines of the fork through her lips to get every last taste. Our eyes meet. She knows what I'm thinking.

We take our time and when we're done, we step out onto the sidewalk into the cool night air. The area is still lively. "How about we walk a bit?"

"Sure."

We stroll along the sidewalk, taking in the energy of the nightlife—restaurants, bars, and shops still open. When I see Big D's Pleasure Emporium, I stop. "Let's go in."

Everly eyes the sign and bursts out laughing. "Nuh-uh!"

"Why not?" I nudge her with my elbow. "It's a sex shop."

"I realize that."

"You don't like sex?" I look her up and down. "Pretty sure you were into it that night you had your tongue in my mouth."

"I like sex."

Christ. Just hearing her say that makes my dick thicken.

"Fine, let's go in."

We peruse the selection of toys. I'm enjoying embarrassing Everly by picking up anal plugs and a three-way dildo that has me first puzzled, then intrigued. "Look," I say. "Think what you could do with this."

"Oh my God."

Then we get into the kinky stuff and even *I'm* embarrassed about puppy play. I mean, to each his own, though.

"Hey," Everly calls to me. She's over in another area. She holds up something. "This would look good on you."

I choke on a laugh. It's a black and red neoprene one-piece shorts thing with a cut-out over the abs. Not my style at all, but hey, two can play this game. "Yeah, it would. I should go try it on."

I remove it from her hand.

"Oh no . . ."

I start toward an area that has dressing rooms.

"No . . ." Everly's tailing me, tugging at my shirtsleeve. "You can't do this."

"Oh yeah?"

Trying on crazy outfits in the rough trade section of a sex store is . . . crazy. But this is one of those moments I don't give a shit. I just want to have fun.

The guy working in the store gives me a subtle up-and-down look as he shows me into a dressing room. He's dressed in black neoprene too, but without cutouts.

I'm laughing as I strip down and maneuver into the garment. Huh. This is a workout. I eye how the front pouch outlines my junk. Jesus. My legs look especially hairy against the shiny neoprene, my bulky thighs stretching the little shorts to the max. Then I step out of the room to show off for Everly. She's hovering near the entrance to the change rooms, her cheeks flaming.

"That looks amazing on you," the dude says, this time his appreciation not so subtle. "Really shows off your abs. And those legs!"

I do a ridiculous pose and Everly cracks up.

"You could model for us," the guy adds. "Your body is perfect."

The guy working here is all serious about this. I kind of feel bad. So I sling an arm around his shoulders. "Thanks, man."

"It does look good," Everly agrees. "You should get it. I bet Chad would love to strip you out of that."

Now I'm sputtering. Chad? What the fuck?

The dude sighs. "Chad's a lucky guy."

Everly has to turn away, shoulders shaking, and I head back into the change room to strip out of the garment.

We emerge onto the sidewalk, both laughing like lunatics.

"You're awful!" Everly wheezes, hanging on to my arm. "But I have to admit, you did look good."

"Chad!" I choke out. "Who the fuck is Chad?"

"Your boyfriend, dummy. I had to say that because the sales guy was looking really smitten."

I'm laughing so hard, but I curl an arm around her waist and sweep her up against me to plant a long, hot kiss on her mouth.

She stares back at me when I lift my mouth from hers and we're caught like that, in a moment full of heat and sizzle.

10

EVERLY

I stare back at Wyatt, spellbound. Heat is mainlining through my veins like heroin. Laughter and wine and . . . well, lust are making me dizzy and breathless.

God, he's a good kisser. I could make out with him for hours.

I *have* made out with him for hours.

Gah.

"You're beautiful," he says hoarsely, touching his fingertips to my cheek.

"Thank you. So are you." His eyebrows fly up. "Okay, handsome. Never mind. I take that back. Your ego is big enough." I pull away from him, the spell broken by my lighthearted words.

We continue walking down the street. "Your car is the other way."

"We can't go home already. The night is young. And so are we."

I snort. "I think that's a song."

"Really? Whatever. I'm on holidays."

"Oh right. You are. But *I* have to work tomorrow."

"What are you, forty? Come on." He grabs my hand and pulls me toward a club. It's a dance club I may have been to years ago. So not my thing anymore.

"I'm a mature, responsible adult who has to get up early in the morning."

"That's boring."

There's a line to get in, but Wyatt flashes some cash at the bouncer and has a few words with him and we're inside, surrounded by pulsing music, flashing lights, and writhing bodies.

The DJ is spinning a Tiësto song. The electronic beat vibrates inside me.

"Oh my God, I haven't been to a place like this in years," I shout into Wyatt's ears.

He grins. "Can you handle it?" He tugs me to the dance floor and sets his hands on my hips. The rhythm is strong and throbbing, and I can't help but get into it. A little.

Wyatt's a good dancer. Not flashy, but comfortable, with a good sense of rhythm. His smile tells me he's having fun as we move to the music. The song slides into another sexy, pulsing tune, and Wyatt turns me so my ass is pressed to him. Deliberately, I grind against him. We dance like that, moving against each other. I'm exquisitely aware of his big, hard body, his hands on my waist, my hips. Somehow we know how to move together, and I'm buzzing and so turned on by the sultry music and his touch, I can hardly stand it.

After a few songs, we're both damp and out of breath.

He leads me off the dance floor with a hand on the small of my back. "Let's get a drink."

We head to the bar, lined with more bodies, including a lot of women barely old enough to drink, in sexy short dresses and high heels. I feel old.

I take off my jacket and drape it over one arm, and Wyatt's eyes move over me in my short leopard-print dress. I'm not oblivious to the attention Wyatt is attracting from the other women, with his good looks and athletic body. *He's mine, girls, back off.*

Whoa. Where'd that come from?

Wyatt orders me a glass of champagne (how does he know I love champagne?) and a beer for himself, receiving immediate service from a pretty, young bartender. Then he turns my back to the bar and steps in front of me, setting one arm on a pillar next to us, effectively creating a little privacy for us in the crowd.

I gulp down some wine. The bubbles sting my nose and throat.

"Admit it, you're having fun," he says near my ear.

"Okay, okay, I like dancing. I haven't done it for a while."

"Is that because you've been dating guys old enough to be your father?"

I snort. "No." *Maybe.* It's true that most of my recent dates have been dinner dates or charity events or dinner and a movie. Definitely not sex shops and dance clubs.

"You have to live a little," he says. "Life is short."

He's smiling, but the words sound intense.

"I guess that's true."

"Hakuna matata."

I burst out laughing. "You're crazy."

"Maybe so." He leans in closer and nuzzles my ear. His breath has shivers cascading down my skin. "But I'm having a good time."

"Life's not all about fun."

"Right now it is."

I shake my head, but he's irresistible and I smile.

We dance more. He runs into someone he knows—-a football player? And we hang out with them for a little while, laughing a lot. I can't believe it's two in the morning the next time I check my phone.

I lay my hand on his forearm and go on my toes to speak into his ear. "I really have to go home! It's late."

This time he nods. "Okay. Beam us up, Scottie."

"I wish. Are you okay to drive?"

"Sure. I've only had one beer."

"Really?" How the hell did that happen? Then I realize I've only had two tiny glasses of champagne the whole time we've been here. Every time I mentioned another drink, Wyatt made me dance again.

We say goodbye to our new friends and I dance my way out of the club. The street is a lot quieter now and we start down the sidewalk arm in arm. I'm singing the words of a song the DJ played. "Chop up the beats, chop up the beats."

Wyatt laughs and spins me around. I can't believe I don't fall over, but I guess I'm not that drunk.

"I haven't laughed that much in a long time. My face hurts."

"That's good. Laughter is important."

"I'm not *that* much of an old fuddy-duddy."

"Fuddy-duddy? That must be a term your dad uses."

I giggle. "Yeah, that probably is where I got it."

We arrive at the church parking lot where Wyatt left his SUV and we both stop short at the now locked gate in front of us. A big, black wrought-iron fence with spikes on top surrounds the lot, including his Land Rover.

"Oh my God." I gaze at the locked gate.

"Fuck."

We both stand there staring at it.

"What are we going to do?" I ask.

Wyatt walks back and forth along the fence, as if assessing his ability to climb it. That won't help, though; we still need to drive out.

He blows out a breath and shoves a hand into his hair. "Maybe I can pick the lock."

"What?"

He moves closer to the gate to inspect it and I hover near him as he pulls a Swiss Army knife out of his pocket. "Damn, I can't see," he mutters.

"Here." I pull out my phone and turn on the flashlight, shining it on the lock.

"Great, now the cops can clearly see me breaking in."

"Do you want to see what you're doing or not?"

The sound of voices reaches us, and we both look down the dark sidewalk. A man and a woman are approaching. The guy's hair is bleached blond and spiky. He's wearing a long black leather coat and multiple piercings glint in the streetlight. In the darkness, all we can see of her is black hair, black-rimmed eyes, and black lips. And black combat boots.

I clutch Wyatt's arm nervously.

"Shit," Wyatt hisses, straightening.

"It's your fucking fault!" the woman says. "He wouldn't be in jail if it wasn't for you!"

"Calm down! It's not my fault."

My eyes widen, my stomach clenching.

The dude stops near us and takes in what we're doing. "Hey, man. I can get that done for you."

"Uh . . ."

He disappears back up the street and around the corner.

Wyatt and I exchange wide-eyed glances, then smile cautiously at the goth girl scowling at us, her arms crossed and one hip cocked.

The roar of an engine fills the quiet street, and the dude in the coat pulls up in a white van. He jumps out and opens the back doors. He's got an entire True Value hardware store in there.

He pulls out a power saw and in a few minutes, sparks flying, metal whining, he has the lock cut open. I glance wildly around, ready for the police to race up with lights flashing and sirens blaring,

I'm not even sure what to say. I mean, we could have taken an Uber home and come back tomorrow for Wyatt's vehicle.; we didn't really have to do this. But it seems polite to thank the guy for breaking in.

"Yeah, thanks," Wyatt adds.

"No worries, man, it's cool. You never know when you're going to need to fuck some shit up."

He gives Wyatt's hand a bro shake and then he and Goth Girl jump in the van and roar away.

Wyatt and I turn to each other, stunned, then both collapse into each other's arms, laughing.

"We just broke into a church!" I wheeze, holding on to him.

"I know!"

"Pretty sure we're going to burn in hell for that."

"I feel guilty." He pulls out his wallet, peels off a bunch of bills, and jogs over to push them into a mail slot beside the church door. Then we make our getaway.

"I can't believe that just happened." I lean my head back against the headrest. "I have to say, a date with you is an adventure."

"Of course it is. Life is an adventure."

"I can't believe how late it is. This is really going to mess with my sleep hygiene."

"Sleep what?"

"Sleep hygiene. I try to keep a strict routine, because I have, uh, trouble sleeping. Sometimes." *All the time.*

"Yeah, I know what it is. Sleep is important, but a night of fun is okay once in a while."

"I don't know." I sigh. But yeah, I had so much fun.

When we arrive at my place, Wyatt parks on the street. He jumps out to open my door, and leads me to my condo.

I was all relaxed and mellow until this moment. Now uncertainty grips me.

"You kept me out way too late," Wyatt says. "It's past my bedtime."

I splutter. "What? You're the one who kept *me* out!"

"Nah." He brushes his lips over my cheek. "Now it's too

late to come in and make out with you." He shakes his head. "I know it's disappointing, but you'll survive."

I'm both aroused and . . . yes, disappointed. And relieved. I should be relieved.

I smile, though. He took an awkward moment and made light of it. "Damn. If I'd known, I would have insisted we leave hours ago."

His eyelids lower and his lips part enticingly. "Maybe next time."

There shouldn't be a next time. But my own lips part too, hungry for his kiss, and I close my eyes as well. His mouth meets mine . . . warm . . . firm . . . delicious.

My belly quivers and flips, a little ache starting up low down inside me. I pull in a slow breath as he eases away from me, my eyes fluttering open. I stare into his dark orbs, and he touches my face. I love how he does that.

"Good night, princess. I had fun."

"Me too." I have to be honest. "Good night."

He waits until I'm safely inside, the door locked behind me. I lean against it, listening to his footsteps on the sidewalk, then his vehicle starting.

Wow. That was a crazy date, but . . . I really did have fun.

I'm NOT EVEN HUNGOVER THE NEXT MORNING, JUST TIRED. And yet I seem to have some weird adrenaline thing going, a fizzy, excited, energetic feeling every time I think about Wyatt and the crazy stuff we did last night. So I'm buzzing through my work all morning. I check in on the photo shoot where Wyatt is decked out in Hockey for All gear and smiling at the camera in various poses. All is going well.

At lunchtime, I'm on my way out to grab something to eat. Passing by the front reception counter, I see a group of people crowded around the receptionist Jennifer's computer.

"What's going on?" I pause. Maybe they're watching something from the All-Star Game in Vancouver.

Jennifer looks up at me. "Is Wyatt Bell gay?"

I jerk back, nearly falling over. "Pretty sure he's not," I say casually. "Why?" *Why are you asking me?*

"There's a picture of him online—the On the Town blog. In some kind of gay BDSM fetish-wear."

I blink. My insides go hot, then freezing cold. I grip the edge of the counter. "What?"

"Come see." She gestures.

I round the desk and peer at the screen at which Jennifer; Brenda, the chief HR officer; and Kate, the CFO, are all staring.

"Jesus." I can only gape at the picture of Wyatt wearing that singlet last night.

But it's not just that . . . it's a picture of Wyatt with his arm around the guy who works in the store, and they're smiling at each other, looking for all the world like they're a couple.

"I didn't know he was gay when we chose him to be the ambassador for All," Brenda muses. "Is he out?"

"He's not gay."

I frown. I'm confused and my mind is spinning uselessly. Lack of sleep probably isn't helping.

"Are you sure?" Lisa eyes the image doubtfully. "Wouldn't it be good to have an ambassador who's gay?"

"He's not gay." I keep saying that.

"Then what is this?"

I swallow. I rub my temples. Okay, this is a dilemma. "Who else has seen it?"

Jennifer snorts. "Only about a million people." She leans closer to the screen. "There are nearly a hundred comments on the post."

"Oh my fucking God. I meant, who else from the hockey organization has seen it?"

"I don't know." Jennifer grimaces. "But I'm sure they'll hear about it. Théo and Dave and Brock are in Vancouver. I bet there's talk about it there."

I can just let this go. Hope for the best. Maybe nobody will see it. Talk will die down. It'll be a big nothingburger.

And the Condors are going to win the Stanley Cup this year.

I bite down hard on my bottom lip. "I'm sure it's, um, nothing. But if you hear anything more, will you let me know?"

"Sure."

Instead of going for lunch, I return to my office. I drop into the chair behind my desk.

I need to think. I need to stay calm. On the Town is a pretty popular blog. They post a lot of news about celebrity sightings in Los Angeles. Some of them are tacky and trashy, but not all. They've been criticized in the past for how they get some of the images they run. I wonder how much they paid the person who was in the store last night.

Dammit! I should have known that could happen! I

tried to stop Wyatt, but he went and did it anyway, and we were laughing and having fun and I guess I just lost my common sense for a few minutes.

That doesn't happen to me. Ever. What the hell got into me?

I slump in my chair and close my eyes. Being in the news for the wrong reasons is my worst fear.

Of course, I'm not in that picture and there's nothing about me in the article.

It'll be okay. But nothing like that can happen again. I live my entire life to avoid things like this.

I fish my cellphone out of my purse. I don't like talking on the phone, but sometimes it's necessary. I call Wyatt.

"Hey, princess." His deep, smooth voice greets me. "How are you?"

"I'm . . . oh my God."

"What?" His tone sharpens. "You okay?"

"I'm fine. You're in trouble, though."

"What the hell?"

"Where are you? Are you near a computer? Or can you look on your phone?"

"Look at what?"

"This blog." I give him the URL and wait.

And wait.

"Oh my fuck."

"Yeah."

He cracks up laughing. "Jesus! This is hilarious! Who the hell took this picture?"

I hold my phone away from my ear and gape at it. He's laughing about this? "Must have been a customer who recognized you."

He's still laughing, so hard he almost can't speak. "They think I was trying that on . . . for real? Ahahahaha. And the dude who works there . . . bahaha."

"They think you're gay."

He laughs more, gasping for air. "Jesus Christ."

"This isn't funny, Wyatt." I glare across my office. He thinks everything's a joke. Well, this is not.

"Sure it is. It's freakin' hilarious."

"You were just named the team ambassador to Hockey for All."

"Yeah?"

"You're supposed to support inclusivity and diversity."

"So?"

I grind my back teeth together. "You're not gay."

"That is correct. You figured that out, huh."

"Smart-ass." I close my eyes, my jaw aching. "This could be a huge problem. I don't know how huge. But if management finds out about this . . ." I stop.

"Who cares?"

"You have no idea." He should know something about optics and image and public relations.

"Come on, if people think I'm gay, it's no big deal. Not these days. And I don't give a shit what people think."

"I know you don't, and it wouldn't be a problem if you *really were gay*." I rub my forehead. "Look, never mind. Let's just see how things play out. Maybe it'll blow over without attracting any attention."

"Okay. Whatever. So . . . do you want to come over to my place for pizza tonight?"

My eyes pop wide open. *Now* he's asking me on another date? Good God, I should never have gone with him last night, and this whole shit show wouldn't be happening. "No. I can't. Look, Wyatt, we should never have gone out. Now this has happened . . . I can't do that again. Sorry. I have to go. Bye."

I end the call and toss my phone aside. Elbows on the desk, I bury my face in my hands. That was rude. I feel bad. I'm such a bitch.

It'll be fine.

I'll just spend the weekend imagining the worst, having anxiety dreams, and knitting up a storm. There might be wine involved. It'll all be fine.

It's not fine.

Of course word gets out about the blog post and the picture. Monday morning, when everyone's back in the office, there's a big meeting about it, including Murray and . . . my dad.

I'm not included in the meeting. I don't work for the team. But I'm aware it's going to happen at eleven o'clock. I sit in my office, swiveling back and forth in my chair, my palms sweaty, my stomach churning, debating what to do.

At about five minutes to eleven, Wyatt appears in my door.

I stop my mindless twirling and plant my feet on the floor. "Wyatt." I'm getting dizzy anyway. Or is that the effect of seeing him again? "What are you doing here?" He better not be here to see me and try to persuade me to go out with him again, because that is *not* happening.

"I was asked to come to some meeting. About that blog article." He runs a hand through his hair. "Don't know what the big deal is."

I stare at him. My heart is galloping in my chest. I rub my sweaty palms on the upholstery of my chair.

What should I do?

Throwing up probably isn't a good option.

I know I'm not in the picture, and I'm not involved in this . . . I could just stay here and pretend it's not happening, and let Wyatt fend for himself.

But I was there. I know what was going on. I know the truth. And I also know how bad this could make the Condors look if it gets blown up.

Shit. I sigh and push up out of my chair. "I'm coming with you."

"Huh? Why?"

"I was involved." I start toward him and my heart scampers. Why does he have to look so good? Dressed in casual tan-colored pants and a navy sweater with a brown-and-blue-checked shirt beneath it, he nonchalantly leans against my door. His light brown hair is tousled, his jaw dusted with dark gold stubble, and his hazel eyes gleam as he watches me advance across the carpet toward him. "Let's go."

I assume the meeting is in the boardroom and I start down the hall.

"You know, your ass looks amazing in that skirt," he says from behind me.

I stop dead and whirl around. "Shhh!"

He grins. "There's no one around, princess." He drops a light kiss on my nose.

My chest expands with the deep, fortifying breath I take, my heart giving a couple extra beats. Dammit, his gaze drops to my breasts, which lift as I inhale. "Behave!"

Still smiling, he shakes his head. He's not taking this seriously.

Maybe I'm overreacting. I *hope* I'm overreacting. I hope I'm doing the right thing by crashing this meeting.

11

WYATT

I watch Everly's sexy ass sway as she hoofs it down the hall in her killer heels, tight pink skirt, and silky blouse. Her hair bounces and I can tell her body is filled with tension.

I guess some guys might be embarrassed about that photo being out in the world, but I really don't care. So if this meeting is because they think I'm upset about it, I can just reassure them there's nothing to worry about and get on with the rest of my All Star break.

I'd hoped that I'd spend more of the weekend with Everly, after being gentlemanly enough to leave her at her door Thursday night. Leaving her wanting more. Always a good strategy.

Seems to have backfired right now.

She made it pretty clear that she never wants to see me again when she called on Friday.

I follow her into the boardroom and the atmosphere in there is, shall we say, uptight.

Hmmm.

The office dudes all greet me with big smiles. Everyone treats the players like royalty. I could probably ask for some Russian caviar, a bottle of Dom Perignon, and some Cuban cigars and someone would rush out to get them.

Instead I'm holding a Venti Starbucks cup.

Crap. Bob Wynn is here.

I glance at Everly. For the first time, a little nudge of worry prods me. What is she going to say about all this?

Bob frowns at his daughter. "What are you doing here, Evvie?"

Her lips tighten at his nickname for her. "I was involved in this."

Bob's forehead furrows as Everly takes a seat at the far end of the table.

Everyone else exchanges puzzled glances too.

I feel like there's a rock in my gut as I too sit and wait for whatever shit is about to hit the fan.

"Anyone else coming?" Dave asks, looking around, preparing to close the door to the meeting room.

"This is it," Murray says. "Okay, we need to discuss that blog article and photo of you that's online, Wyatt."

I nod. Not surprised.

"Can you explain to us what that was about?" he asks.

I almost laugh. I'm used to a coach asking me "What the fuck did you do?" and this is so polite. I open my mouth to answer, but Everly jumps in.

"I was with him," she says. "We were out for dinner and we were walking down Melrose and decided to look in the shop."

Bob makes a noise that I think might mean he's having

a stroke. I shoot him a worried look. Then I glance at Everly. She doesn't seem so well either.

"We were just goofing around," she says, clearly striving to keep her emotions in check. "I told Wyatt he'd look good in that . . . um, outfit, making a joke. I didn't think he'd do it, but he tried it on."

I catch her eye. So far this is accurate.

"We had no idea there was someone there taking a picture. That was all it was. But I know how bad it looks."

"It doesn't look bad." I finally speak up. "It looks like we were, uh, goofing around, just like you said."

"You're the ambassador for Hockey for All," Murray says. "Part of the initiative is to include the LGBTQ community."

"Yeah." I nod. "I know."

"But you're not gay," Murray adds.

"No." I shrug. "But if we want to let people think I am, that's okay."

Everly jumps in again. "We can't let people think you're gay. Because you're not. We can't pretend for this campaign. It would be an even worse PR mess if *that* came out."

"I don't get it." I'm confused as fuck and I don't even care about this.

"If we let people think you're gay and don't correct it, the LGBTQ community would be offended when the truth comes out. Which it will . . . since *you're not gay*."

I nod slowly.

"I know what to do," Everly continues. "We'll make a statement, just what I told you, and I'll take responsibility for it."

Murray nods. "I like that."

Bob's face is tomato red. "I don't like it."

Everly turns to her dad. "It's okay, Dad. I got this. It has to be done."

"What would be better is if you two were actually in a relationship," Murray says thoughtfully, rubbing his chin. "Then there'd be no question about his sexual orientation."

I can only shoot him a what-the-fuck look about my sexual orientation.

"We're not in a relationship," Everly quickly puts in.

"But you could be." Murray is still rubbing his chin. It's starting to annoy me. "Make a few appearances together. That way there'd be no question when you tell the story of what happened that it's true. It'll add credibility."

"It *is* true," I snarl. At Everly's wide-eyed warning look, I shut my mouth.

"Of course it is." Murray smiles broadly. Fakely. "But we all know how rumors start and social media can be a nightmare."

I do know this. Not from experience. But I know other guys who've gotten themselves in trouble on social media. Best advice I ever got was from my agent, Steve Walsh. He told me years ago to stay off social media, that it's a tool to brand myself but nothing else. His number one rule: do not read your mentions. I don't know what people say about me and I don't care.

Hell. I was just having a little fun with Everly. And it's turned into a shit show.

I look over at Everly and meet her eyes. Her mouth is puckered up and she looks like she just ate a lot of bad seafood. But then her expression changes to resigned, she lifts a shoulder, and her eyes say to me, *Why not?*

Then it hits me . . . this is perfect!

I clear my throat and try not to appear too enthusiastic. "I don't know . . ."

"Are you seeing someone else?" Murray asks. "I mean, usually it's not my business. But it kind of is. If you have a girlfriend, this could be a problem."

"No. I don't have a girlfriend. But if we're trying to be honest about the situation, this seems . . . deceptive." I don't even care.

"I know what you're saying," Dave jumps in. "But we won't make a big deal of it. Like Murray said, you two just go out a few times, hit some events so people see you together, you don't even have to talk to the media or say anything."

"Well." I twist my mouth up like I'm thinking about it. "I guess I could do that."

Bob still looks like he has an aneurysm. He rounds on Everly. "This is—"

"Would you like to talk about it in my office?" Everly interrupts her dad sweetly.

He snaps his mouth shut, but is still frowning.

Everly rises gracefully. She places her hands flat on the boardroom table and gazes around at everyone. "Anything else?"

I'm surprised they don't all bow to her, Princess Wynn.

"Good. I'll be in my office if you want to talk more, Dad."

I hide my grin. "Let's go make a plan, Ms. Wynn."

She shoots me a skeptical look.

I open the door and hold it for her.

"Thank you."

I let her lead the way back to her office.

She closes the door and throws herself down into the chair behind her desk, shoving her hands into her hair. "Shit!"

I perch my ass on the edge of her desk. "It's not that bad."

"Maybe not for you! My dad's having a heart attack and when my mom hears about this, she'll freak out too."

"Why?" I regard her steadily. "We didn't do anything wrong. I get that it's a bit of a PR issue, because of Hockey for All, but otherwise it's not a big deal. We went out on a date and we were having fun."

She blows out a heavy sigh. "It's a long story."

"Are you okay?" I gnaw on my bottom lip, studying her. Her face is shiny, like she's sweating, and her hands are shaking.

"Of course I'm okay."

I don't believe a word of that. But I admire her ability to rise above whatever is making her look freaked out.

She swallows, sits up straight, and clenches the armrests of her chair. "I'm fine," she repeats.

"Okay. So when should we go out again? I'm off until our next game on Monday in Toronto."

She presses her lips together. Clearly she's unhappy about this. "We need to be strategic about it."

"What does that mean?"

"If we're going to do this, we have to be seen somewhere for maximum exposure."

I open my mouth, and she holds up a hand. "Don't

make this about something dirty. Exposure doesn't mean nudity."

I have to laugh. "You know me so well already."

"I don't know what's coming up . . ." She scoots her chair forward and clicks the mouse on the desk. I peer over at her computer and see she's brought up her calendar. "We don't have any big events planned." Her eyes rove over the screen. "Oh . . . there is something next weekend."

"*Next* weekend?" Disappointment settles like a rock my gut. "That's too far away."

"Hmm. Maybe so. Well, we could just do something really public like . . . Hey, I know. My dad has courtside tickets to the Cougars." One of the local pro basketball teams. "We could go to a basketball game. We'll let it leak to the media that you're there, and they'll put us on camera for sure."

"Excellent." I rub my hands together.

She's already checking the basketball schedule. "Perfect. Saturday night there's a game."

"The stars are aligning."

She frowns at my flippant comment.

"What?" I give her an innocent look.

A sharp knock sounds on the door.

She gives me a shove to move me off her desk. I take a few steps away as she calls out, "Come in!"

Bob enters. His face is still ruddy, his lips turned down. He eyes me like I'm something that fell out of a dog's ass. Eeesh. Clearly he blames me for involving his princess in this mess.

"I know what you're thinking," Everly immediately says to her father. "Relax, Dad."

"Your mother's going to shit a brick," he says in that famously gruff voice.

I do like a man who's blunt.

"Do you want me to talk to her?" Everly asks.

"I should go . . ." I edge toward the door.

"No, it's okay!" Everly waves me back. "We should, uh, go out for lunch!"

"You don't have to do this, Evvie," Bob growls. "Murray's lost his mind. I'm going to fire him."

"No, you're not." She stands and pats her dad's shoulder. "It was a reasonable suggestion."

I'm watching, agape.

"It's crazy." Bob shoots me a cutting look that I swear I can feel slicing across my skin.

Okay, enough of this shit. I straighten my shoulders. "Mr. Wynn, I know Everly and I aren't really dating, but you can rest assured that I will treat her with the utmost respect."

"You're a ladies' man," Bob says.

I want to smile at the old-fashioned term, despite the contempt in his voice. "I'm a single guy, and yes, I like ladies." I put on my most guileless face. "But I'm a good guy." I lay my palm on my chest.

He still scowls. "You don't date anyone else until this whole thing is done. I sure as hell don't want rumors about you cheating on Evvie. And no more shenanigans in sex stores."

"Of course not."

"Anything you do to her—"

"Dad. Stop." Everly steps closer. "I'm a grown woman. Give me credit for having been brought up well enough that

I can know how to look after myself when it comes to men. Do you say things like that to the women Noah and Archer and Harrison date?" She pauses. Bob doesn't answer. "No, you don't, because I've seen you with them. You're all flirty and complimentary. Well, don't treat me any different than you treat the boys. It's insulting."

Go, Everly. Admiration for her heats my chest. I kind of want to kiss her right now.

Bad idea in front of her dad.

"Okay, okay. I get it." Bob points at me. "But I'm keeping an eye on you."

"I totally understand."

He leaves and I turn to Everly. She has her hand over her eyes, her thumb pressing into one eyebrow. I move closer. "Headache?"

"Yeah. And his name is Bob Wynn." She looks up and sighs. "So. Where should we go for lunch?"

EVERLY

I'm freaking the fuck out.

On the inside. I think I'm doing a pretty good job of keeping it on the inside.

I need to reel it in. Chill down. Settle the kettle.

We climb into Wyatt's Land Rover. As he drives, I focus on breathing, without being obvious about it.

This is my worst nightmare. The media getting hold of something and turning it into something it's not. Broadcasting my mistake to the whole world.

One stupid mistake almost ruined my life years ago. I can never screw up like that again. That was why I'd decided I can't date Wyatt again, and here I am . . . forced into it.

"How about Lard Boy?"

"Uh . . . sure." It sounds like a dive, but it's actually a new and trendy restaurant on Wilshire. I guess if we're going to do this, might as well make sure people see us, even if it's just lunch.

When we're seated, Wyatt leans forward. "I'm really sorry. I feel responsible for all this."

"It's not your fault." Although I kind of have been blaming him in my inside voice. In fairness, though . . . "Who knew there was someone there taking pictures?"

"Yeah. But I guess I should have known it's a possibility."

"I should have known too." I sigh. "It's done. We have to make the best of it. I just don't want this to be negative PR for the team or for the league."

"Neither do I. Seriously, I don't care about myself. If people want to start stupid rumors, I don't care." He scrunches up his face. "Maybe I'm not the best person to be the ambassador."

"Too late now. We've already put your name in and done the marketing photos. Your name is on everything now. And next week we're filming the video we're making."

His smile melts my panties. "Well, it's not exactly a hardship to spend time with a beautiful, sexy, fascinating woman."

My heart bumps with pleasure, but I ignore it. "That's laying it on a bit thick."

He puts on an affronted look. "I mean all that."

"Oh." I drop my gaze. "Well. Thank you."

"Does your dad get that upset about every man you date? Or just me?"

"Pretty much everyone," I admit.

"Even Dan Diaz?"

"Especially Dan Diaz."

I beam a smile.

"He thought Dan was too old for me."

"He's not the only one," Wyatt mutters.

"And even though he keeps saying he wants grandchildren. Apparently I'm supposed to produce them through some kind of immaculate conception." I make a face.

"Hmm. Don't think that's gonna happen."

We pause our conversation to order lunch.

"What if your dad fires Murray?" Wyatt asks.

"He can't. Théo's in charge now."

"Ah. Okay. Have you talked to your dad about going to the doctor?"

I grimace. "No. I'm waiting for the right moment. Today he seemed fine . . ."

"If by fine you mean furious."

I smile, relaxing a little. It's hard to be wound up around Wyatt. He's so laid back. I wish I could be like him and not give a shit. "Yeah."

"I hope his blood pressure is okay."

"He should probably have that checked too." We share a look—amusement and understanding and acknowledgment of how weird this is.

"A lot of guys would be upset about a picture like that being public," I say. "About the comments."

"I don't read the comments. Jesus, princess, don't ever read the comments."

I laugh. "I know."

"And I'm not upset. It doesn't matter what anyone thinks about me. I live life for myself."

"I guess that's a good philosophy." I trace a finger over the tablecloth. "I think I care too much what other people think." I look up at him hesitantly, through my eyelashes.

He reaches out to take my hand. "Why is that?" he asks quietly.

I can't tell him. "I grew up with a lot of public attention. I suppose it was drilled into me that any trouble a Wynn gets into will be broadcast for the whole world to see."

"That's a lot of pressure."

"Tell me about it," I mutter.

Our server brings our lunch. Wyatt ordered "truck stop" eggs, sausage, bacon, and potatoes. I guess he burns a gazillion calories a day. But my salad looks delicious—gem lettuce topped with beets, feta, sumac, and a Meyer lemon vinaigrette.

"I like food," he says with satisfaction, cutting into a sausage.

"Me too. I wish I could eat as much as you."

"You should eat however much you want."

"If I want to weigh two hundred pounds, sure."

He shrugs. "You'd be gorgeous if you weighed that much."

My jaw drops. "You lie."

He regards me with a puzzled notch between his eyes. "No."

"Your privilege is showing," I mutter, forking up a piece of beet. "You don't know what the pressure on women to look good is like."

"I guess I don't." He nods. "You don't have to be perfect, you know."

I pause. *Oh yes I do.* But I just shrug. "Can I try your potatoes?"

"Sure." He moves his cutlery out of my way.

I reach over and fork up some potatoes, lifting them to my mouth. I close my eyes as I savor them . . . seasoned perfectly, crispy on the outside, melting soft on the inside. "Mmm. So good."

When I open my eyes and look at him, he's staring at me with a hungry expression and dark eyes. "Christ," he mutters, then bends his head and stabs another sausage.

Oh. That must have sounded . . . orgasmic.

Oops.

12

EVERLY

"I guess we should be clear about what we're doing," I manage to say, my face hot.

"What do you mean?"

"These 'dates' we have to go on. They're just for show. Right?"

"Wrong." He eats his sausage, meeting my eyes with a bland expression.

"What? What do you mean, wrong?"

"Okay, they are for show. But that doesn't mean we can't have fun together."

"Oh no." I shake my head, waving my fork. "This isn't about fun. It's about saving the team and the league from bad PR."

"Come on, princess." He leans forward, his lips curving downward in annoyance. "Why are you so against having fun?"

"Fun is dangerous. That's what got us into this mess, remember?"

One corner of his mouth hitches up.

"Fun is only safe if it's carefully planned and controlled."

"That's bullshit." He calmly takes a bit of toast.

"Nope. Those are my rules."

"I don't think you're in a position to be setting rules here."

I gape at him. "What do you mean?"

"I'm the one who doesn't care what happens with this little incident. You, however, do. Therefore, you need to play by my rules." He smiles.

My breath sticks in my chest. My heart bumps against my breastbone. God, that smile . . .

"You know what Vince Lombardi said," he continues.

"What?"

" 'Winning isn't everything, it's the only thing.' "

"Vince Lombardi didn't say that."

"What?"

I shrug. "Everyone thinks he did. It was actually Red Sanders." I narrow my eyes at him. "Do you really believe that?"

"Of course."

"Is this a game to you?"

"Everything is a game, princess. And if winning isn't everything . . . why do we keep score?"

I've stopped eating, my fork poised in midair. I don't know how to deal with this man.

"So," he says, continuing to eat, as if we're talking about the weather. "We're going to have fun together."

"Define 'fun.'"

"Really?" He arches an eyebrow. "Here?"

My inner muscles squeeze up, my thighs tightening. "That's what I thought you meant."

He laughs.

"We're not having sex." I lean forward to whisper the words fiercely.

"That would definitely be fun."

I sit back in my chair and grind my back teeth together. I want to scream! "That's not what this is about," I insist.

"True."

I frown.

"But there's no reason it can't be part of it. Like I said, we can do this and put on a show, but what we do behind closed bedroom doors is our own business."

I gasp. "And like I said, we're not having sex."

Oops. I might have said that a little too loud. I glance around.

What is he doing to me? I don't lose my composure like this.

"We'll see. How's your salad?"

I blink and look down at it. "Uh. Good."

At that moment, a woman approaches our table with a hesitant smile. "Hi there. I'm sorry to interrupt. My husband and I are just leaving, and I wonder if I could get a quick autograph? My son is a huge fan of yours." She holds out a tent card from the table, folded inside out, and a pen.

Wyatt flashes a charming smile. "Of course." He takes the card and the pen. "What's your son's name?"

"Brandon."

He nods and writes on the card. He's left-handed.

Gah. I don't know why, but I find left-handed men *so* attractive.

The woman catches my eye and returns my smile, then takes the card and pen back from Wyatt. "Thank you so much! He's going to love this!"

"Does he play hockey?"

Gah. More feels. He doesn't have to be so sweet to her, but he is.

"He does! He wants to play for the Condors someday. Maybe he will! Thank you. Enjoy your lunch."

She disappears with a wave.

Now other people in the restaurant are looking at us. Maybe they wonder who Wyatt is, or maybe they recognize him, but nobody else comes over, though I sense their interest as we finish eating.

"I'd better get back to work," I say, my salad done.

"I thought this *was* work for you." He says it mildly, not snidely.

"It is."

He jerks back as if he's been stabbed, slapping a hand to his chest. "Ouch."

"Oh, all right. It was . . ."

"Fun?" he suggests helpfully.

"Maybe a little."

It was more than fun. It was . . . exciting. Frustrating. Energizing.

He seems to have that effect on me.

But we're not having sex.

WYATT

"Hilarious." I shake my head, looking at my phone.

My buddies, who are partying it up in Tahoe, have seen the blog pics of me and the sex shop dude.

New boyfriend?

Jabber texts me.

Something you want to tell us?

Bergie asks, followed by,

It's okay, we aren't judging.

Jimmy texts,

Wish you'd trusted us enough to tell us.
Hate finding out this way.

"Ha-ha."
I text them back

Glad there's no judgment.

Let them ponder on that.
Jabber then texts,

Why the fuck aren't you here anyway?

I stare at my phone for a long moment before I answer that one. *I hate snow.*

I'm also being tagged in all kinds of social media posts and comments. It nearly makes my head explode. The homophobia, I mean; not the fact that they're being dickheads to me. I've got women telling me "such a waste" and men coming on to me and then there are the ones that say "homosexuality is a sin" and "you should be punished." I want to respond to those so badly, but I've been strictly ordered not to. In fact, I shouldn't even be reading them.

I've had haters on social media before. Shit, all you have to do is miss a shot when you're down one goal, or accidently have the puck go in your own net off your skate, and people are all up in arms. They say shit on social media they'd never say to your face. I've learned to ignore it. But this is a bit of an eye-opener what it would be like for a player who's actually gay to come out in this environment.

I was a little ambivalent about being the ambassador for Hockey for All, but this whole situation is making me embrace it. If there's any small thing I can do to improve things for the LGBTQ community in this role, I'll do it. I'd let people think I was gay, but I get where the team is coming from; pretending to be gay to advance LGBTQ rights is the exact wrong thing to do.

I can find other ways, though.

EVERLY

"This is freakin' awesome!" Wyatt gazes around the Coliseum, where we're sitting watching the California Cougars play. We're right on the floor.

I've been to a few games, and I admit it's cool, but I'm not a huge basketball fan. Wyatt seems thrilled, though.

"We're close enough to smell the sweat," I remark dryly.

He laughs.

The lights are bright, gleaming off the wood floor. The crowd and the music are loud, the atmosphere electric as the Cougars lead the Phoenix Suns by only four points.

"Traveling!" Wyatt shouts, leaping to his feet and pointing. "Come on! That was traveling!"

The crowd seems to agree with him, judging by the roar.

I tug at his shirtsleeve. "Sit down."

He subsides back into his seat. "Jesus. These refs are letting all kinds of shit go."

My lips twitch with amusement. "I had no idea you were such a basketball fan."

He shrugs. "I like it okay. Don't watch it much. Yeah!" He shouts and jumps up again as the Cougars sink the ball into the basket. "Woo-hoo! Way to go, Zay! Woop!"

Oh my God, he's loud. He's pumping his arms in the air and cheering. Everyone is cheering. I'm clapping too, of course.

The player who just scored, Isaiah Brown, jogs past and actually gives Wyatt a high five.

Wyatt's face splits into a huge grin and he claps enthusiastically. His passion is infectious, and I find myself eagerly watching the play. He sits again, but in two seconds he's yelling, "Let's go, Jones! Ahhhhh! Come on, boys! Come on!"

"There are assists in basketball, too?" I ask.

Wyatt turns and gives me an affectionate smile that damn near melts me. "Yeah. You get an assist if the scoring player takes two or less dribbles. Regardless of how long they have the ball or what move they used to score."

"How the hell do they keep track of that?" I frown. "Two or less dribbles? Jeez."

"It's not as objective as hockey. In basketball, it's kind of a subjective stat and it depends on the official stats person at the game. Sometimes players get rewarded for assists even if the scoring player does most of the work."

"Huh." I hitch one shoulder and sip my beer. "I'd rather watch a hockey game."

"I like hearing that." Wyatt turns, leans in, and kisses my nose. "Hockey players are better than guys who play with balls."

I choke on a laugh. "Um, yes."

Surprise jolts me at his affectionate gesture, but then I remember we're out in public and on full display. And no doubt Wyatt's antics during the game have garnered a lot of attention.

The team mascot comes our way, a giant cat wearing a Cougars' jersey. He stops in front of Wyatt and puts his hands . . . er, paws . . . out. Wyatt stands and gives them a smack. There's a time-out or something. The music is a peppy song by Shawn Mendes, and Court the Cougar starts dancing with Wyatt.

Sweet smiling Jesus. I can only shake my head and laugh as Wyatt boogies down with the huge cat, people cheering him on around us. Then Court gives me a high five too.

It's the last few minutes of the game, and the crowd starts chanting "defense, defense!" and of course Wyatt's right in there, fist in the air. When the Suns score, there's a huge groan from the crowd.

"Damn!" Wyatt drops his head forward briefly. "It's okay, it's okay. We got this. *Go Cougars!*"

Everyone is on their feet as the game winds down. Even I'm holding my breath when the Suns make another attempt but miss. And even I throw my hands in the air to cheer when that happens and the Cougars get the ball and Isaiah Brown dribbles it up the court. The crowd goes crazy as he shoots . . . and sinks it with two seconds left.

Wyatt cheers and grabs me, picking me right up off the floor in a jubilant hug. Then he plants a hard kiss on my mouth, draws back, and smiles down into my eyes. "That's what I'm talking about, baby!"

He's such a force . . . energetic and enthusiastic and engaging. He pulls me into his web of excitement. I'm as joyful as he is, and I don't even care that much. I've never had so much fun at a basketball game. I grin back at him, holding on to his shoulders as he spins me around.

We make our way out of the arena, Wyatt's arm protectively around me. Then we leave the crowd behind, because of his security pass that takes us out to the parking garage, where he was able to use his parking spot tonight. He nods at the vehicles we pass. "Ever wonder why the hockey players get the shittiest parking spots here?"

I laugh. "Because the Cougars players get the best ones?"

"Yep." He shakes his head. "We know where we rank here."

"Hockey's getting more popular."

"True. Not popular enough to give us prime parking spots and pay us thirty million dollars a year, though." He opens my door for me.

"Five million's not enough?"

"Hey, I'm not complaining. Wait. Don't tell your dad that. Or Théo. Because they should definitely pay me more."

I can't help but laugh. When he's in the driver's seat I say, "Thirty million does sound obscene."

"It's crazy. Where to now?"

"Home?" I ask hopefully.

"My place or yours?"

"That wasn't what I meant."

"No way, princess! We need to celebrate that win. And it's early."

"Here we go again," I mutter. "Okay, it's Saturday night. Where do you want to go?"

"I thought you'd have this all planned out for us. Maximum exposure, right?"

"Sorry to disappoint you."

"You never disappoint me, princess."

"Except if I want to go home too early."

"I'm fine with that as long as I get to come too."

"Wyatt. We talked about this."

He roars out of the parking garage. "We're playing by my rules, remember?"

Shit.

It wouldn't be a problem, except that I'm so damn attracted to him, I want to unfasten my seatbelt, climb across the console, and straddle him. I'm weak. I want him. I know I shouldn't, but he keeps making me like him, and looking at me like I'm beautiful and fascinating, and making suggestive comments that have me think he wants me just as much, and how the hell am I supposed to resist that? *How?*

"Okay, we've done our duty tonight. Let's head back closer to my condo. There's a little place near there I like."

"A bar?"

"Yeah."

"Okay."

He was right; usually I'd be planning things out and making sure we were going to the best place to be seen. I said I want to go home; but the truth is, I want to spend more time with him.

Dammit.

"You're a pretty crazy basketball fan," I comment.

"I figured it would get us some attention."

"You mean you did that on purpose?"

"Well, sort of. I was having fun. But it did cross my mind."

"Oh, you're good."

"Why, thank you," he says with false modesty.

A short drive later we pull into a parking lot behind a little place on Washington. Inside, it's dark and crowded, lots of patrons standing at a long center table, the tables along one wall full, and more people at the bar.

"Yikes." I survey the busy place.

"No worries. Hang on." He disappears into the crowd and a moment later reappears, beckoning me to follow him. I make my way through the people and he leads me to a small table in the corner.

"Hi," the pretty woman with him says to me. She obviously works there, as she's holding menus, but she doesn't look pleased to see me. She lays the menus down on the table. "Your server is Cam. He'll be right with you."

I raise my eyebrows at Wyatt as I shrug out of my jacket and drape it over the back of my chair. "Special treatment?"

"I'm a regular." As usual, he helps me with my chair before sitting himself.

"A regular here? Or with that woman?"

"That woman's name is Abby, and she works here, and since I'm a regular here she knows me." He holds my gaze steadily. "But that's it."

I flatten my lips together briefly. "It's doesn't matter."

He still holds my gaze.

"Okay, that was snippy. I'm sorry."

"She flirts with me. She'd probably go out with me if I asked her. I haven't."

"You don't have to explain to me."

"I *want* to explain to you."

I regard him for a long, heated moment. Okay, yes, I felt a pang of jealousy.

What is wrong with me? This shouldn't be happening! I shouldn't have all these feels . . . the good ones and the bad ones.

"D'you want something to eat?" Wyatt picks up a menu,

"Mmm, sure. Maybe a snack."

He nods. Cam arrives with a much more welcoming smile than Abby had and takes our order of beers and pizza fries, which are waffle fries topped with marinara, mozzarella, and pepperoni. He removes the menus, which is good because the table is tiny.

Wyatt reaches across and clasps both my hands with his. "That was fun. Thanks for the tickets."

"Thanks to my dad. They're his."

"Uh . . . does he know we went to the game together?"

"Yes. He's in on this, remember?"

"Yeah, but he hates it. Or maybe he hates me."

"He doesn't hate you. He told me he likes you."

Wyatt straightens. "He did?"

"Yes. When you were named the ambassador for Hockey for All."

He grins. "Why didn't you tell me this?"

"Because your ego is big enough."

His smile widens. "This is good to know."

I can't help but laugh. "You're terrible."

His fingers tighten around mine and he smirks. "You don't know that. I'm actually really good."

I make a noise kind of like a cough and a laugh. "See what I mean about the ego?"

"I still want a chance to prove to you that younger guys can be better in bed than older guys."

I remember the comment he made about making me come faster than some old guy . . . My lower belly flip-flops and heats. Daaaamn. I want to find out.

Our eyes meet and sizzles slide down my spine.

"Hey, for once you didn't shut me down," he murmurs.

I hold his gaze and his eyes darken.

He leans across the table. "Damn, princess. You got me hard without even saying a word."

My inner muscles squeeze. "I like that."

He closes his eyes briefly as if he's in pain. "You need to feel what you're doing to me."

I let a smile play on my lips. "That would be really inappropriate right now."

"Okay, let's go."

"We can't. We just ordered food."

"Who cares."

Cam brings our beers at that moment and we reluctantly release our hands and sit back.

"Can we get those pizza fries to go?" Wyatt says to Cam. "Something just came up."

I nearly choke.

"Sure!" Cam smiles. "No problem."

"And the check," Wyatt adds.

Cam disappears.

"Something just came up?" I pick up my beer.

"Oh yeah. Something big. And hard."

"I was just setting you up for that."

"I know." We both grin, the eye contact sending sparks through my veins again. "Thanks."

"Anytime."

"We're a good team." He drinks his beer.

"You think so?"

"I do. You just need to let loose a little."

I purse my lips. "Really. And what about you? Maybe you need to take life a little more seriously?"

"Nah. I know how serious life can be. That's why I'm determined to make it fun."

I'm not entirely convinced that life should be all fun, but maybe I'm moving that way . . . a little. Because there's no denying that being with him is . . . fun.

It's more than that, though. It's exciting. It's invigorating. Irresistible.

Cam brings our appetizer, boxed up in a Styrofoam container, and Wyatt deals with the check. I'm only about half done my beer, so I take a couple of big swallows, then push the glass away to reach for my jacket.

"In a hurry?" Wyatt's eyes gleam as he picks up his glass to drain it.

"Can I get a picture with you?"

We both turn to see a young woman standing next to our table. She's smiling nervously at Wyatt, holding up her phone.

"I'm a big fan," she adds.

"Sure." Wyatt stands and moves beside her, smiling. She holds her phone out in front of them and takes a selfie.

"Thank you so much!" She looks at me and says, "Sorry to interrupt."

"No problem." She's kind of cute in her admiration of Wyatt, letting out a little squeal and a hop as she turns away.

"Does that happen a lot?" I ask as we make our way out.

"All the time."

"You love it."

"I'm kidding. It doesn't happen *that* often. And I always appreciate fans."

"Especially young, pretty ones."

He chuckles

"Like you were appreciating the Cougar Corps earlier." The cheerleaders in sparkly, skimpy outfits had definitely attracted his attention as they danced on the basketball court. "I saw them trying to make eye contact with you."

We're outside on the sidewalk now, and he turns to face me, cupping my cheeks with both hands. "I noticed them, yeah. Not gonna lie. I'm a red-blooded guy, of course I'm going to look. But I wasn't making eye contact with any of them. I was with *you*." He brushes a kiss over my mouth.

My chest goes soft and warm.

There he goes again, making me like him.

13

WYATT

I'm dying.

Dying for Everly.

I'm pretty sure I've never been this hot for a woman, and believe me, I like women. Something about her just *gets* to me. I don't know if it's her smile, her sexy body, her scent . . . or her smart mouth. Maybe it's the way she laughed and cheered during the game, grabbing my arm when the Cougars sank a basket. Maybe it's the way she looked at me when I acted like a goof, laughing with me, not at me. I can tell the difference.

I could spend all night sparring with her, but right now I'm desperate to get my hands on her. And my mouth . . .

I make the short drive to my place as if I'm a NASCAR driver, zipping into my garage and throwing the SUV into park. I lead the way into my condo, flicking on lights as we go.

"Here we are again," she murmurs in my kitchen. "I remember this place."

"That's good. You were pretty hungover." I frown. I've been keeping an eye on how much she drinks and fortunately there haven't been any more drunken incidents. Maybe I was wrong . . . maybe she doesn't have a drinking problem.

"I was." She sighs. "But you looked after me."

"Why do you sound surprised by that?"

"I was surprised." She trails her fingertips down my chest. "You seemed like such a player . . . when I woke up in your bed, I wasn't sure what had happened."

I grab her hand and curl my fingers around it. "I would never do anything without your consent. I hope you know that." I meet her eyes directly.

The moment stretches out, full of thickening tension.

She nods. "I know that. You proved it that night."

My chest is full, heat expanding inside me. "Like I told your dad, I'm a good guy."

Her smile is wonderful. "Actually, you are."

"Again with the surprise! Jesus." I'm teasing. Sort of. I don't like it that she thought I was an asshole. But then again, I know I *have* been an asshole to her—baiting her, arguing with her, flirting with her.

She laughs softly, her fingers now sliding back up my chest to my face. "I just needed to get to know you better."

"You're about to get to know me *very* well." I pull her up against me and bend my head to kiss her.

Soft, warm lips meet mine. She makes a little sound and opens to me and I go in deeper, licking into her mouth. Her arms wind around my neck as she presses herself against me. Lust pulses in my balls, my cock thickening.

I slide my hands down to her ass, firm and round in her

snug jeans, urging her even closer . . . into my aching groin. My eager dick loves it and wants more . . .

"You taste amazing." I kiss her cheek, then her jaw. "You feel amazing."

"Oh, so do you." She whimpers, her fingers slipping through my hair. That turns me on even more. "Amazing."

"Do you remember my bedroom?" I kiss her ear.

"Mmm . . . vaguely. Maybe you should refresh my memory."

"Okay." I lift her by her ass. She gasps and wraps her legs around me. I turn and head to the bedroom. I lower her to the floor next to the bed, and reach to turn on the lamp. It's a tiny spotlight with a flexible stand and I turn it so it's pointed at the corner of the room, diffusing the light to a softer glow. "I want to take your clothes off."

Her breath hitches and her eyelashes flutter.

She doesn't stop me.

I lift the hem of the pale pink chunky sweater she's wearing and draw it up and over her head. I suck in a breath. I'd caught glimpses of pink lace in the V-neck of the sweater, but now that I see the silk-and-lace camisole, I'm staggered. I trace a tiny strap over one smooth shoulder, then follow the scalloped edge of the lace with my fingertip, down to the center of her breasts. She's not chesty. Her tits are . . . let's call them . . . dainty. No matter, I love them. I love how they're pushing at the thin silk, her nipples like pebbles. I remember my hands on them, that night . . . how she gasped and whimpered and writhed . . .

Dying. I'm dying.

Gotta get her out of these clothes.

Next, I move to her jeans. I open the button and pull

down the zipper, then shimmy them down her hips. They're ripped to shit in that cool, expensive way, so I have to be careful I don't accidentally destroy them. She's still wearing her boots, ankle boots with a chunky heel, so I gently push her to sit on the edge of the bed while I get those off her feet along with her socks, then the jeans.

"Gorgeous." My voice is hoarse. I run my hands up and down her calves, and she shivers, watching me intently. I reach for her waist, lift her up, and sit her down farther on the bed. She falls back onto her elbows.

I raise her feet to the bed so her knees are bent. Her pink panties match the silky camisole and I press my hands to the inside of her knees to push her legs apart and study the panties closer. "Pretty," I manage to say.

She's watching me, her eyelids half-lowered, lips parted.

Moving between her legs, I stroke up and down the insides of her thighs. She shivers, her nipples hardening even more.

"You need to take off your clothes too," she says in a husky tone.

"Yeah. I do. Don't want to move, though." I lean in and press my mouth to her panties.

She whimpers.

I breathe in her scent, spicy arousal. It's intoxicating. Reluctantly, I stand and unbutton my shirt, not taking my eyes off her. She's gazing at me too, as I shrug out of the shirt and toss it aside. I take my time unzipping my fly, lowering my jeans, enjoying the heat in her eyes and the hitch of her breath. I get rid of my boxer briefs too, and unlike her, I'm totally naked.

The corners of her mouth tilt up and she reaches out a

hand as I climb back onto the bed. She trails her fingertips over my chest, then down my abs. My skin heats to scorching, my dick already hard as a goalpost. She brushes her fingers over the sensitive head and I suck in a sharp breath. My dick twitches.

"Want this, baby?" I grip it and give a firm tug.

"Yes."

"Be patient."

"I'm not patient."

I smile, leaning in again to kiss her smooth inner thigh. "You want to take over?"

"No." The word is a sigh. "I want you to . . . do whatever you want to me."

I pause. I lift my head and meet her eyes. "Yeah?"

"Yeah." Understanding flows between us.

Fuck, yeah.

"I want soft and slow," I murmur, brushing my mouth over her panties again. Her abs tighten. "I want to make you come on my tongue. Then I want to pound into that sweet pussy and feel you squeeze me, and fuck you until you come again and scream."

"Oh Jesus." Her head falls back and her eyes close.

"That sound good?" I lick her hip bone.

"Good . . . yes . . . please."

I kiss her center again over her panties, then crawl up her body, pushing the camisole up, and up, revealing those sweet, sweet tits. She falls flat on her back. "Jesus fuck," I croak, studying them. "Gorgeous." Tight pink nipples beg to be sucked and I cup her with both hands, plumping her flesh and pulling one tip between my lips.

Her back arches and she throws her arms up over her head.

Excellent. I suck and pull at her tender nipples. I fucking love how they feel against my tongue and the sexy little noises of pure enjoyment she makes. Then I shift higher still and kiss her—deep, long, tongue kisses. She opens to me, kisses me back, and sensation radiates through every nerve ending in my body. Her hands touch my face as we kiss . . . and kiss . . . and kiss.

I lick down her throat, between her breasts, over one nipple. "You like this," I say. Not a question.

"I love it. That makes me so hot . . . I'm aching."

"Good. I want that pretty pussy to ache for me."

"Sadist."

"Maybe a little." I suck a nipple again. She writhes. "It'll be good for you too, though."

"Confident."

I guess that did sound kind of cocky. "Tell me what you want. Want to make you feel so good."

"You are." She gasps.

"I want to taste your pussy."

"Yes. Do that."

I kiss my way down her abdomen, my hands still caressing her tits, pinching her nipples. She's panting in breathy little puffs of air. As I open my mouth on the soft skin beneath her bellybutton, her hips lift. "Mmm. I can tell you want it."

"Please. Lick me."

Christ. My dick strains, my balls ache, and the rush of my blood is scalding my veins.

I'm taking my time and maybe torturing her a bit, but I'm torturing myself too.

I spread her thighs wide, curl an arm beneath one, and tug her panties aside. Fucking beautiful. My blood on fire, I taste her, a long, slow slide of my tongue over the softest flesh.

She pushes back up onto her elbow, one hand landing on the back of my head and rubbing over it as she watches me eat her, licking, sucking her, sinking a finger deep inside her.

"Are you aching here?"

"Yes . . ."

"Good. Wanna take care of that." I lick right over her clit.

"Oh Jesus," she gasps. As if she can't stay still, her hips move, her belly muscles contract. "Not already . . ."

I do it again. And again. I curl my finger inside her. Cries fall from her lips in a stream and she drops back down, raising her pussy to my mouth. I close my lips around the quivering nub and suck.

I feel her contract, her thighs tensing, her abdomen hollowing. She almost weeps as she comes, and my chest fills with effervescence. Gently, I lick her, tasting her orgasm on my tongue, and lay one more soft kiss on the patch of dark hair on her mound.

"Oh God." She's flat on her back, trembling, eyes closed.

"Okay, pretty princess?" I climb up over her again, wiping my mouth.

"I'm . . . yes."

"I need a condom. Be right back."

"'Kay."

I don't have to go far; they're in my bathroom. I grab one and roll it on. When I return, she hasn't moved. I smile.

I hook my fingers into her panties and drag them off, then help her lift up so I can pull off the camisole. I'm careful because it's delicate . . . and so is she.

"So beautiful." My eyes eagerly devour her—smooth skin, soft curves, her mouth a fantasy.

She opens her eyes to smile lazily at me. "You're beautiful too." She lifts a languid hand to trace my abs again, right down to the root of my cock. "Fuck me."

"Oh yeah." On my knees, between her thighs, I guide myself to her entrance and ease in. She's so wet, it's a slow, sweet glide of pleasure, but I'm careful anyway. I watch her face. She tips her chin up and her eyelashes flutter down as I fill her. "Okay?"

"Yes," she whispers. "Do it."

I'm holding back, adrenaline flooding my body, wanting to take and take . . . I think it's what she wants, but I don't want to hurt her. Seated inside her, my balls pressed against her, I plant one fist into the mattress beside her and caress her breast with my other hand, then touch her face. I drag my thumb over her bottom lip and she sucks it in. Our eyes meet in a burst of heat. Her tongue swirling over my thumb damn near makes my cock explode.

I lower myself over her to kiss her, openmouthed, my tongue licking inside, and then I move . . . my hips slowly rocking forward and back, my cock tunneling in and out of her slick channel. I rise back up and lift one of her legs so her ankle is on my shoulder, then I squeeze her breast again as I move faster. I can't take my eyes off her beautiful, expressive face . . . her lust-blown pupils, swollen lips, pink cheeks. She watches me too, our gazes connected in some kind of powerful link that neither of us can break. I've never done this before. Eye contact like this is . . . scarily intimate. But right now, it's breathtaking. Epic. Unescapable.

I plunge into her again and again, not holding back now, fucking her hard and fast. Her soft cries pick up tempo and volume. I love how noisy she is.

Goddamn, I want to go all night like this, watching her, listening to her, feeling her pussy around my cock all velvety and hot, but I can't. Pressure builds, tension torquing inside me. Heat sizzles up my spine, then back down, centering in the small of my back.

I find her clit with my fingers. She jolts at my touch, still sensitive, but whimpers her encouragement. I circle wet fingers over it. "There?"

"Not quite . . . higher . . . a bit more . . . ohhhhhh *God*, yes, there . . ."

She contracts around my dick, rippling, squeezing, and I shout as my own orgasm roars through me. My vision goes black, my ears buzz, and I hold myself deep inside her as I release in in thick, heavy pulses.

"Fuuuck," I groan, and pant. Jesus. I think I just died. I hope not, though, because I want to do this again.

I kiss her knee, then slowly lower her leg to the bed. Holding the condom, I ease out. For a second, I'm afraid it broke, because she's so creamy, but it looks okay. I drop down beside her and lay my hand on her stomach. "I'm just gonna go get another condom."

She laughs breathily. "No."

"What?" I turn my head to smile at her.

"Already?"

"Sure." I smirk. "That's why being with a younger guy is so great."

She snorts.

"Also I'm a hockey player." I kiss her nose. "Good endurance. I can go at least sixty minutes."

She laughs and stretches. "Okay, fine, you've convinced me."

"Good."

14

EVERLY

I drift half-asleep, awash in lovely, warm sensation as Wyatt kisses his way down my back—soft, openmouthed kisses, his tongue lingering in the small of my back. My eyes flutter open and close again. Then fly open as the numbers on the clock beside his bed come into focus.

What day is it? Sunday . . .

"Oh my God!" My head snaps up and I roll away from Wyatt.

He sits back on his heels, staring at me. "Uh . . ."

"I have to get up!" I roll off the bed, nearly falling on the floor. I stand with my hands in my hair, disoriented, looking around Wyatt's room. "Shit! I'm going to be late!"

"Late for what?" His forehead creases. "It's Sunday morning."

"I know!" I grab my clothes, still lying on the floor from when he undressed me last night. This isn't a sexy, graceful moment as I struggle into my panties and bra.

166

Wyatt moves off the bed too, and hands me my jeans.

"I have to be somewhere." I fight my way into the skinny jeans, my feet catching in the blown-out knees. "Argh!"

"Where? I'll take you."

"In the same clothes I wore last night?" I close my eyes briefly.

"Where are we going?" he asks again, patiently.

I take a breath and blow it out. "I don't . . . okay, fine. I volunteer Sunday mornings at a homeless shelter." I pull on my camisole.

His mouth drops open. "Oh. Okay."

"It's not far from my place. I can change quickly. I'm supposed to be there by ten, but if I'm a few minutes late, they won't kick me out."

"Okay." He grabs a pair of boxers out of a drawer, steps into his jeans, and dons a clean T-shirt. "I didn't know you did that."

"Nobody does," I mutter.

He shoots me a curious look and waves me out of the bedroom ahead of him. Soon we're cruising along Pacific Avenue. It's sunny but wicked windy, palm trees blowing and tossing.

Shit, shit, shit. I hate being late. I'm never late. I'd rather be somewhere way too early than be late.

"Relax," Wyatt says, shooting me a sideways glance. "What's wrong?"

"I hate being late."

"Yeah, I hate it when a woman is late too."

I scowl at him. "You're disgusting."

He laughs. "Lighten up, princess. What are they going to do? Fire you?"

"Ha." I wrinkle my nose. "I don't know why I hate it so much."

"Could it be because you have to be perfect?"

"I don't . . ." I shut my mouth, and he laughs softly.

"So why the secret volunteer work?"

I sigh. "It's not secret, exactly. I just don't like to talk about it. I started doing it about a year ago."

"Yeah?"

"I know the work I do every day gives back to the community, but it feels . . . distant, sometimes. I sit in an office and manage a bunch of people and we raise lots of money. Then my dad hands out a giant check and makes people happy. But I hardly ever get to see the results of giving that money. So I found something I can do myself. Nobody at the shelter knows who I am."

"Ah."

"I know I'm privileged. I grew up with money and everything I needed. My parents were both pretty firm about making sure we didn't totally take it for granted, but even so . . . I don't want to live in a bubble and not know how tough things are for some people. And maybe give back in some small way."

He nods slowly.

At my place, I hurry inside, Wyatt following me. I quickly change into clean clothes, jeans with a Hope Home T-shirt. I wash my face, still wearing remnants of last night's makeup, pull my hair back into a ponytail, and smash a baseball cap down onto my head.

Wyatt grins when he sees me.

"What?"

"You look cute. Ready to roll?"

"Yup."

I give him directions to Hope Home. He parks in the lot beside it, turns off the SUV, and opens his door.

"What are you doing?"

"Coming in to help."

"Oh." I bite my lip. "You don't have to do that."

"I want to."

"What if they recognize you?"

"I don't care."

I nibble my lip.

"Oh. *You* do."

"Just . . . please don't call me princess. Everyone knows me as 'Ev.' You won't be able to help cook—you have to go through a screening process. But they'll probably be fine if you help serve."

He follows me in. I'm greeted by a couple of the staff there—Joan and José—and other volunteers. On Sundays, it's quite often me, Layla, Robert, and Rufus. I introduce Wyatt as "my friend, who'd like to help serve" and Joan and José shake hands with him, neither of them giving any indication they know who he is.

I head into the kitchen where Layla, Robert, and Rufus are already working.

"Sorry I'm late!" I call to them as I tie the big apron around my waist.

"No worries. We figured you'd show up." Rufus gives me a big smile.

I put on a pair of latex gloves and set to work chopping up vegetables for a big salad. Rufus is mixing up a bowl of chicken salad to make sandwiches, and Joan is stirring a huge pot of soup. "That soup will be popular today. It's cold out there!"

I'm aware of Wyatt up front, probably setting tables. I have no idea what he thinks of this, except . . . he's here. That's kind of sweet. He doesn't have to do this. My heart feels full in my chest and I'm smiling as I work.

I think about last night . . . about how careful he was with me, and yet when he realized what I like, he gave it to me. He's generous and thoughtful . . . and oh God, so sexy. Sex with him was indescribable, more than just a physical experience. I feel like I've been changed, like I never knew what sex and intimacy really were, sharing our thoughts and feelings and desires.

Also, my thighs hurt and every time I move it reminds me of everything we did, and I want more.

It's actually a little scary.

We were just supposed to go on a few dates and maybe get our picture taken a couple of times.

It's okay. I can do this.

The kitchen is warm and I'm sweaty. I wipe the back of my hand across my forehead, then pick up a huge stainless-steel container of food and haul it out front to the big table where we set up the lunch.

There's Wyatt . . . he's wearing gloves and a hairnet—oh my God!—and sitting at a table talking to Tiana. She's a regular here, and in the last year her life has totally changed.

"I got sick," I hear her telling Wyatt. "My doctors couldn't figure out what was wrong with me. Then I couldn't get out of bed anymore and I missed time from work and I lost my job."

He shakes his head, listening intently, and my heart does a flip in my chest. I set the tray on the table, but pause to listen.

"I had doctor bills and no money coming in," she continues matter-of-factly, although I know how hard this has been for her. "I had to give up my apartment. I went to a lady on the street and asked her to give me lessons on how to be homeless." She chuckles, her dark brown face crinkling as she smiles.

Wyatt's eyes flash and the corners of his lips turn down. I can tell her story moves him. Hell, it moves *me*, my throat thickening.

"I lived in my car for a while," Tiana continues. "Then I found this place. I got medical help. Figured out what was wrong with me. And next month . . . I move into my own place. They helped me find a home." Her voice breaks with emotion now too.

Wyatt squeezes her hand. "That's fantastic."

"It really is. This place saved my life. I finally had a roof over my head and a support system. Everyone here treats me with respect and dignity. They helped me rebuild my life."

Emotion swells in me and I duck back into the kitchen to bring out the pot of soup.

Wyatt strides toward me to relieve me of the heavy pot. I show him where to put it. As he ladles up soup into bowls, he flashes his magnetic grin at everyone. There are people I know in the line and some I don't, and I chat with all of them as I use tongs to lift sandwiches onto plates, Layla, next to me, is dealing with the salad.

"Thanks, Ev," says Zion, a regular. "You're a sweetheart."

I smile at him. "Aw, get out."

He laughs.

I catch Wyatt's eye and he smiles.

My heart bumps.

Damn.

When everyone has eaten, I stay to help put away food and clean up so the place is ready for the volunteers who'll come in shortly to start dinner prep. Nobody objects when Wyatt comes into the kitchen and scrubs some pots. I can't believe he's doing this.

Finally, I take my apron off. "Okay, we're done," I tell him.

"You know what? I'm starving."

"Oh my God, me too. We didn't even have time for breakfast."

"Let's go get some food."

We head out to his vehicle. It's warmed up a little outside, and inside his SUV it's toasty from the sun.

"Where are we going?" I ask.

"My place."

"Oh. I guess we're not exactly dressed for somewhere nice."

"Well, that too. It just doesn't feel right . . . to go somewhere and spend a bunch of money on food."

I eye him. "I know." I'm taken aback that he feels the same. He gets it. "We can go to my place, if you want. It's closer, and I have food."

"Okay, sure." He pauses. "Now I know why you do that."

I nod.

"When I was talking to Tiana, I damn near started bawling."

I swallow hard. "I know. She's amazing."

"So are you." He reached for my hand and squeezes. "Do you go there every Sunday?"

"Pretty much. I also, uh, help clean up the beach sometimes."

"Like, you just go out and pick up garbage?"

"I meet up with a group who does it."

He slides a glance my way. "So when you were going off on me about caring about the environment, you weren't kidding."

"No."

"Huh." He stares out the windshield.

I don't know what he's thinking.

He parks on the street outside my building and I lead the way in. I did pick up groceries yesterday, so I'm sure I can find something to make us.

"Did I tell you I like your place?" he says, following me through the living room toward the kitchen.

"Um, no."

"It's very . . . calm."

I smile. "Thank you! That was my goal."

"You seem like a calm person." Then his eyebrows pull together. "Except in bed."

"Ah." If only knew how *not* calm I am on the inside. "Is that bad or good?"

"That's good. *Very* good." He pulls me against him and

loops his arms around me. "Thank you for letting me help out this morning."

"I don't think I 'let' you do anything." I smile up at him. "Thank *you*, for doing it."

He kisses me, a soft but lingering kiss that melts my brain. Everything inside me goes soft and weak. I rise up onto my toes and wrap my arms around his neck and kiss him back. I can't help it; I just feel I have to. On some level I know this isn't good, but I don't even care right now. I just want to kiss him and show him my gratitude and appreciation and admiration and . . . oh God, I'm in big trouble.

He pats my butt. "Okay, what are we eating? Besides you, later."

My belly flips. "I have some ham . . . how about Denver sandwiches?"

"Sounds great. What can I do?"

I get him chopping onions while I whisk up some eggs and dice the ham. We chat about the shelter and more about the game last night as we cook together, then sit down at my table to eat.

"This is great." He finishes off two sandwiches easily.

"Mmm." I wipe my fingers on a paper napkin. "I was hungry."

"Now I need a nap." He stands and picks up his plate. "After we clean up."

My mind is jumping around, trying to decipher what that meant. Is he going home? Is he staying? Did he mean he really wants a nap?

He helps me wash the omelet pan and load the dishwasher. Drying his hands on a towel, he prowls up to me. He drops the towel, plucks my baseball cap off my head, and slides the hair tie off my ponytail. My hair falls around my face and he threads his fingers through it, holding the back of my head, peering into my eyes. "Let's go back to bed."

My heart leaps and my belly flip-flops. "Oh, you meant a 'nap.'" I make air quotes.

He laughs. "You know what I meant. Although truthfully, there may be sleep involved because I sure as hell didn't get much last night. You just wouldn't leave me alone."

My first reaction is to gasp with outrage, but I'm getting to know how he pushes my buttons, so I simply smile and rub my fingertips over the stubble on his jaw. "And you loved it."

"I did." He takes my hand and leads me upstairs to my bedroom.

WYATT

"Wyatt?"

"Mmm?"

"Who was that little boy I saw you with? New Year's Day . . ."

I stiffen, then force myself to relax. Since she's pressed up against me in her bed, she probably noticed, though. I'd forgotten that day I ran into her at the pier. "He's a friend's kid."

"Oh. I was wondering if you had a son."

"Jesus! Uh, no, he's not mine. I have no kids."

"That you know about."

I groan. I made that joke on New Year's Eve. No wonder she thought Owen was mine. "Seriously. And if I did, I sure as hell would know."

"Okay."

We lay snuggled together. A few minutes later, I ask, "Why do you have to be perfect all the time?" I stroke her arm.

She sighs. "I don't really want to talk about it."

"I know your secrets. I know about your volunteer work. I know you're worried about your dad. You can tell me."

After a pause, she says slowly, "When I was a teenager, I got in some . . . trouble. I wasn't arrested or anything," she adds hastily. "But it was a potential scandal that had my parents really upset. They were so disappointed in me. My dad had to . . . well, he got involved and saved my ass, and I guess I feel like I owe them. Ever since then I've tried to make it up to them."

I think about this. When I was sixteen, I got caught with having alcohol underage. The cops called my parents and told them. I didn't get arrested or anything either, but I knew my parents were disappointed in me. "I think every teenager goes through that. Every teenager screws up somehow."

"I suppose. But not every teenager is a Wynn."

"That makes it worse?"

"Well, some teenagers get in trouble and nobody ever knows about it. With us . . . it's hard to keep stuff like that out of the media."

"That's a lot of pressure on a kid."

She lets out another short sigh. "Yeah. It can be. There

are a lot of benefits that come from wealth and privilege, but there are some negatives too."

I call her princess. And in a way she is. But she's a lot more than that.

She volunteers at the shelter. Nobody knows who she is. She does that for no reward. Nobody knows about it. She helps clean up the beach.

She grew up with a shit ton of expectations and pressure and now I'm starting to see why she's so perfect . . . she thinks she has to be.

But nobody's perfect and it worries me that she puts that much of a burden on herself.

I roll her under me and kiss her, slow and sustained and sweet. "You don't always have to be perfect," I murmur against her cheek. "Around me. I just want you to know that."

"Oh." Her eyelashes flutter and her bottom lip quivers. "That's the sweetest thing anyone's ever said to me, I think."

Holy shit. What does *that* say?

"I like you when you're not perfect . . . when you're messy and aching and wet. I like messing you up and having dirty, messy, fun sex with you."

She wraps her arms around my neck and kisses me again, a deep kiss full of emotion. My heart expands hard against my sternum at the vulnerability she just revealed to me. I want to protect her. Take care of her. And . . . fuck her.

15

EVERLY

I'M SITTING IN MY OFFICE MONDAY MORNING WITH Murray.

Pictures of Wyatt and me are all over TV and social media. Sitting courtside at a Cougars game will do that. And Wyatt's antics helped; him dancing with the mascot provides entertaining clips. The sports commentators on the big networks are getting a kick out him cheering on the Cougars, and other blogs are posting a picture of him kissing me. That one's being retweeted and shared on Facebook and Instagram over and over.

I don't know why I didn't think of this, but of course I'm inundated with texts from Lacey, Taylor, and . . . my mom.

Ack. Dad didn't tell Mom what was going on?

Then my stomach cramps as I realize there's a definite possibility he forgot to.

"This is perfect," Murray says. "We don't even have to

make any statement to counter the rumors that started after the picture from the sex shop."

I rub my forehead. "Great."

"Just a couple more outings," he adds.

Great.

"This weekend will be a good time," he says. "At the presser to announce Wyatt as our ambassador—you should be there too. That would get some media attention."

"Right. Sure." Blergh.

Murray leaves and I drop my head back against my chair.

Wyatt stayed at my place the rest of the day yesterday. We fooled around a bunch, slept a little, ordered pizza, and fooled around more before he went home.

He was right—his endurance is impressive.

It's also impressive—no, that's not the right word for it . . . exciting? Maybe flattering?—that he wants me that much. Like he can't get enough of me. Touching. Kissing. Fucking.

Oh God. I'm getting that low-down, achy feeling again. Like I can't get enough of *him*.

Just a couple more outings.

I better figure something out for our next date. I guess we could hit some other trendy restaurant where the celebs go to be seen. Ugh. This idea doesn't appeal to me, but hey, that's what I signed up for! I open my browser and start clicking, my chin resting on one hand.

I bookmark a couple of sites and I'll check with Wyatt about when he wants to go. It's still All Star week, so he's off until practice before their next game a week from today. Other than the press conference on Friday.

Tonight, I better set up dinner with Taylor and Lacey. But first, I have to call my mom.

"Hey, Mom! I saw your texts." Plural.

"Evvie! What's going on? You said there was nothing with you and Wyatt Bell."

"There isn't." Okay, I'm totally lying now. We had sex, pretty damn amazing sex, so there's . . . something. "I'm sorry I didn't tell you . . . I thought Dad would."

"Tell me what?" Confusion shades her voice.

"Well, this is top secret, but I know I don't have to tell you that. Last week Wyatt and I were out one night, and someone took a picture—"

"A picture of you and him?"

"No, just him. It was a little, um . . ."

"Compromising?"

"No, not exactly. It just started some rumors—"

"Tell me where the picture is. I'll figure it out."

I grin and give her the name of the entertainment blog. "So we thought if he and I were seen together a few times, it would dispel the rumors. Not that it's a big deal, and Wyatt doesn't care himself, but he's going to be our ambassador for Hockey for All this year, so we don't want negative attention for that."

"Of course not," she murmurs dryly. I think dryly. "Oh, I see the picture." She makes a little noise as if repressing a laugh. "I'm not even going to ask what you were doing."

"Yeah, it was really nothing. Wyatt has a weird sense of humor. So Dad was part of this plan, although he wasn't thrilled about it."

"He didn't say anything."

I know we're both thinking the same thing. I pull in a

long breath. "Well, maybe he just wanted to keep it on the down low."

"He knows I'd never reveal confidential information about the team."

I don't know what to say. "Did you talk to him again about going to the doctor?"

"Yes. I blamed you. I said you're worried too."

"Great. And . . . ?"

"Now he's being passive aggressive. He says he'll go, but he hasn't done anything about making an appointment."

"You make it. Go with him."

"Ugh. I hate treating him like a child."

I bite my lip. I guess being so much younger than him, she probably knew something like this could happen in their marriage. But that doesn't make it any easier. What happens when the person who's your partner becomes someone you have to treat like a child? I rub the sharp ache in my chest. "Do you want me to do it?"

"No." Her voice is soft but firm. "That's not your job as his daughter. I'm here. I'll deal with it."

"Okay. But I'm here to help. With anything."

"I know. I love you. Um . . . as for Wyatt . . . you two looked like you were having a lot of fun."

"Wyatt's an expert at fun. I'm just along for the ride."

"You could use more fun in your life. You're a young woman, not an old lady."

"I have lots of fun!"

"Uh-huh. You work long hours. You don't date much. You go to the odd yoga class and spend your spare time knitting. You might as well take up bingo."

I choke on a laugh. "Mom! I have friends. I'm planning to see them tonight in fact."

"I'm just saying. Fun isn't a bad thing."

"Fun can get you in trouble."

"Oh, Evvie." The sadness in her voice undoes me.

"It's okay, Mom. My life is great. Anyway, now you know what's going on. I better get back to work."

"Okay, sweetie. Talk to you soon. Love you."

I send a message to Taylor and Lacey suggesting dinner, to which they eagerly agree. We make a plan to meet at Food for Thought Bar and Grill for Appie Hour (yes, that's spelled correctly; they have five-dollar appetizers from four till seven on Mondays).

In the meantime, I have this charity watchdog group snooping around. Not literally, but they've emailed me a few times with requests for information and they're making me nervous as hell.

"What is happening?" Lacey demands once we're all seated at the wooden table in Food for Thought. Her eyes bug out. "What were you doing with Wyatt at the basketball game?"

I've already decided I'll tell her and Taylor the truth, because they're my best friends and I trust them, but . . . "I have to swear you to secrecy."

They exchange wide-eyed looks, then nod solemnly.

The waiter arrives to take our drink order, drawing out

the suspense. I can see Lacey's impatience and I have to grin.

We order different kinds of beer from the many they have on tap so we can try one another's.

Once that's done, I relate the story to them. They listen, mesmerized, then kill themselves laughing.

"Jeez, you're so funny," Taylor says, wiping her eyes.

"Did you see the picture of him in that neoprene singlet?"

"Nope." But Lacey's already got her phone out and it takes her no time to find it. Her eyes pop as she stares at it.

Taylor leans over for a gander as well. "Holy shit!" She throws her head back to laugh again. "I have to say, he looks amazing in that."

"I thought so too. Oh my God, it was so crazy."

"Okay, so I'm not sure I totally buy this whole PR thing," Lacey says. "But the more important point, which you skimmed over, is *why were you out with him before that?*"

"A moment of weakness." I smile as the waiter arrives with cold, frosty beer glasses. We pause again to order food.

"Go on," Taylor says.

"Okay, I'm attracted to him. He asked me out, and I knew it was a really bad idea, but I just . . . wanted to. Then I had second thoughts and I tried to get out of it, only he wasn't having it."

"It sounds like you had fun, though."

I sigh. "Yes. It was crazy. But fun. And hey, you know what? He doesn't have a son."

They both frown.

"Oh, right," Lacey says. "You saw him with a little boy."

"It's a friend's kid."

"Ah. You believe him?"

I jerk back. "Yes." I divide a look between them. "Wyatt's a smart-ass and a partier, but he's not a liar."

Once again, they slowly nod in unison.

"What? You think he is?"

"No, no," Lacey says quickly. "I like Wyatt."

"He's extremely bangable," Taylor adds. "And I mean that in an objective way. Not that I personally want to bang him."

"Oh. Yeah . . . he is." I say it with such heartfelt emotion, they both straighten and fix their gazes on me intently. I realize what I just gave away.

"You banged him?" Lacey gasps. "Already?"

"What do you mean already? We've been having foreplay for months."

Taylor bursts out laughing. "That is so true."

"I didn't mean to sound judgey," Lacey says apologetically. "There's not a waiting period before you can bone someone."

I laugh. "Okay, thanks."

"Um, that could make things messy, though, if you're only doing this for the PR." Taylor's eyebrows slant down.

"I know." I sip my beer. "I thought of that. Apparently my determination to never screw up isn't that robust. My vagina betrayed me."

"Fickle bitch," Lacey says, and we all laugh.

"I'll deal with it, whatever happens." I shrug. *I hope.*

"Was it worth it?" Taylor eyes me over her glass.

"Oh, hell yeah."

They both reach across the table to high-five me.

We gorge ourselves on too many appies—truffled parmesan fries, wings, mozza sticks, and roasted Brussel sprouts.

"What's happening with Byron?" I ask Taylor.

Byron is her dog. When her parents split up last year, they didn't know what to do with him, which was heartbreaking for Taylor, because she loves that dog. She had to move to an apartment that didn't allow pets. JP, her boyfriend now but at the time he wasn't, offered to take Byron. Hey, they may have to make Byron the best man at their wedding to thank him for bringing them together. Assuming they get married. Anyway, Taylor's dad recently bought a new house and is supposed to take Byron.

"Oh! Good news." Taylor beams. "I talked to Dad and he was fine with letting Byron stay at JP's."

"Oh, that's great! You'll see him a lot more there." She has to help look after him because JP travels a lot, obviously, with the Golden Eagles.

"Yes! Although Dad was hesitant. He didn't get a very good impression of JP, since the first time he met him was when Byron ate chocolate and he was so sick. He thought JP wasn't doing a very good job looking after him."

"Ugh." I grimace. "JP felt terrible about what happened."

"I know. And Dad's getting to know him better and he can see that JP really loves Byron."

"So you're probably spending even more time at JP's place now."

"Yep." She smiles, contentment and love softening her features.

Love. How sweet.

Okay, okay, it is.

"How's your dad doing?" I ask.

"Fine, I guess."

"Not seeing anyone?"

"Not that I know of. Honestly, I think he's still in love with my mom." Taylor swipes at condensation on the outside of her beer glass, her lips drooping.

"Aw. That's sad."

"It is." Taylor sighs. "And it makes it really hard to be happy for my mom. I don't want to take sides, but . . . I feel so bad for him."

Lacey, sitting beside Taylor, bumps her shoulder into Taylor's in sympathy.

"I was feeling bad for *my* mom today," I tell them.

"Why?" They regard me curiously.

I told Wyatt about my fears for my dad before I told my best friends. That's really weird. But having talked about it once, it feels easier now. So I tell them the things I've noticed, my worries, and the fact that my mom shares them.

"It's weird when you're at an age where you worry about your parents, isn't it?" Taylor says sympathetically. "Our whole lives, they looked after us."

"I looked after my mom when she was dying," Lacey says. "It's really hard. But we have each other. I'm here for you guys, whatever you need."

My throat aches. "Thank you. And same goes for me. Hey, Lace, have you been able to talk to Aline?"

"No, I haven't. But we're seeing Matthew and Aline this weekend. I'll see what I can do."

"Okay, good."

"What about you? Have you talked to your mom about the money?"

"Yes." I wrinkle my nose. "She wasn't informative. I'm sure she knows exactly what's going on, though. She just basically told me to keep my nose out of it."

"Ugh." Lacey purses her lips. "I have a feeling she knows everything."

"Why do you say that?"

"Just my intuition. Théo is even coming around to that idea."

"Really?" My mouth falls open. "I thought he hates my mom."

"No!" Then she stretches her lips into a grimace. "Well, not hate, but there were bad feelings. That's no secret. But I'm an outsider and I guess I'm seeing things differently, and kind of opening his eyes."

"JP says he's always liked Chelsea," Taylor adds.

I smile. "Well, *I* think my mom is awesome."

"I agree," Lacey says firmly. "Whatever happened to that money, I'm sure she wasn't involved."

"Then how does she know what's going on?"

"Well, I could come up with several different stories that I could make up. One of them might be true."

I laugh. "I've imagined a lot of different scenarios too." Usually lying in my bed at night when I can't sleep.

"Okay, back to Wyatt," Lacey says with determined cheerfulness. "Are you going tell us about the sex?"

"No. Who's going to yoga Saturday morning?"

"Oooh, me, me!" Taylor says. "I want to. Come on, Lacey. You're so stubborn about this."

"I will fall in the water."

We go to a stand-up paddleboard yoga class in Marina del Rey. It's really cool. Being on the water adds an extra soothing component to the yoga poses. Lacey refuses to try it, though.

"Fine." I sigh. "I think you'd like it, though."

"Lace, tell us about doing Rielle Simpson's makeup," Taylor urges her. Rielle is an up-and-coming young African American actress.

"I really want to hear about sex with Wyatt," Lacey pouts.

I laugh. "Absolutely not. Because if you two tell me about sex with my nephews, I'll be grossed out forever."

WHEN I GET HOME, I TOSS MY COAT IN THE CLOSET, KICK off my heels, and grab my phone. I throw myself down onto my couch and prop my bare feet on the coffee table, and scroll through my social media.

But first . . . there's a text from Wyatt.

A silly smile tugs at my lips as I open the message app. God. I can't believe how happy a text from him makes me feel. This is ridiculous.

I have an idea for our next date.

Huh. I push out my bottom lip and reply.

Yeah? What is it?

He answers right away.

Hiking!

I frown.

I don't think so.

What? Why not? It'll be fun. We can do a trail in the hills.

First of all, nobody will see us. That defeats the purpose of the date.

It takes him a few minutes to reply.

Oh yeah.

I was thinking about a fancy dinner.

I know.

I mean, I like having dinner with u.

I smile.

Fine. When?

Saturday?

Hell no! Not waiting that long to see u.

My chest heats. I don't know what to say to that.

We could go for a hike anyway. Just for fun.

I have to work.

U can take an afternoon off. Ur the boss.

I grin. I don't do things like that—take an afternoon off just to have fun. Take advantage of the fact I'm the director of the Foundation. But he's tempting me . . . again. I tap in my reply:

Okay.

Pick u up at ur place at 1 tomorrow.

Tomorrow? Eep! I inhale and slowly let the air out of my lungs.

Okay.

Sure, it'll be fun. But you never know who might see us hiking in the hills.

WYATT

"WHERE ARE WE GOING?"

"Hollywood, baby." I grin as I drive. I made sure she had on appropriate clothing—no four-inch heels or a tight skirt. I approve of her snug cropped black leggings, performance layers, and Nike shoes. Her hair is in a ponytail and big sunglasses perch on her nose.

I park on Wonder View Drive and we get out to begin our hike. It's a perfect day for it—sunny but cool. I've got a backpack with water and snacks in it and we set off along the paved road. The views of the downtown skyline and the Hollywood Reservoir are spectacular.

We reach the end of the street and find the path. It's steep and uneven. We both have to watch our footing, and in a few minutes, Everly is breathing hard. I pause. "You okay, princess?"

"I'm fine." She narrows her eyes at me. "I work out. Of course, I'm not a professional athlete like you."

Pro athlete or not, it's a workout, and even I'm feeling it by the time we get to the ridge.

"Let's go see the tree," I say, pointing to the sign with an arrow directing us to Burbank Peak.

"You've done this before," Everly puffs.

"Once. Don't tell me you haven't. You're a native Los Angeles . . . Angelesian."

She laughs. "Angeleno. And no, I haven't done this hike."

"We can sit for a while when we get there."

"Great."

We arrive at the Wisdom Tree. We're not alone here, with small groups of people walking around to check out the view.

"It's nice," Everly says, wiping her brow when we get to the top.

"Want some water?"

"Yes, please."

I pull out an insulated bottle and hand it to her, then grab the second one to take a drink.

We stroll over to the big pine tree and take a seat on a couple of the rocks.

"Glad I'm not afraid of heights." Everly surveys the view stretched out far below us.

"How about snakes?"

She actually jumps to her feet. "Where?"

"Relax." I reach for her hand and tug her back down. "There could be snakes, though, so good to keep an eye out. Oh hey, look." I point to a bird soaring, circling over us. "A hawk."

"Oh." She sits again, eyes darting around.

I slide my arm around her. "I'll protect you from snakes. Just enjoy the view."

"It *is* beautiful."

The sky is clear blue above us, the city hazy beneath us.

Everly lets out a slow sigh and I feel tension ease out of her body. She hands me back her water bottle and I stow them in the pack again.

"Like it?"

"Amazing."

I reach for her cheek and turn her face toward me. "Good." And I kiss her.

We're on top of the city, the world spread out around us, and I'm kissing her. Things don't get much better than this.

Well, getting her in bed again would be better.

But there's a lot to be said for moments like this . . . just a moment in time, but overflowing with something so beautiful and special and . . . Jesus, I'm getting so sappy.

We point out various landmarks in the panorama in front us and sit for a while, before deciding we're ready to continue on our hike by retracing our steps then heading east to climb to the Cahuenga summit. Once there, we pause to enjoy the view of the San Gabriel Mountains to the north and Los Angeles on the south.

As we round a corner, the Hollywood sign comes into view.

"There it is!" Everly points like a little kid. "Cool!" She pulls out her phone. "I have to take a picture!"

The trail gets steeper and windier, although the views make up for it. This path is even scrubbier, dry and dusty gold, with leafless shrubs and tree roots here and there. At one point we have to go down, then back up. Finally, we're there, hopping onto a paved road that goes behind the Hollywood sign.

"Ugh. This fence is in the way." Everly frowns at the chain-link barrier.

"If you can climb a bit farther, we can get a better view."

"I can do it!"

I lead her to the hill, where we negotiate a shorter, dusty path to the top, where we're now looking down on the back of the sign. Again, we're part of a crowd.

"Ah! This is amazing!" Everly stares. "Not just the sign . . . look!" She waves a hand at the city below us, the buildings of downtown L.A. and the mountains in the distance. A thin layer of haze or maybe smog softens the vista. "It's so beautiful!"

It really is, so much natural beauty as well as the city.

"Can you imagine what this was like before there was a city here?" she asks, surprising me. "It's so . . . rugged. I feel that there must have been a lot for people to overcome—the weather here is amazing when it's good, but there are droughts and then floods, even earthquakes."

"Yeah. So different from where I grew up on the east coast."

Standing behind her, I wrap my arms around her middle and look over her head. She leans back into me. It's another moment. For a few minutes, we're actually alone up here.

"It's so quiet," she comments. "Just the wind and the birds."

Yes, the quiet is striking . . . away from the noise and hustle of the city.

She turns her head to peer up at me. "Thank you for bringing me."

"You're welcome." I kiss her nose. "I still can't believe the California girl hasn't been here."

A group of tourists arrives behind us, chattering in a language I don't recognize—Japanese, I think. They're all excited about the view and Everly and I exchange a smile at their delight.

We walk around a bit, holding hands now.

"Let's get a selfie," I suggest. "You can post it on Instagram and everyone will see us on our date."

"Oh. That's a good idea. I kept thinking we had to go places people would see is, but we can do it ourselves."

We position ourselves and snap the pic, then do a few more. Then I take a couple of her alone with my phone, without her even realizing it, as she gazes over the vista. She looks beautiful—the wind tugging strands of hair out of her ponytail, her skin glowing in the sunshine.

Eventually we make the trek back to the vehicle, Everly bounding ahead of me, full of energy. She may not be a professional athlete, but she's got a lot of get-up-and-go in her. And she may be a perfect princess sometimes, but right now she's got dirt on the ass of her leggings, sweat and dust on her face and chest, and her hair is windblown. She doesn't seem to care. In fact, she seems to be loving this, and for some reason the fact that I get to see her like this, all imperfect and dusty and smiling, makes me weirdly happy.

I take my time driving back to her place. When I park, she looks at me. "Coming in?"

"Sure."

"I can make us dinner, if you want to stay."

I gnaw my bottom lip briefly. I'd told Heather I might come by tonight. But I still have the rest of the week off to spend time with Owen. "Okay, that would be great."

She unlocks her door and we step inside. A faint scent greets us, something clean and sort of . . . oceany.

"I could use a shower." She grimaces and runs a hand over her hair. "I feel like I'm coated in dust."

"Great idea. Let's go."

"Um, what?"

Smiling, I take her keys from her and hang them on the holder near her door, a pale blue starfish with hooks, then reach for her hand and lead her upstairs. "I saw your shower. It's big enough for two."

She gives a breathless laugh. "I guess it is."

In the bathroom I pull her up against me and sniff her hair. "You smell fantastic. Warm, like sunshine and wind."

"Mmm. And sweat."

"You don't stink, if that's what you're worried about."

She leans in to me and inhales. "I love how you smell too." Then she presses her mouth to the side of my neck.

I close my eyes and curve my hands over her ass cheeks. They fill my palms with satisfying firmness. She continues to kiss me, soft presses of her mouth on my skin, then a little tongue action on my throat. A groan climbs in my chest.

I pull her closer, my dick thickening in my shorts, and she makes an aroused noise as she feels my growing erection. I slip my hands under her tank top and up her back, lifting the top as I go until I need to pull back and tug it off over her head. Her sports bra is pink, thin straps crisscrossing her shoulders and back. With her eyes on mine, she pulls it off too.

My gaze drops to her tits—so sweet and pretty, I have to touch them. As I cover them with my palms and gently squeeze, she pushes down her shorts and panties and steps out of them. She lifts one foot, then the other to drag off tiny socks and then she's naked, right in front of me.

I step back and quickly get rid of my own clothes as she steps into the shower and turns on the faucet. Water rains down from a showerhead and she holds her hand under it to wait for it to warm up. I join her and close the glass door.

I can't wait to touch her and I crowd her up against the tiled wall to kiss her, one hand sliding down her front and between her thighs to cup her. Warm water pouring down on us, I curl my other hand around the nape of her neck, and she kisses me back, running her hand up my wet chest and into my hair. Warm water rains down on us, around us, the enclosure slowly filling with steam.

We start with our hair, Everly handing me a bottle of shampoo. I watch her tits lift as she raises her arms to wash her hair, soapy rivulets running down her smooth body. Then I reach for a sponge hanging from a hook. Everly picks up a bottle and squirts thick liquid onto the sponge. The scent is incredible . . . it's Everly, warm spicy flowers. I use the sponge to wash her, starting at her shoulders, her arms, her stomach. I turn her around so her back is to me, to wash that expanse of silky skin, then drop the sponge to use my soapy hands. I slide them around to her front to cup and squeeze her tits. Her nipples are tight points, and the feel of her flesh in my hands all slick and slippery is such a turn-on, I almost can't stand it.

My hands wander down over her belly, between her legs. My dick leaps with excitement when she bends over to pick up the sponge.

"You little tease." My hands on her hips, I soak up the view she's offering me, and it's fucking hot.

She straightens, tossing a little smile over her shoulder. "I need to wash my legs and feet."

She does that, slowly turning to face me, tipping her head back into the shower spray. Then she squirts more body wash and starts washing me. After she's scrubbed over my shoulders, chest, and abs, I pluck the sponge away from her so she too can continue with her hands.

My cock is stiff and when Everly lays her hands on my chest to push me back, then reverse our positions, it leaps in delight. Now my back is pressed to the tiles. She kisses me, pulls back, and bites her lip, then, with her eyes fastened on mine, her sudsy wet hand glides down over my chest and abs and closes around my shaft.

"Jesus," I groan.

Her lips tip into a half smile and she lowers herself to the shower floor, kneeling in front of me. I fucking love it, but . . . I open the shower door, grab a towel, and toss it to the floor for her knees. It gets wet, but who cares, those pretty knees need cushioning.

She tenderly lifts my cock, kisses my pelvic bones, then the crease of my groin, her eyes still raised to mine. Water streams from her hair and she slowly licks over the head of my cock.

I slide a hand into her hair, cupping the back of her head, and she slides her mouth lower onto my shaft. The tingles start at the soles of my feet, rocketing up through me in a sizzling rush.

She glides her lips up and down, slowly, deeper, then lets my cock fall from her mouth. Lifting it, she licks my balls. It's almost unbearable, need building in my body, my skin tightening.

I'm watching all this like it's my own personal porn movie, and nothing could be hotter than Everly on her knees in front of me, that beautiful mouth sucking me, smiling, her eyes moving from staring at my cock in awe, to meeting my eyes and sending sparks shooting down my spine.

She pulls my testicles into her mouth, slowly, gently, one at a time, then drags her tongue up the underside of my shaft and takes me into her mouth again.

Sensation twists inside me, pleasure climbing, lust making me dizzy. "That's fucking amazing," I groan. "Jesus, Everly."

"You like?"

"I love it. Goddamn, I love it."

She works me more, sucking, licking, her hand gripping the base of my cock, and I'm getting so close I have to stop her. I reach down and lift her up, hoisting her by the backs of her thighs.

She squeals out a laugh and wraps her arms around my neck. Our mouths meet in more long, hungry kisses. I grip her ass with one hand and my cock with the other, find her entrance, and slide home.

"Awwww fuck." Her tight heat around me is unbelievable. I lean back against the wall and plant my feet into the floor, holding her butt with both hands to bounce her on my dick. She cups my face and kisses me, although the jolting motion of her body makes it hard. Breathy whimpers and moans fill the steamy air as we move together.

"You're so strong," she gasps. "Are you okay?"

"Yeah. Hell yeah." I pause. "Are *you*? Can you come this way?"

"I . . . think so." I watch, fascinated, as she closes her eyes, a little crease between her eyebrows, a look of intense focus on her face. A few seconds later, her fingers dig into my shoulders, she lets out a high-pitched wail and clamps around me.

"Ah yeah, baby, that's it . . . Christ, I'm coming too . . ." I shout as heat explodes in my center, zipping up my spine, burning in my chest. My balls squeeze, pleasure slamming through me as I burst in long, nearly painful spasms.

"Wyatt . . ."

I gasp, "What?"

"We didn't use a condom."

"Aw, shit." My lungs are still heaving, desperate for air.

"It's okay . . . I'm on the pill. But . . ."

"It's okay. I've been tested. All good."

"Okay." Relief lightens her voice. "Me too."

"Sorry." I kiss her forehead and slowly lower her to the floor. "So sorry."

"We're good." She smiles. "So good."

17

―――

EVERLY

After our shower, I pour us each a glass of Cabernet and we cook dinner together, making a stir-fry with the chicken and vegetables from my fridge. Then we settle on my couch, a fire crackling in the fireplace and my TV turned to a Netflix show neither of us has seen. It's so easy and comfortable and . . . right.

I try not to hyperventilate.

My Instagram and Facebook posts have gotten a ton of attention, unusual for me. I know it's because of Wyatt being tagged in them. He's got a way bigger social media following than I do. I rarely post pictures of myself; I prefer to keep my life private. Or as private as I can, given who my family is. So I guess our outing was unconventional but it accomplished a purpose.

It also accomplished me having all the feels about Wyatt. Inside, I'm a swirling maelstrom of emotions, many of which I can't or won't identify. He keeps surprising me. He may be a vagina hunter, and he may give off attitude

201

like he doesn't give a shit about anything, but he has a romantic, almost poetic streak. Up there in the hills, with those amazing views and gusts of air scented by the sun-warmed grass and earth, he seemed as moved by it all as I was. It was an incredibly sensory experience that soothed something inside me and yet excited me too, and I felt a connection of spirit I don't know if I've ever felt with a man before.

This was alarming!

So I also have nerves jittering in my belly, which is pretty normal for me.

After three back-to-back episodes of the TV show, we call it a night.

"You have to work tomorrow." Wyatt picks up our wineglasses and carries them into the kitchen. "I'll head home and let you sleep."

"Damn." I make it sound like I'm joking, but I'm sort of not.

He laughs.

I follow him to the door and we spend long moments kissing good night, which doesn't help my disappointment that he's leaving. I'm turned on and breathing hard by the time he walks out the door with a promise to talk soon.

I drift back into the kitchen to slide the glasses into the dishwasher, my body humming, my mind teeming with images and sensations, my chest full of cotton candy.

I float up the stairs like I'm filled with helium.

God. I need to get a grip on my emotions. I need to settle down and be smart about this whole situation. It was supposed to be a media stunt, go on a few dates, make sure people know we're seeing each other. That's it.

After the press conference on Friday, we probably won't have to see each other again.

And that makes me really, really sad.

I can't screw this up. There's enough about this family in the media already, with that stupid lawsuit Mark and Matthew have filed against Dad.

I can't let my heart get involved in this.

But I'm having so much fun.

I change into my pajamas, a pair of flowered shorts and a tank top. I never even blow-dried my hair or put on any makeup after our sexy shower. That's also weird for me, because I don't like people to see me when I'm not looking my best. But Wyatt looked at me no differently, touched me and kissed me and snuggled with me on the couch despite me not looking perfect.

I slide into my bed and pick up my Kindle to read a bit before going to sleep, to distract myself from thinking about Wyatt and about how dangerous it is to let go and have fun, and how I might be making another huge mistake in my life.

I DON'T SEE WYATT AGAIN UNTIL FRIDAY MORNING AT THE Hockey for All press conference, although we've texted back and forth. He hasn't arrived yet, and I'm hanging out at the front of the media room with Murray and Théo while reporters and photographers file in. Our team videographer is set up at the back, along with a few cameras from sports networks.

And in walks my brother Asher.

Smiling, I push away from the wall I'm leaning against and scamper toward him. "Hey, Ash!"

He holds out his arms and we hug. "Hey, Ev, long time no see. You weren't at Mom and Dad's for dinner on Sunday."

"Oh. No. I was, uh . . . busy."

His eyebrows lift and he smirks. "So I've been seeing. Pics of you and Bell are all over the place."

My cheeks heat. Since he's a sports reporter, I don't want to tell him the truth about what Wyatt and I are doing. "I know." I roll my eyes. "What's new with you?"

We chat a couple of minutes until Théo takes the podium and greets everyone.

"I'm going to set up another family meeting!" I whisper to Asher. "I'll be in touch!"

He nods, and I make my way back to the front of the room, carefully keeping to the side. Wyatt's there now, looking handsome and relaxed in a pair of dark gray dress pants and a button-down shirt. He catches my eye and smiles. I lift a hand in a tiny wave, smiling back.

Théo talks about the mission of Hockey for All, the role of the ambassadors, and then introduces Wyatt. Wyatt steps up to the podium. "This is such an important initiative," he begins. "And I want to thank the NHL and the NHLPA for their commitment to inclusivity in the sport of hockey, as well as the management and leadership of our team." He nods at Théo. "It has to start at the top, and when leadership supports something, the players follow. We know that it's up to us to create an environment in the team, in the dressing room, where anyone feels safe no matter their religion, culture, ethnic background, sexual orientation, gender identity, physical and mental ability. And not just in the sport, but also in our everyday lives, we have to be aware of it. I'm honored to be an ambassador for Hockey for All, but I'd be an ambassador for it unofficially anyway."

They bring up Casey Gregg, who played for the US women's national hockey team, and Brian Mankowsky, a sledge hockey player, who also say a few words. Then the media has a chance to ask questions.

Sure enough, it's not long before that douche from the *L.A. Journal* asks, "Wyatt, there was a photograph of you taken at a local sex shop that appeared in a popular entertainment blog."

The crowd snickers. I keep my face expressionless.

"The picture had people speculating about your own sexual identity, especially since you attended last year's Pride Parade in St. John, New Brunswick. But you've never given any indication that you're a member of the LGBTQ community, so were you mocking the community?"

Wyatt's eyes widen briefly. "Mocking it? Uh, no, man. I'm a supporter of LGBTQ rights. The reason I participated in the parade last year is because a good friend of mine who I played hockey with in Rimouski came out last year, and I went to support him. The reason we were in that store . . ." He refers to me but doesn't name me, a smile flickering on his mouth. ". . . is none of your business."

The crowd chuckles again.

"But I wasn't making fun of anyone. Except maybe myself."

I can tell his answer and his charming self-deprecation has won over the media people there; in fact, I get the feeling that most of them didn't like it that Foster had asked that question.

Wyatt meets my eyes again across the room and we share a small smile. I give a tiny nod to show my approval of how he handled that.

He deals with a few more questions and then Murray ends the conference, thanking everyone for coming. People start filing out. Wyatt's chatting with Casey, Brian, Dave, Théo, and Murray. Casey is a very pretty blonde, who's hanging on Wyatt's every word. Ugh.

I guess I've done my part by being here, but before everyone's gone, I approach Wyatt and touch his arm.

He turns to me and his smile is . . . intimate. Just for me. He runs his hand down my arm, barely touching me, and brushes his fingertips over mine. "Hi."

"Hi. Good job up there."

"Thanks." We're standing close together; closer than any others are. He bends his head. "I'll come by your office in a bit, okay?"

"Sure."

As I walk back to my office, I check my phone for messages or emails. Another email from that watchdog dude, telling me that they've completed their work and will be publishing their findings in a month.

I don't know why I'm so nervous about this. Okay, I do know. I'm afraid they've found something heinously bad that I've done and will tell the whole world, and everyone will know I'm a complete fraud and have no idea what I'm doing.

Yes, yes, this is crazy, but that's how I think. Imposter syndrome is real.

I can't do anything about it, though, other than worry, which sometimes is an actual strategy I use to keep something bad from happening. I know that's a waste of energy, though. So I distract myself with other work, reviewing the proposals that my assistant, Beth, has deemed worthy of my attention, out of the thousands we receive.

A while later, I look up at Wyatt's voice saying, "Hey, princess."

I smile as he saunters in, all big and beautiful, the door swinging shut behind him.

"Hey." I push back from my desk and rise. "Did you write that little speech yourself?"

I meet him in front of my desk, and he sets his hands on my waist, frowning. "Why would you ask that?"

I suck briefly on my bottom lip. "Because it was good?"

"You think I can't write a good speech myself?"

"That's not what I meant." I give his chest a little shove. "I was just asking!"

"Okay, okay. Yes, I did write it myself. I mean, I didn't actually write it all down, I just thought about what I wanted to say."

"Well, you did great."

"Whew. So . . . where should we go for dinner tonight?"

"Uh . . . tonight?"

"Yeah."

"I, uh, thought . . . well, I think we've done enough fake dating for the PR thing."

"Fake dating?" His forehead creases. "You thought this was fake?"

I stare at him. "We both knew it was fake."

"Was that fake fucking, too?" His voice is edged with annoyance.

I close my eyes. "No."

"Everly. Look at me."

I lift my eyes to his.

"I don't care who sees us or what they say about us. I want to have dinner with you tonight."

"For real?"

"Fuck, yeah. Look, maybe we had to go out on those dates, but I wasn't faking the fun I have with you." He pauses. "Were you?"

I slowly shake my head. I can't lie. "No. I was having real fun."

His lips twitch. "And fun fucking."

"That too."

He slides his hands around behind me, down to my ass, and pulls me to him. "Come here." Then he kisses me, tilting his head and capturing my mouth with his.

I melt into him, winding my arms around his neck, letting his tongue slide over mine. I press myself against him, wanting to feel him everywhere I can, and a little moan rises in my throat.

"Seven o'clock?" he murmurs against my cheek long moments later.

"Okay." The word comes out all breathy.

He draws back and smiles at me. "I'll pick you up. See you then."

I watch him leave my office, my lips throbbing, my nipples peaked, aching low inside, and my heart rocketing around in my chest.

What am I doing?

WE GO BACK TO THE CELLAR, WHERE WYATT TOOK ME after the Cougars game. We sit in the bar, but this time Abby's not here. It's dim and crowded and noisy, and I check over the menu, looking for something that's not too carbolicious.

I settle on a salad, a Niçoise with rare tuna, and a glass of wine. Wyatt orders an Angus beef burger and a beer.

"I'm getting fat and lazy," he says, patting his abs. "Being off all week."

My eyebrows shoot up. "I don't think so."

"Okay, I've worked out nearly every day." He grins. Then his attention is diverted.

I look around to see a bunch of guys headed our way . . . Jimmy Bertelski, Arvid Bergström, and Derek Jablonski.

"They're apparently back from Tahoe," Wyatt mutters. "Okay if they join us?"

"Uh . . . sure." I don't think I have much choice, as they all greet Wyatt with bro shakes and backslaps, and start pulling up another table and chairs.

It's not that I don't want them to join us, but hanging out with his friends makes this seem . . . like we're really dating. And I kind of wanted to talk to him about that, to make sure we're on the same page. Only I don't even know what page I'm on.

I'm not really good at going with the flow. Letting stuff

happen. I like to be in control and have a plan. I'm freaking out a little.

Wyatt, now sitting beside me, leans in and whispers in my ear, "Sorry."

Great. He can see I'm freaking out. I shake my head. "It's okay."

"I know you don't like surprises." He squeezes my hand. "It'll be fine. You know I've always got your back."

My heart quivers, and my breathing slows. I nod. I got this.

His buddies don't seem surprised to see me.

"Hey, Everly," Jimmy greets me, and the others say hi too.

"Hi, guys."

"No broken bones?" Wyatt asks.

"Nah, man. I'm not allowed to ski, it's in my contract." Derek grins.

"How about snowboarding?"

"That is not specified," Derek smirks.

"If you came back with a broken leg, you'd be so deep in fecal matter."

"I know, I know." He grimaces and holds his hands up. "I'm fine. We're all fine. Had tons of fun."

"I assume that involves women."

Arvid laughs. "Oh yeah."

"I don't get why the chicks go for the Swedish guy," Jimmy complains. "Swedes are boring."

"We're not boring. We're just reserved. She thought I look like Alexander Skarsgård."

I nod. "You do!"

"And I play hockey," he adds modestly.

I laugh.

"Also, *you* can't talk," Arvid says to Derek. "You were with a different woman every night."

Derek shrugs.

"That chick you were with last night," Jimmy says to Derek. "What was her name?"

"Lola."

"Right."

Derek sighs. "Man, she could suck a bowling ball through a cocktail straw."

I choke on my tuna.

"Oh, uh . . . sorry, Everly," he says.

I wave a hand. "No worries. I have three brothers."

"Don't remind us," Jimmy says. "We're trying to pretend you're not a Wynn."

"Keep it up," I encourage them. "I'm fine with that."

"You gonna see her again?" Wyatt asks Derek.

"Maybe." He shrugs. "Still don't understand why you didn't come with us."

Wyatt's face tightens and his eyes flicker. He smiles, but it's a little strained. "I told you I hate snow."

"I seem to remember that you love snowboarding," Jimmy says. "But guys, shut up, we can see now why he didn't want to leave town." He waves a hand back and forth between me and Wyatt.

I know that's not the reason he didn't go with them, and I'm curious. But I keep that to myself.

The guys share funny stories from their trip, including how Derek met the woman who can suck bowling balls through cocktail straws, when she was too afraid to let go of the lift and was swinging through the air before dropping to the ground. He was on the lift right behind her and skied right over to rescue her. Luckily, she wasn't hurt.

Then Wyatt tells them about our crazy night out that ended with us breaking into a church, and they howl with laughter. I'm laughing too, reliving it.

The guys order food, we get more drinks, we're all laughing our asses off and I realize, once again . . . I'm having fun.

Wyatt has his arm around my shoulders, resting on my chair back; we're close enough together that our thighs are touching. He's very handsy, brushing fingertips over my hand, my cheek, squeezing my shoulder. It's so affectionate and heart-melting, and I'm just a big squishy pillow, listening to him and his friends trash-talk one another with genuine friendliness. It's all the more impressive when I recall that he hasn't even known these guys that long, having joined the team last season.

When we finally call it a night, Wyatt murmurs to me, "Come to my place?"

And I nod yes.

18

WYATT

"Last day of the break," I say the next morning. It's nearly eleven, and we're still in bed. "We practice tomorrow."

"You need to practice, since you're so fat and lazy."

I laugh and pin her to the bed. "You calling me fat?"

"You said it yourself."

I lean down to kiss her, enjoying her teasing, enjoying the feel of her beneath me in my bed. But I have something to tell her. Ask her? And I'm glitching a little about it. I draw back and gaze into her eyes. "Are you going to yoga class?"

"I should . . . but . . ."

"I have something I have to do today."

"Oh. Okay."

She thinks I'm brushing her off. "I want you to come with me."

She blinks. "Where?"

"To see a friend of mine and her son."

A tiny notch forms between her eyebrows. "A friend?"

"Yes. I promised I would take Owen to the zoo."

She gazes back at me. "Okay."

"We can stop by your place if you want to change. Heather lives on Franklin Avenue, it's not far."

"That would be good. My heels wouldn't be the best for the zoo."

Am I doing the right thing? I've never even told people about Heather and Owen, let alone taken anyone to meet them. I don't really know why I'm doing it.

We stop at a café and get coffees and bagels to go, then continue on to Everly's place. I sit at her table with my phone, sipping my coffee, while she goes upstairs to change. Again, I feel that sense of calm that her condo creates, with all the light and the fresh scent and lack of clutter.

I smile when she returns, now wearing jeans, a black-and-white-striped T-shirt, and bright red Converse sneakers. Very zoo appropriate, and yet totally pulled together and polished. That's Everly.

She sits too, to eat her bagel. "I haven't been to the zoo in years."

"Owen loves it. That day we ran into you, we'd been at the aquarium. He likes that too. He's really into animals."

"Cool. How old is he?"

"Just turned six." I tip my head. "The night of the Birds Banquet?"

"Yeah . . . ?"

"It was his birthday party. That's why I was late."

"Oh." She sinks her teeth into her bottom lip briefly. "I was a bitch to you about that."

"Nah, not a bitch. You were doing your job."

"I didn't know. I'm sorry."

I shrug. "It's fine. I know I have responsibilities to the team. But I'd promised him I'd be there, and Heather needed help with a rowdy bunch of five- and six-year-olds. We changed the time of the party, so I managed to do both."

She eyes me over her coffee cup. "Owen must be very special to you."

"I know what you're thinking. Heather is just a friend. Actually, her husband was my friend." I pause, my throat squeezing as it often does when I think about Hank. "He was my best friend. He died a couple of years ago." I cough. "So I help Heather and Owen."

Her eyes warm and her mouth softens. "I'm sorry. What happened to him?"

I give my head a sharp shake. "Rather not talk about it." The air in the room has grown heavy and thick. "You know what they say . . . life is short. So smile while you still have teeth."

She laughs, but I can see she's still thoughtful.

We make the short drive to Heather's place and park in front of her little bungalow, Spanish-style stucco with a red tile roof.

"Should I wait here?" Everly asks.

"No, come in. You should meet Heather."

She follows me up the sidewalk. The yard is getting overgrown. I should come trim back some of these shrubs. I ring the doorbell and Heather opens the door as Owen zooms up behind her and skids to a stop in his sock feet. "Wyatt's here! Wyatt's here!"

"Hey, buddy!"

"Come in!" Heather beams a smile at me. Then her gaze lands on Everly behind me and her smile disappears.

I step inside and take Everly's hand, tugging her into the small foyer too. When I look back at Heather, the smile is back, dimmer but determined. "Hello . . ."

"Heather, this is Everly. Everly, my friend Heather, and . . . my best little buddy, Owen."

"Nice to meet you," Heather says, extending a hand. "Everly Wynn, right?"

"Yes. Nice to meet you too." They shake hands. Everly turns to Owen. "And nice to meet you, Owen."

"Hi." He studies her intently. Kids.

"Everly's going to come to the zoo with us, buddy."

"Okay."

"Here's your backpack," Heather says, now frowning faintly.

"I don't wanna take my backpack."

"I'll carry it, bud," I say. "Sunscreen? Hat? Water?"

"Check, check, check," Heather says, smiling again. Her gaze darts between me and Everly and I sense the curiosity on both their parts.

Heather's a beautiful woman—long golden-blond hair, big blue eyes. I know this, but I've never been attracted to her. She was married to my best friend. I hope Everly isn't jealous, because there's no reason to be.

And I hope Heather likes Everly. Owen too.

"Okay, the zoo closes at five today, so we'll be back around then."

Heather nods. "Sounds good. Have fun!" She hugs Owen, who then hurtles down the sidewalk toward my SUV.

Owen chatters about the animals he wants to see at the zoo, entertaining us. At least, Everly seems entertained, laughing and asking Owen questions with what seems like genuine interest.

We approach the entrance, Owen skipping along.

Everly points to the condors' rescue zone. "Look. They rescue hockey players like Wyatt."

Owen giggles. "That's not rescuing hockey players!" he tells Everly. "Condors are real birds. They used to be exkinked."

"Ah." She nods.

I pay our admissions and we head in through the gates. It's a sunny day, nice and warm, and we get him sunscreened up and a hat on his head before we move too far.

I hold up the sunscreen bottle to Everly. "Need some?"

"I'm okay. I put on sunscreen at home." She slides her big sunglasses onto her nose.

Owen's enthusiasm always makes the zoo fun, and Everly seems to feel it too. He doesn't like to spend too long at each exhibit, dashing on to the next one. We pause to watch keepers feeding Tasmanian devils, which fascinates Owen.

"They're really aggressive," I comment as they attack some kind of small animal and make scary noises.

"They're going crazy!" Owen says, wide-eyed.

"They look like Wyatt when he gets a steak," Everly says to Owen and he laughs.

I shoot her an amused glance. "Ha." I nudge Owen. "They have no table manners."

He laughs again.

After that, we move on. "I wanna see the grillas!" Owen says. "I like grillas."

We stop for a late lunch of tacos, and a bathroom break, then wander on. Owen's pace is slowing, so I carry him on my shoulders for a while.

"I learned about giraffes at school," Owen tells us when we arrive there. "Their tongues are this long!" He holds his arms wide. "And their tongue is black!"

"Wow." Everly looks impressed.

"Also, giraffes only sleep a little bit. And they sleep standing up because if they lay down they might be attacked."

"He's smart," Everly murmurs to me.

I squeeze her hand. "Yep."

"Can we feed them? Please?"

"Sure, buddy." It costs extra, but only a few bucks. And it's a cool experience.

When we're done there, we move on.

"Look, Everly!" Owen tugs her other hand. "Monkeys!"

"Chimpanzees," I correct him.

"Right. They're funny!"

"They are," Everly agrees. "Oh my gosh! What's happening?"

A fight has broken out. One chimp is chasing another with a stick and screaming.

"Looks like a hockey game!" Everly says, cracking Owen up again. Okay, and me.

Everyone around is laughing at the animals and the show they're putting on. One chimp stops and beats his chest. Owen dies laughing.

We take one more rest and buy some ice cream before

heading out to get a tired boy home. He falls asleep in the backseat.

"He's adorable," Everly says quietly. "He really loves you."

I smile. "I think he's in love with you, actually. He wouldn't let go of your hand."

She laughs softly.

I wake up Owen when we're at his place. "I was just resting my eyes," he says, rubbing them.

"That's good, buddy."

Heather greets us with big smiles for Owen and more reserved smiles for Everly and me. Often Heather asks me to stay for dinner after I've taken Owen out, but she doesn't today, so I hug my little guy. He wants to hug Everly too, and she kneels down to give him a squeeze. "I had fun," she tells him. "You taught me a lot about animals."

"Everly is funny," Owen tells his mom.

"It was lovely to meet you both," Everly says, standing and facing Heather. "He's a great kid."

"Thanks." Heather's smile is tight.

"He's so smart. He knew how long a giraffe's tongue is." She grins. "And elephants are the only animals that can't jump. I love his curiosity."

Heather's pride shines on her face. "He is very smart."

"See you soon, Heath." I set my hand on the small of Everly's back to usher her out of the house. We wave goodbye and leave.

Everly is quiet in the vehicle.

I glance at her as I drive. "Tired?"

"Yeah. All that fresh air and sunshine." She smiles. "I

could fall asleep like Owen." She pauses. "Are you and Heather really just friends?"

"Yes." I hesitate, then ask, "Why?"

"She didn't seem very happy to meet me."

"Sure she did."

Her smile is skeptical. "Well, maybe I'm wrong. Just a feeling I got. Thanks for bringing me along, it was fun."

EVERLY

I'm a mess.

I think I'm falling in love.

The last time I thought I was in love with someone, it turned into an epic disaster. It terrifies me. Excites me. Makes me want things I'm not sure I can ever have.

Because, like the last time, I'm falling for the wrong guy.

Ever since Wyatt took me to the zoo, I've been messed up. Seeing him with Owen made my heart swell up huge in my chest. He loves that boy. His best friend's son.

His best friend died, and he can't talk about it. That makes my swollen heart ache for him.

The fact that he trusts me enough to tell me about Heather and Owen makes my feelings for him expand. But he's not telling me everything, and I wish he would.

I'm seeing past the front he puts on for everyone—the jokester, the partier. He's the honey badger of the hockey world—he just doesn't give a shit.

Except he does.

I've seen how much he cares about his friends. I've now seen how much he cares about Owen and Heather. Clearly he cared about his dead friend.

Maybe . . . he even cares about me. A little. He does things for me, like bringing me coffee, and cleaning my kitchen. When we're in bed (or the shower) he's thoughtful and generous and focused on giving me what I need.

But thinking thoughts like that will get in me in trouble. He doesn't care about his reputation. He thinks life is a big party. Well, okay, knowing that his friend died so young, I get that now. But still, life is about goals and accomplishments and making people proud of you.

I miss him.

How pathetic.

We saw each other a bunch of times during the All Star break, and now the team is off on a road trip to Toronto, Montreal, and Ottawa. They'll be back tomorrow, Friday, and it's crazy that I can't wait to see him.

I have lots to keep me busy at work, meetings with stakeholders, proposals to review, reports to write, so I'm putting in some long hours. I do go to yoga class on Wednesday night because I know yoga's good for me. And I've set up our next family meeting to discuss progress on ending the stupid family feud. Tonight I'm going out with Lacey. I need to talk to someone.

Wyatt texts me a few times while he's away, so I know he's thinking about me too. His parents flew to Montreal for the game there, and he's clearly happy to spend some time with them. I'm trying to keep things casual and breezy, though, sending him funny GIFs and memes instead of sad face emojis and telling him how much I miss him.

I meet Lacey at Food for Thought again, one of our favorite places.

"I need a big glass of wine," I announce, picking up the menu.

"Uh-oh. Bad day at the office?"

"Nah, just busy. I'm kind of stressed about something else, though."

"Wyatt?"

My head snaps up. "Why do you say that?"

She smiles. "Wild guess."

I choose a Sauvignon Blanc and she orders the same.

"Okay, what's up?" She eyes me expectantly. "Why are you stressed?"

"I have a little problem."

"Mmmhmm."

"I think I'm falling for him."

"Is he why you bailed on yoga class Saturday? Taylor told me."

"Yeah. He asked me to go to the zoo with him."

"Aw. So why is this such a problem?" Her forehead furrows. "He doesn't feel the same?"

"I don't know. We haven't had that conversation yet, and I don't know if we should. I mean, I think he likes me. We didn't have to keep seeing each other once we'd done our duty for the team." I roll my eyes. "But . . ." I drop my eyes to my hands on the table. "There's something I've never told you about."

I don't speak for so long, she asks dryly, "Are you going to tell me now? Or you just wanted to let me know you have a secret . . ."

I give a short laugh. "I'll tell you some of it." I sit back so the waiter can place my wineglass in front of me. I reach for it and take a gulp. "Lovely," I say, though I barely tasted it.

Lacey snorts.

"Okay. When I was sixteen, I got involved with a . . . a man."

Her eyebrows shoot up. "A man?"

"Yes." I clear my throat. "He played for the Condors."

"You were *sixteen*?"

"Yeah." I sigh. "I know. I was a crazy teenager."

"I have a hard time picturing that," she says slowly. "I don't believe you were *ever* young and crazy. You're so together and mature."

"Well, maybe I wasn't young and crazy. Maybe I was just trying to be. I thought I was in love. It was . . . glorious. You know—passionate, obsessive, teenage love."

"Mmm."

"He was older, obviously."

"Um, how old, exactly? I mean, there *are* guys who play in the NHL who are teenagers . . ."

"Twenty-eight."

Her eyes pop open.

I nod. "I know. Anyway. I don't really have daddy issues, even though it might seem like that. I do like older men, but it's not to fill an emotional void left by my father. He was mostly there for me."

"Mostly," she says in that dry tone again.

"Okay, he was gone a lot. He was busy. Also, he was busy with the boys . . . because they played hockey."

"You've been to therapy, I take it."

"Yes."

"Well, I don't know your therapist, but that sounds a lot like an absent father to me."

I nod slowly in agreement. "Yeah. I don't want to blame him for my weird hang-ups, though. He's a good dad, really."

"So . . . you've always wanted a protective, older male figure as your romantic partner."

"Apparently. I really I thought I loved this guy. And there's more. He was . . . married."

"Oh my God."

"I was a stupid kid." I plead with her with my eyes to not judge me. "I know it was a mistake."

"*He* was a fucking assbucket. What kind of man would do that? Jesus! You were a child!"

"Yes. I know that now."

"You're not going to tell me who it is."

"No." I wrinkle my nose. "It's enough to say that obviously when my dad found out about it, he went berserk."

She closes her eyes. "I can only imagine."

"So there's the problem . . . Wyatt's not an older guy, but he plays for my dad's team. And he *is* someone who doesn't care about his reputation, so dating me . . . no big deal. He doesn't care what people say. The media loves it right now, but . . . what if . . . what if . . . we try to have a real relationship and things go wrong? I can't do that to my family again."

Lacey's brows pull together. "Did it get out the last time? When you were a teenager?"

"Not so much." I bite my lip. "My dad threw some money around and things got buried."

"And I bet a certain player got traded."

I nod slowly. "My parents were so disappointed in me. It was the worst time of my life. I knew I'd messed up, but I didn't want to admit it, and I was pissed off at them for ending things with the man I loved, who I thought was leaving his wife to be with me." I drop my head forward, the remembered shame scalding inside me. "I wasn't exactly a joy to deal with. I even tried to run away."

"Wow." She lets out a long breath. "Wow. Okay, first of all, you're not sixteen. You're twenty-seven. Wyatt's what . . . ?"

"Twenty-six."

"Phhht." Lacey waves a hand. "This is not a big deal."

"I can't screw up again! I can't fall for a guy who plays for the team my dad owns! I let this go too far, it should have just been a few very public dates and now emotions have gotten involved and it's a big mess."

She studies me across the table. "Ah, Ev. I'm sorry. Maybe you should talk to Wyatt about it."

"I can't." I shake my head. "I can't tell him about that."

She sips her wine, clearly pondering. "Well, here's what I say. If you love him and want any hope of a relationship with him . . . you have to tell him. That's what a relationship is . . . honesty." She sips her wine again. "And if you tell him and he can't handle it, then you couldn't have had a relationship anyway."

I think about her words. I'm not sure I buy in to them, though. "Okay, I'll think about that."

19

WYATT

We get back from our road trip in the middle of the night. I slept on the plane, but I still go straight to bed when I get home. I'm sore and tired and horny.

I can't wait to see Everly.

We text when I get up, and make plans for dinner. This time those yahoos aren't crashing my dinner date. We'll go somewhere else, not the place we all hang out. I make a reservation at The Fig Tree.

I arrive early at Everly's place, because it seems stupid to sit at home waiting to see her. She might still be getting ready, but that's okay, I can hang out.

She doesn't answer the door right away and I'm almost going to ring the bell again when finally the door opens.

Not only is she not ready, she looks like hell. I step in. "Hey. What's wrong?"

"I'm not feeling well. I'm sorry." With a hand on the wall as if she needs it to balance, she makes her way into the living room, then lowers herself carefully onto the couch. "I was going to text you. I was hoping it would pass."

"Pass?" I frown, following her. "What's wrong?"

She doesn't answer, her eyes closed. Her face is flushed and shiny.

I perch on the edge of the sofa and touch her forehead. "Fever?"

"No." She swallows.

"What can I get you?"

"Um. Some ice water?"

"Sure." I hasten into her kitchen to fill a glass with ice and water from the fridge dispenser, then return.

She gulps down half of it and hands it back to me. I set it on the table, worry jabbing at my insides.

"I'm sorry," she says again. "I don't think I can go out."

"That's okay. We'll just stay here. I can order something in."

"Sure."

She's probably not hungry.

This is just what she was like that night of the banquet, when I had to bring her home. I thought she was drunk.

I gnaw my lip. "Have you been drinking, sweetheart?"

Her eyes open and her eyebrows snap together. "What? No." Then her eyes widen. "You think I'm drunk?"

Telling her I thought she had an alcohol problem might not be a good idea right now. Come to think of it, I haven't seen any signs of that since then. "No, no."

She gives me an incredulous glare, then closes her eyes again. "Shit." She takes a few deep, even breaths. "Okay, fine. I'm having a panic attack."

I frown. "Huh?"

"I know I don't look like I'm panicking or freaking out. But this is how it is. I get a buzzing in my ears. It gets worse and then I get dizzy and nauseous. My heart is racing." She lays a hand on her chest. "It almost feels like I'm choking, my heart is beating so fast."

"Oh man." I stare at her with concern. I have zero experience with something like this. "Does this happen often?"

"Not as much anymore. I'm on a medication. It helps. Usually."

"What happened? I mean, what caused this?"

"Nothing." Her lips twitch as she almost smiles. "It's never one specific thing that triggers it. It just happens at random times."

"Is this what happened at the banquet?"

"Yeah. I didn't want to tell you what was happening. It's stupid."

"It's not stupid," I object. "I don't know much about panic attacks, but I don't think you can control them."

"That's true." She sighs. "The first time I had one, Mom took me to the emergency room. I was so embarrassed. I thought I was dying, and they told me it was a panic attack. I was all, 'I don't have panic attacks.'" She snorts. "But that's what it was. I figured I should be able to just get over it. But . . . I can't."

I pick up her hand and hold it. "I know." I pause. "What can I do for you? Anything?"

"I . . . uh . . . would really like a Slurpee. It's nice and cold." She bites her lip adorably.

"I'll go get you one." I jump up and pull my keys out. "Where's the nearest 7-Eleven?"

"Santa Monica and Sixteenth, I think."

"What kind do you like?"

"Lemonade, if they have it. Or orange."

I could probably walk there just as fast, but I make a speedy trip there and back, returning with a jumbo Slurpee.

"That's so nice of you." She sips through the straw. "Mmm. So good."

I make a quick call to cancel our dinner reservation, then ask her, "Anything else I can do?"

"No. I just need to rest until I feel better. I know how it goes. In a while, it'll settle down, but I'll have a killer headache and need to sleep."

"Oh man. Okay, I can do that. Do you feel like eating?"

"Not really. You go ahead, though."

"I'll order pizza. I can heat some up for you later, if you feel up to it."

"Okay."

Christ, I hate seeing her like this. She's clearly miserable, and miserable because she's miserable, frustrated that she can't control this. I wish I could do more to make her feel better. At least I can be here with her and make sure she's okay.

"How about a back rub?" I offer.

Her eyes open. "Really?"

"Sure."

She rolls over. I ease her loose T-shirt up to reveal the curve of her back. No bra. (I already noticed that, to be honest.)

I slide my hand up and down her back, slow and gentle, over and over.

"That's so nice," she whispers. "Thank you.

I keep rubbing for a while, fighting back a stubborn erection. This is *not* the time to molest her. Then I tug her shirt back down and tuck a soft blanket around her. I hang out, eating pizza, drinking a beer, watching TV. She snoozes on the couch. I keep an eye on her.

Not my typical Friday night. But right now, I don't want to be anywhere else.

IT'S BACK TO THE GRIND, AND WITH THE ALL STAR break done, all sights are set on making the playoffs. We have a home game Saturday against Philadelphia, and Sunday I head over to Heather's to tackle some of the vegetation that's taking over her yard.

"You don't have to do this," Heather protests when I arrive.

"I know. Just thought I could help out." I find her garden tools in the small shed out back and set about trimming and weeding. She comes out to help, and I know it's because she feels guilty that I'm doing this. Owen is "helping" too, although he gets in trouble when he pulls up some kind of flower that apparently isn't a weed.

"Is Everly your girlfriend?" Owen asks me.

I shoot him a startled glance. "Uh . . . yeah, I guess she is."

"I saw pictures of you together online," Heather comments, not looking at me. "You hadn't even said anything about seeing someone."

"It's pretty new," I admit.

"Moving quickly."

"Well, it's not like we're getting married next week," I joke.

"Are you serious about her?"

I'm taken aback by the question. "I don't know. Maybe."

"Oh." She yanks a weed out of the ground. "I see. You haven't had a girlfriend since you moved here."

"Nope."

She says nothing, moving away to pull more weeds. I keep trimming the shrub, tossing branches to the ground. "Hey, Owen. You could pile up these branches for me."

Heather asks me to stay for dinner, but I'm sweaty and itchy. Something scratched my arms and it's turning red. "I better head home and shower," I say, frowning at the scratches.

"You probably have plans with your new girlfriend," she says with a smile.

"Uh, not tonight. We have a practice in the morning."

"You played great in that game against Ottawa. I watched it on Saturday night."

"Thanks. I felt really good that whole trip. Got a little banged up, though." I ruefully rub my hip, which was turning shades of blue when I got dressed earlier.

"You should have rested today."

"Actually, it was good to move around. It felt stiff earlier, but it's loosened up a bit now." I pull my keys out of my jeans pocket. "Hey, Owen! Come give me a hug!"

He bounces over, gives me a tight squeeze, then disappears. I grin. "Bye, Heather."

"Let me know when you have a night off you can come for dinner. I'll roast a chicken—you love that."

"Yeah," I agree. "Sounds good."

I drive home, once again with that uncomfortable feeling that Heather is coming to rely on me too much. Maybe "rely" isn't the right word. She's always asked me to stay for meals as a thank you for helping her or taking out Owen, but lately she seems disappointed when I say no. Could be I'm imagining things. We're just friends.

Maybe I shouldn't have come over to help clean up the yard.

But I can't just drop out of their lives. I want to be in their lives. I *have* to be in their lives.

20

EVERLY

I was so mortified that Wyatt saw me having a panic attack. I didn't want to answer the door, but I had to.

But he was so understanding. He didn't freak out about it. He went and got me a Slurpee. He gave me the best back rub. He asked me what else he could do for me. When I tried to tell him how stupid I felt it was that I had these, he just shrugged and said, "It's not like you can control it."

Which is so true. Also something that frustrates me, because yes, I like to control things.

I don't tell many people I have them. Definitely not co-workers. So many people still look down on any mental illness as a sign of weakness. I know I should be open about it, to break the stigma, but I'm not one to draw attention to myself. Maybe one day I'll be brave enough to do that.

But Wyatt knows and he doesn't seem to think any less of me for it.

Tonight is the Condors' game against Calgary, and Wyatt and his friend Baz Chadha are doing an interview for

CBC for Hockey for All. We're going out with Baz and his agent for drinks after the game. And it's Valentine's Day. Wyatt hasn't said anything about that, and I'm not going to. It's kind of a silly, made-up holiday.

I watch the game from Dad's box on the press level. I don't go to many games, but I've been watching them on TV—okay, I've been watching Wyatt on TV—so I figured not only would I get to see the game live, and then meet up with Wyatt and Baz after, I'd get to spend time with Dad.

I arrive while the warm-up is going on. Dad's already there, along with Théo and Scott. I meet Théo's eyes as I greet them, both of us remembering the troubling discussion the other night. Dad looks sharp in his suit and tie. I guess I'll see how sharp his mind is tonight. My stomach is tight with anxiety.

Théo and Scott are also wearing suits, and since I'm sitting up here with them, I dressed up a bit too—black trousers, a fitted black turtleneck, and high-heeled boots. I hang my fluffy ivory faux-fur jacket over the back of my chair and set my purse on the floor beneath the counter.

I lean on the counter to peer way down at the ice, immediately searching out Wyatt. He's feeding pucks to Jimmy to shoot at the net, one after another. I smile.

We haven't told anyone that we're dating for real. Mom and Dad still think it's just a PR thing. I asked Lacey not to say anything to Théo about our conversation where I spilled my guts about Gage, warning her that nobody else in my family knows that sordid story and I want to keep it that way.

Everyone thinks I'm perfect. The perfect daughter. The perfect student, when I was in high school and college. The perfect director of the Foundation. They don't need to know that the reason I try so hard to be perfect is because I know I'm the exact opposite.

I listen to Théo, Scott, and Dad talking hockey business. The trade deadline is Monday, so everyone is focused on that. I know Théo has been working long hours, involved in top secret discussions with other teams, trying to strategically make the best deals possible. It's like putting together a puzzle—trying to get the best player possible while staying within the salary cap, mindful of the players on the team he wants to keep and how much that will cost.

If anyone's up for it, it's Théo. He's super smart and analytical, and I think Dad made one of his best decisions ever hiring him as GM. Lots of people think he's too young, but I think his analytics background, plus being a former hockey player, make him perfect for the job. He made some amazing deals over the summer, and already the team is doing better than they ever have.

"I don't know," Théo says. "Boston hasn't done much for Jackman since they got him in December. He's only suited up for one game."

"But he's got a lot of potential," Scott says. "He's young."

Théo shakes his head.

"You can never have enough defensive depth in the playoffs," Dad says in his distinctive craggy voice. "And Jackman is on a cheap deal that expires after this season, so there's no risk in getting him."

I watch Théo's face, because I have no idea if Dad's statement makes sense or not, but Théo nods. "That's true."

Hmm.

The warm-up is ending, so I pull out my phone to check social media. Taylor has sent a hilarious Snapchat picture of Byron sprawled on his back on the floor, sleeping.

I scroll through Twitter, check out a few hashtags I follow, laugh at @dog_rates.

I need a dog.

What? I'm too neurotic to have a dog. But it would be nice . . .

"Want a drink, Everly?" Théo asks, standing.

"Um, sure. I'll have a vodka and cranberry."

Scott goes with him, and I'm alone with Dad. As usual, it feels stupid to bring up memory problems when he seems fine. "Dad?"

"Yeah?" He turns affectionate eyes on me.

"I love you."

He blinks in surprise. Then he smiles, his face crinkling up. "I love you too, sweet girl."

I study him, his legendary crystal blue eyes, his tanned face, his thinning gray hair. My heart squeezes with love and I reach out and grab his hand briefly, smiling back at him.

I want to ask him about the money, to see for myself if he knows what I'm talking about, but it's not the time or place. Théo and Scott return with drinks for all of us and I take mine and set it on the counter.

Pierre Lalonde, GM of the Flames, sticks his head in the door. "Hey, Bob, how are you?"

"Pierre!" Dad stands and greets his colleague (adversary?) with a strong handshake. "How are you?"

They make small talk and I lean closer to Théo. "He seems fine tonight," I murmur.

"Yep." Then Théo joins Dad and Pierre, and I can tell from the conversation that Théo and Pierre have already had discussions this week.

The game is an exciting one, with end-to-end action and scoring going back and forth. First the Flames are up by a goal. The Condors score a goal to tie it and then another to go ahead. Then the Flames even the scoring, and get another. It's crazy but wildly entertaining, both teams playing hard and fast. The game is tied four all with only forty-four seconds left in the third period, seriously looking like overtime, when Baz scores for the Flames.

The wild atmosphere in the arena dims, the crowd falling silent. I drop my head forward. This might as well have been sudden death overtime, because the chances of tying it up in forty-four seconds are slim.

And . . . they don't. We lose five–four.

Ah well.

I hang around a few minutes to chat with other people who stop by the box. Now Dad looks tired, and I can tell he doesn't remember the name of someone he's talking to. It's not a huge deal . . . it's someone from the Flames, not a person he knows well, but he's always been so personable, remembering people's names and their spouses' and children's names and . . . I learned how to do it from him.

My throat constricts but I keep my smile in place, making sure the people we're talking to have no idea Dad doesn't know Sheldon's name.

This is probably what Mom does. All the time.

Now my heart aches for my mom. I can't imagine what it would be like to be dealing with this, the man you love slowly losing his mind.

I pull in a long breath and let it out slowly. I have to get through the rest of this evening.

I take the elevator down to ice level and make my way to the family lounge just outside the dressing room. There are still media interviews going on, so I duck into the lounge. The players are starting to come out in their game day suits, finding their wives or girlfriends in the lounge to head home. I text Wyatt that I'm in here so he'll know where to look, then spend a few minutes socializing with Elle and Anna, two of the players' wives. I feel a bit out of place down here, because I'm not a wife or girlfriend—at least not officially—but everyone talks to me and is friendly to me because of who I am. They know I've been watching the game with the owner of the team up in the press box. I could think it sucks that they're only nice to me because of who I am, but I decided a long time ago not to feel that way. I'm just happy they're friendly to me, and I figure if I'm a nice person back to them, then maybe it's *not* just because of who I am.

My phone pings with a text, and I check it to see Wyatt is showered and changed and out of the dressing room, waiting for me outside. "Well, I have to go," I say. "So nice to see you again!"

"You too, Everly!"

I meet up with Wyatt in the corridor. He gives me a tired smile, leans down to smooch my lips, and we start walking toward the exit. "Baz will meet us at the Beach Bistro," he says, naming a bar that's in the Fairmont, where the Flames are staying. We decided to meet there for a drink to make things easy for Baz.

"Sounds good. Sorry you lost," I say, slipping my hand into his. "It was a really good game."

"Fuck." He shakes his head. "So fucking close." He makes a frustrated noise in his throat.

"It really was."

I've learned that he likes to talk about games after. Some players don't; I know this from my brothers. But I've also learned that Wyatt doesn't expect me to say much. He just wants to unload. So I let him, with the occasional, "I know!" and "That is so true."

Then we're at the Fairmont. The Beach Bistro is a cool indoor/outdoor bar here. It's a nice evening and there are heaters, so we head outside.

"Oooh! Let's sit there!" I point at the fire pit with Adirondack chairs arranged around it.

Wyatt strides over and we sit and order drinks while we wait for Baz and his agent. Lights glow in the big fig trees around us on the wooden deck, more lights shining on the tables, palm trees silhouetted against the midnight blue sky. I lean toward the flames leaping up, gold and orange and blue.

There's actually live music on a small raised stage, a quartet playing smoky, bluesy jazz.

"Oh my God, I love this place." I relax into my chair.

The waiter brings our glasses of Pinot Noir. I sip and it's delicious.

"This is so perfect." I let out a sigh and relax.

"It'd be more perfect if we'd won." But Wyatt leans over and touches his wineglass to mine.

"I know." We sip our drinks.

"Oh hey, there's Baz." Wyatt stands and waves.

A dark-haired man waves back and heads our way, smiling. I saw him earlier, at the interview, although we didn't speak. I stand too, smiling, so Wyatt can introduce us.

Then my gaze lands on the man behind Baz. A tall, muscular man, dressed in an expensive suit. He's smiling too . . . until he sees me.

My heart stops beating.

Our eyes meet.

I haven't seen or heard from Gage in nearly eleven years.

"Baz, this is Everly Wynn." Wyatt touches my lower back. "Everly, Baz Chadha."

"Nice to meet you," I murmur politely, a practiced smile in place. "I saw you earlier during the interview but didn't get a chance to say hi. Thanks for doing that for the Hockey for All program."

"Of course. Happy to. And good to meet you also." He half turns to the man now standing next to him. "This is my agent, Gage Gregoire. Gage, have you met Wyatt Bell?"

"Haven't had the pleasure." Gage extends a hand to Wyatt and they shake.

"And his girlfriend, Everly Wynn."

We face each other. Heat suffuses my body, my heart now galloping. I don't know what to say.

"We *have* met," Gage says. "A long time ago when I played for the Condors."

"Small world," Wyatt quips and we all move to take seats.

I'm trying to breathe. I pick up my wine and take a quick sip. I have a strong urge to get up and run.

"Gage and I wanted a chance to meet up while we're

both in L.A.," Baz says. He looks up as our waiter pauses beside his chair, then requests a sparkling water with lime. Gage orders a Manhattan. "So thanks for letting him tag along."

Gage snorts, grinning.

"No worries," Wyatt says easily. He doesn't seem to have noticed that I'm dying of awkward. Hopefully I can keep it that way.

I let them talk, keeping a smile and an interested look on my face, trying to gather my thoughts and act appropriately.

The man sitting across from me is a reminder of the worst mistake I ever made. Not only do I hate making mistakes, and I relive them for way too long all by myself, I hate being reminded of them.

I glance at him and our eyes meet.

I look away immediately.

I drain my wineglass and look around for our waiter. Wyatt notices and gets his attention. He's such a sweetheart.

Fuck.

"Thanks," I say to him with a smile. "I'm just going to use the ladies' room." I pick up my purse and stand.

I have no idea where the ladies' room is but I stumble blindly across the outdoor deck. I pause at the bar to ask, and they direct me down a corridor just inside the bar, to the left.

I lock myself in a stall and sit there. Okay. I got this. I don't need to be so freaked out by it. Yes, I thought I loved Gage. Yes, I thought he loved me too, when basically he was a lying, cheating pedophile. Sixteen wasn't even the legal age of consent in California. He was fucking a sixteen-year-old girl.

I inhale slowly. He got traded away and his career never took off after that. My dad was responsible for trading him, obviously, but as for his career tanking, I don't know how much Dad had to do with it. I'd bet my condo Dad had *something* to do with it, though. I was stupid and immature and looking for attention from my dad, and I'll regret all of it to my dying day. But I also hate Gage for his part in what happened. He should never have come near me. He should never have led me on.

He probably hates me too, and I guess he'd have every right.

I'm reliving what happened back then, until I realize I've been gone a while and everyone's going to wonder what happened to me. I wash my hands, touch up my lip gloss, and swipe a bit of smudged mascara from beneath one eye. I fluff my hair and then I can't put it off any longer.

With my chin up and my spine straight, I walk out of the ladies' room. And there's Gage, standing there, apparently waiting for me.

"Everly." He gives me a cold smile. "I can't believe we ran into each other like this."

Fuck, fuck, fuck. "Well, like Wyatt said, it's a small world. Especially the hockey world, I guess."

"I hear you're working for your dad now."

"Not really. I'm the director of the Condors Community Foundation. It's a separate organization."

"Sure."

"I should get back . . ."

"Wyatt Bell, huh? Does he know what happens to guys Bob Wynn's little girl dates?"

My jaw drops in outrage. "Are you kidding me?"

"Not really." One corner of his mouth deepens. "I could tell him."

My eyes pop.

"He doesn't know about us, huh."

For a moment my blood is bubbling so hot through my veins I can't speak. "How many people have *you* told about 'us'?" I fix my most forbidding look on him. "Are you proud of dating a sixteen-year-old girl when you were twenty-eight? And married! Because I think most people wouldn't be very impressed by that."

His face tightens. "You were a very willing participant."

"Hey." Wyatt's voice has us both jumping around. He tilts his head, a notch of concern between his eyebrows. "Everything okay?"

"Yes." I'm sure I look guilty and panicked and terrified. "Everything's fine. I was just on my way back."

He nods, his gaze sliding back and forth from Gage to me. He slaps a hand on Gage's shoulder. "I'm following you to the bathroom, man." And he almost shoves Gage down the dimly lit corridor.

I walk back to the table slowly, my hand over my mouth. I feel like crying. I can't cry.

Baz is there, relaxed in his chair, surveying the patio bar, his foot moving to the music. He smiles at me as I take my seat. "Nice place," he says. "I love coming to L.A."

I smile too. "Yeah, I guess Calgary's a bit different in February."

"No kidding."

"Where did you grow up?"

"Toronto. My parents emigrated to Canada before I was born, and that's where they ended up."

"They're still there?"

"Yeah."

"They must be proud of what you've accomplished."

He laughs. "They don't get hockey at all, but yeah."

I cast a worried glance toward the inside bar, where Wyatt and Gage still are. Wyatt looked annoyed. And Gage . . . is he telling Wyatt about us? It reflects even worse on him than it does on me. He wouldn't. Would he?

21

WYATT

I DON'T KNOW WHAT THE FUCK THIS DUDE WAS DOING talking to Everly in the hall and looking like he was pissed at her. I don't like it and I'm glad I interrupted. Everly looked petrified. But why?

He's a big guy, but I'm bigger and stronger. I can tell. Pretty sure he hasn't played hockey in years, and it doesn't look like he works out either. So I kind of use my physicality to separate him from Everly and hustle him into the men's room.

I don't look at him as we stand at the urinals. "So you and Everly met before, huh?"

"Yeah."

"That was what . . . ten years ago?"

"About that. Maybe eleven. That's when I got traded to the Wild." His tone has an ugly edge.

"Huh." There was something about the way he'd looked at her that I don't like. Eleven years ago, Everly was sixteen.

And I remember what she told me, about some trouble she'd gotten into when she was a teenager.

My stomach heaves.

We wash our hands side by side at the sinks.

"Be careful with her," Gage says. "Her dad's pretty protective."

I tug paper towels out of the dispenser and dry my hands. "And you know that how?"

His face ruddies. "Everyone knows it."

I react without thinking, adrenaline flashing through my veins. I shove him up against the tile wall. "Did you touch her?"

He eyes me defiantly. "Ask her."

I stare him down. "You better not have touched her. It's not only her dad who's protective of her." I give him a hard thrust against the wall and step back. As he winces, I straighten my suit jacket, eye him with disdain, and walk out.

Back at the table, the fire flickering from the center, I sit. I'm tense. Edgy. Pissed. I don't even know for sure why. I turn to Everly. "We need to go."

She has her arms wrapped around her stomach, her lips tight. "Oh. Okay."

Baz seems surprised but stands as we do. He holds out a hand. "Great to see you, man."

I take it and slap his shoulder with my other. "Yeah, you too. I'll take care of the bill on my way out."

"No, no . . . I got this."

"You don't even drink, dude." I shake my head, my lips curved into a smile that is not happy. "No worries. Hope you and Gage have a good talk."

I take Everly's arm and lead her out with long strides that nearly trip her up. I slow my roll and take more care with her.

We stop at the valet parking out in front of the hotel and wait for the attendant to bring my car around. I turn to face her. It's cooler here, the ocean not far away. I grasp her upper arms. "Are you okay?"

Her eyes are big and shiny, fastened on mine, her head tipped back. She nods. "Are you mad?"

"Mad? Uh . . . fuck. I don't know what the hell I am." I shake my head. My insides are clenched and my chest tingles with dread. I don't even know why.

The valet helps Everly into the SUV. I see how the guy looks at her. She looks smoking hot tonight, expensive and classy, the black turtleneck and pants outlining her slim figure, gold and diamond accessories glinting at her ears and wrist. I take a deep breath.

She was sixteen.

I rub my mouth as I pull out of the hotel driveway, hanging a left onto Ocean Avenue. I blow past Wilshire, then Santa Monica, and Everly tentatively says, "Where are we going?"

"My place."

"No." She lifts her chin, her lips tight. "I want to go home."

For a moment, I don't answer. Then I say, "Fine."

I make a left at the next intersection and zoom up whatever street it is. I control my frustration enough to check out some street signs and get my bearings. I haven't gone that far out of our way, so a few turns get us back on track and soon I'm pulling up in front of her place.

She unfastens her seatbelt and shifts so she's facing me. "You don't have to come in."

My jaw clenches. "I don't *have* to?"

"What is wrong?"

"I saw the way he looked at you."

She gapes at me, and the look of pain and repulsion on her face makes me feel like an asshole. "Who?"

"Gage. I gather you two . . . knew each other."

Her lips tremble but she lifts that stubborn little chin and tosses her hair back. "That was a long time ago. Look. I think we've taken this too far. We were supposed to go out a few times and get some media attention. We both know there can't be any more than that. So we can't see each other again."

My molars are grinding and I force myself to relax my jaw. "What the fuck?"

"You're all bent out of shape over nothing." She waves a hand. "Come on, you're Mr. Fun. Clearly you're not having fun."

She's right. Dammit. But she's not making sense. I don't want to have fun right now, I want to punch someone. Preferably Gage Gregoire. My life isn't just about having fun all the time, for fuck's sake.

"Okay, so we're good." She attempts to suck in a breath and nearly sobs. "Thanks for lots of fun, Wyatt. See you around."

Incredulously, I watch as she opens the door and hops out of my vehicle. Even in her high heels, she runs lightly along the sidewalk to her door.

What the hell just happened? I think I've been dumped.

I also don't think I've ever been angrier in my life.

I watch her unlock her door and enter the condo. The outside light extinguishes. I sit there longer, my body buzzing, my hands clenching and unclenching on the steering wheel. I don't even know what to do. Chase after her and argue with her?

I don't want to end things with her.

I slam the vehicle into drive and pull away from the curb. My vision is hazy. I probably shouldn't be driving. I only had one drink, so it's not that.

Why am I so pissed? She's right. Mr. Fun. Ha. Good one. But that's me. Life is too short to be miserable. And unlike hockey, there's no replay in life.

I focus on the road so I don't screw things up even worse by crashing into someone, and drive home.

There, I pour myself a big glass of scotch and throw myself down onto my couch.

I can't stop thinking about Gage Gregoire. The way he looked at Everly. The way she looked guilty and afraid.

The connections I'm making in my head make me want to puke.

My chest and stomach are burning inside, and once again my jaw aches from clenching it without even realizing. I gulp down some scotch. That heats me up nicely, sending a tingle all the way to my fingers.

I'm . . . pissed. Furious. I think . . . nah.

That can't be my heart breaking. That shit doesn't happen in real life.

More scotch sears its way down my throat.

I don't like this. I don't like feeling like this. These

intense emotions remind me of when Hank died. I didn't want to analyze my feelings then, and I don't want to now.

So I wallow in agony as I try to drown my emotions in scotch.

It doesn't really work.

IT'S A GOOD THING WE'RE FLYING TO VANCOUVER TODAY. I won't think about Everly or Gage fucking Gregoire or the shit that went down last night. I'll just have fun with the guys. Road trips are great for hanging out together and bonding.

It's pissing rain when we land in Vancouver. Fine with me. We check in at the hotel and don't have much time before we get back on the bus to go to the Rogers Arena for a game day skate. I'm pumped. Humming with energy. I can't wait to get on the ice and burn off some of these damn feelings.

Our opponents don't know what hit them. I'm slamming guy after guy into the boards, playing the body, standing up in the neutral zone. I even score a goal, beating their goalie clean with a sizzling wrist shot from the blue line. And we win, three—one.

From Vancouver we fly to Calgary. I settle down Sunday between games, but Monday, the day we play Calgary, is the trade deadline, and everyone else is on edge about that. You never know what can happen on the trade deadline. Teams that want to make a push for the playoffs are looking to bolster their team; other teams, who know they're out, might want to clear up some cap space by getting rid of someone. I have to admit I'm a little tense myself. Last year, it was me being traded, except I'd asked for it, hard as it was to leave the bunch of guys I was so close with in Detroit.

The team doesn't escape unscathed, with Théo making a few moves. They don't have a huge impact, though; two of the guys play for the Pasadena Condors, although they've been up and down; and in a surprise move our backup goalie is gone, which kind of sucks. He's a good guy. But we have a lot of depth at the goalie level, with a couple of guys in Pasadena that can take over that role. It's probably good for Bolton; he'll get to play a lot more in Pittsburgh.

That night, playing against Baz again revives my muddled feelings. It's not his fault his agent is an asshole; it just reminds me of Thursday night, and I'm flying up and down the ice again. And we win again.

Hell. If this is heartbreak, I should experience it more often.

Except, alone in my hotel room after the game, phone in hand, staring at social media pictures of Everly and me like a sappy teenage boy, the ache in my chest returns full-on, eclipsing the soreness of my body after two extremely physical games. Coldness seeps into my bones, my arms and legs heavy. Jesus. I should be listening to an Adele song, or something.

I pause on an Instagram image of just Everly. She's so beautiful. Inside and out. I called her a perfect princess, and yeah, she damn near is perfect, but I've seen she's not afraid to get messed up and dirty. Damn, in more ways than one. Sure, Everly hot and sweaty in bed is fucking fantastic, but she was also sweaty that day she was cooking lunch at the homeless shelter. And the day we went hiking in the hills. And she was still beautiful. My lungs burn as I breathe in.

She's my boss's daughter. And she's right. We let this go too far. It should have just been a few very public dates, and now emotions have gotten involved and . . . .and . . . I'm all fucked-up. Shit.

I lean my head back against the headboard and close my eyes.

I WALK INTO HEATHER'S HOUSE A FEW DAYS LATER. THE roast chicken smells fantastic. I take off my jacket and drop it over the arm of a chair. I look around. The place is quiet, other than some music playing. "Where's Owen?"

"He's over at a friend's place."

"Oh. I could've picked him up. Do you want me to go get him?"

"No." She shakes her head. She's holding a wineglass and now I notice that her fingers are trembling a little and her face is tense. "He's staying there for dinner. I'll go get him a bit later."

"Well, damn." Disappointed that I don't get to see him, I sit down in a chair. "You should have told me. We could have made it another night."

"Would you like a drink? I have this red wine." She holds up her glass. "Or beer."

"Uh, okay, a glass of wine would be nice."

She moves into the kitchen and pours from the bottle

sitting on the counter, then returns to hand me the glass. The ruby liquid is sloshing in her shaking hand.

"Is everything okay?" I eye her with concern as she sits, too, on the couch, turned to face me.

"I'm, uh, yes, fine. Fine." She gulps some wine. "I didn't change the plan for tonight because I wanted to talk to you. Alone."

"Oh." I sip my wine too. "Are things okay with Owen? Did something happen at school?"

"No, nothing happened. I wanted to talk to you about . . . Everly." Her voice shakes and she swallows.

"Everly?" My eyebrows shoot up and heat stabs through my chest at hearing her name. "Why?"

"Are things serious with her?"

I shift in my chair. "Uh . . ."

I haven't got a hot clue how to answer that. She dumped me. And I'm miserable as hell about it. I can't stop thinking about her. I keep remembering moments, when she made me laugh, when she pissed me off and then made me laugh, when she served dinner to homeless people, and when she got down on her knees in the shower and looked like she loved what she was doing. . .

I suck air into my lungs.

"You don't need to worry about that," I tell her, my voice scratchy, not exactly sure where her question is coming from and wanting to reassure her. "I've told her that you and I just friends. I told her that you were married to my best friend and I help look after you and Owen now that Hank's gone."

"Oh." Her lips quiver. "Just friends."

"Yeah." I study her. "Heather . . ."

She presses her lips together and lifts her chin. "I'm not just friends with you, Wyatt. Since Hank died, you've been around so much, and . . . I mean at first I was grieving for Hank . . . but now . . . I'm in love with you."

Holy shit. I stare at her, trying to keep my mouth from falling open, trying to keep my expression calm . . . but inside I'm a freakin' typhoon.

"I thought maybe you were feeling the same," she continues in a soft voice. She scoots to the edge of the couch and leans toward me. "You do so much for us. You haven't had a girlfriend since you moved here. You love Owen. I thought maybe you were developing feelings for me too . . ." She swallows. "We get along really well, and have a lot in common."

What do we have in common? Besides Owen and Hank. Okay, Heather likes hockey. And she has a pretty good sense of humor, and she's a great mom, but I've never felt anything more than sympathy and affection for her. I still haven't said a word, flabbergasted.

"You've been seeing Everly Wynn," she continues. "You didn't tell me about her. I didn't think much of it until you showed up here with her. I was . . . hurt."

"I'm sorry." My response is automatic. I had no idea. I rub the back of my head and look away.

"I thought about it and realized I have to tell you how I feel if I ever want to have a chance with you."

My head is spinning. This is insane. I don't know what to say. I don't want to hurt her—again—but I don't feel like that about her.

I do feel like that about Everly.

Before I can say a word, though, she goes on. "Owen

needs a dad." Her voice trembles. "And he looks up to you so much. You've been there for him, since Hank died. You've really helped him deal with his father dying. You're a huge part of his life."

Jesus. Guilt slams into me like a slap shot. It knocks the wind right of me.

I'm the reason Hank is dead.

That's why I do so much for them. I mean, I really do love Owen, and Heather's great, a good mom, a nice person. But I realize that selfishly, everything I do is to try to make myself feel better.

I gaze helplessly at Heather as more guilt pummels me.

She's right. Owen needs a dad. And I'm the one who took his dad away from him.

Owen does love me. It would be easy. There are times Heather, Owen, and I *are* almost like a family. That time we went to Disneyland, people *did* think we were a family. We could make it official and I could spend the rest of my life trying to make up for how I let them down.

Now Heather's waiting. Watching me, clutching her wineglass, her eyes flickering.

How much am I willing to do to make up for the heartache I've caused them?

I keep thinking about Everly.

I think I might be in love with her. Fuck it, I know I am. I never planned on having that. I don't feel like I deserve it. But she doesn't feel the same.

If I can't be with Everly, maybe I should think about what Heather's saying. Hank, wherever he is, would be happy that I'm taking care of his family. Or would he be pissed? I don't really know, and I guess I never will, but I think I need to live life for the living. It would make sense. It would help assuage my guilty conscience and make up for my failings.

But my insides are rebelling, my gut churning, my lungs burning. I know what I should do . . . but can I?

22

EVERLY

Our second family meeting is at Théo's place, because it's a little more central for everyone coming from different directions—Harrison from Pasadena, JP from Long Beach, Noah and Riley driving up from San Diego together. This time Lacey joins us too.

When I walk in, Lacey focuses on me and her forehead creases. "Are you okay?"

I nod brusquely. I'd rather eat my own foot than tell her about my broken heart with the whole family here, especially my three brothers.

She clearly doesn't believe me, but lets it go. For now.

"Okay, check in time," I announce, sitting at Théo's dining table. "What have you all learned?"

Théo slaps some papers on the table. "Here. This should answer some questions."

"What's that?" I eye the papers.

"The lawsuit." He shakes his head.

"Whoa."

"It's public information. I don't know why we didn't think of just looking at it sooner."

I make a grab for it, but JP gets it first. "Okay, Théo, give us a synopsis."

"Here's the deal. Grandpa didn't steal the money . . . exactly."

I stare at him.

"He borrowed it. He used the money to fund the purchase of Steve Holbrook's share of the Condors. He wrote out the loan contract and agreed to pay interest using installments."

"That's not stealing!" My eyes pop open wide.

"But . . ." Théo holds up a hand. "He didn't repay it as per the stipulations in the contract. According to that"—he gestures at the papers JP is now scanning—"they tried to talk to him about it and even sent him written notices, but he still didn't pay up. So they sued him."

"He failed to timely cure such defaults and accordingly . . . the entire balance of the note would become immediately due and payable," JP reads.

We all fall silent.

My mind whirls. Well, this isn't as bad as outright theft, but . . . I swallow.

"Mom knows about this," I say, my voice scratchy. "She wouldn't tell me anything, but I know she knows." I relate my conversation with my mom.

"I talked to Aline," Lacey adds. "She wouldn't say much either. She thinks it's a 'misunderstanding,' but she supports Matthew and Mark."

"Obviously," I add.

"But she doesn't believe your mom had anything to do with it," Lacey adds. She meets my eyes and smiles.

"She's been coming to pretty much every meeting with Grandpa," Théo says. "And I saw her meeting with Kate."

The chief financial officer of the Condors organization.

I wrinkle my nose. Why would that be?

I'm not the only one wondering that. "What the hell?" Riley snaps. "Why would she do that? Is she trying to get more money?"

I turn and level her with a narrow-eyed look. "Excuse me?"

JP waves his hands. "Stop. We aren't going to solve things if we keep acting like our parents." He focuses on Riley. "That was kind of uncalled for, Ri."

She purses her lips. "I'm sorry."

I inhale a fortifying breath as I check my notes from our last meeting. "Harrison and Asher . . . what happened when you talked to Dad?"

They exchange a loaded look. Asher sighs. "I don't think it was a good day for Dad."

My stomach clenches. I don't even need to know what he means. "Oh." I meet his eyes. "Mom's trying to get him to go to the doctor."

The air in the room thickens.

"He won't go," I continue, trying to keep my voice from trembling.

"I'll talk to him," Théo says quietly.

"No, I will," JP speaks up. "I know you two are close because you work together, but he and I talk . . . quite a bit."

"Have you noticed problems?" I ask him.

"Yeah." He purses his lips. "Sometimes. But other times he's totally fine."

"He either didn't know what we were talking about," Harrison says, "or he was pretending not to know. I'm not sure which is worse."

"Shit." I rub my forehead, feeling the tension gathering in my shoulders. "JP? Théo? Did you learn anything from *your* dad?"

JP grimaces. "Dad is still super pissed about it. I get it. It's a lot of money. I think he's worried they'll never see it again. And apparently he needs the money. Purchasing the Golden Eagles was a huge risk for him."

"Well, he didn't need to buy a hockey team," Asher says. "He only did that because he was pissed at Dad."

The air snaps with tension, but JP answers calmly. "He always thought he'd have that trust fund there if he needed it, and now it's gone." He and Asher have a stare down.

Asher nods. "Fair point."

"My dad doesn't need the money," Riley adds, looking around. "I asked him about it. He's okay financially. I think he's more worried about Grandpa than angry. But he *is* pissed about it."

"He has a right to be," JP adds. "Does he think Chelsea was involved?"

"No." She makes a face. "He says he doesn't totally trust her, but apparently she talked to him about it and . . . he wouldn't tell me what exactly was said, but I got the impression she was trying to fix things."

"That's the impression I got too," I put in. "My poor mom. She's dealing with Dad and his . . . health issues."

Wow, that's a euphemism for my worst fears. "And the money issues."

"I think that's why she sits in on meetings," Théo says quietly. "I suspect she wants to know what's going on in the business so she can, er, remind Grandpa. Or help him understand."

"Oh my God." I bury my face in my hands. "Oh my God."

Lacey gets up and moves around the table. She rubs my back. "I'm sorry, Ev."

My dad. This can't be happening to my dad. I know he's not young, but come on, seventy-two isn't old either. And he's still so fit and agile. Physically. *Oh my God.*

I've been so worried about this, hoping and hoping it's not really happening. With so many others confirming my own fears, it's hard not to feel devastated. But we still don't know for sure. He hasn't gone to the doctor and gotten a diagnosis. There's still room for a tiny bit of hope.

But Mom wouldn't be involved in the hockey team if she didn't think there was good reason. She knows how that could be perceived by Mark and Matthew . . . that she's taking over or interfering, trying to get money. She wouldn't do that unless she had to.

Oh my God.

I lift my head and look around the table, my eyes burning. "What do we do next?"

"I wonder if they've tried mediation," Théo says, rubbing his chin. "If we got everyone in a room together—I mean Uncle Mark, Dad, and Grandpa—and tried to get them to talk it out, maybe that would help."

"It won't help if Dad doesn't even remember what he did," Harrison says quietly.

"Yeah." Théo nods. "What would end this?"

"If Dad and Uncle Mark got their money back," JP replies.

"Maybe we should talk to Chelsea." Théo looks at me.

I roll my lips inward while I consider that. "Maybe."

"Who should do it?" JP looks from me to my brothers.

We all exchange glances as well. "All of us?" Harrison suggests.

"I told you, I tried to talk to Mom," I say.

"What if we tell her that we all want this stupid feud over, and we're trying to figure out how to do that. Ask for her help," Harrison says.

I nod slowly. "Maybe. Or maybe someone should talk to Mark and Matthew. Do they know that Dad is . . . maybe not well?" Pain slices through my chest. "Maybe *they* should make an effort to resolve things before it's too late."

"I'm sure they've noticed too," Théo says. "Although they don't see Grandpa very often anymore."

"This is ridiculous." I'm losing patience. "We're talking about a fight over stupid money, when my dad is . . . is . . ." I can't even say it. Alzheimer's is fatal, although it can take a long time. I slide my gaze around the table. "We all have more than enough money to be comfortable. Family is more important than money."

Heavy silence fills the room, and then everyone murmurs agreement.

"Okay," I say to Harrison, Asher, and Noah. "Let's talk to Mom. Let's start with that. How do we get her alone?"

"I'll figure out something," Asher says. He looks as

pained as I'm sure I do, his mouth tight and his eyes dark, and yet he asks, "You okay, Ev?"

I am so far from okay. I was a mess before I got here, after ending things with Wyatt. After falling in love with him, which I knew I shouldn't do. After coming face-to-face with my ugly past. And now I feel sick about Dad.

"No." I attempt a smile. "But we have to deal with it."

I want to go, but we sit around talking for a while longer until Riley and Noah say they have to get going. Everyone else stands, making the move to leave. Lacey hugs me, and I pick up my purse to head out too.

Outside Lacey and Théo's place, I stand on the sandy sidewalk for a moment. It's dark, and a chilly, salty breeze is wafting in off the ocean. I shiver and walk down the sidewalk, but instead of going to my car, I turn, make a loop around the back of the building, and look up at Wyatt's place. His living room window is faintly illuminated.

My heart reaches out to him with a yearning that hurts. He's so close. As in physical proximity. But I ended things with him.

I wander farther down the sidewalk and step onto the beach.

It's dark, although lights along the path and from the houses lining it keep it from being completely black. The sky is a clear, deep blue, stars glinting out over the ocean. The distant hushed whoosh of ocean waves onto the sand carries on the soft breeze. I kick off my ballet flats and dig my toes into the cool sand, wandering a bit. Then I lower myself onto the beach, sitting cross-legged.

I gaze at the building where Wyatt is. The sliding doors onto his terrace glow yellow. He's in there.

My chest constricts and my stomach is quaking.

Why did I end things with him? It all seems so meaningless now. What does anything matter, when we're all just going to die?

Okay, that sounds melodramatic, but it's true. Dad could have a heartbreaking illness that will steal him away from us. Why am I worried about what could happen if I'm with Wyatt? What difference does it make in the big scheme of things? He's not Gage and I'm not sixteen.

And I don't have to be perfect.

I'm not perfect. And there's no such thing anyway. And . . . Wyatt knows I'm not. He's seen me at my worst and still seemed to like me. With him, I feel like I can be myself instead of the person I'm supposed to be. I thought I knew who that was, but now I'm not so sure.

Wow, I was so afraid of screwing up that I . . . screwed up.

Okay. Now it's time to be brave.

I stand and dust the sand off my butt. I trudge through the sand, pick up my shoes, and step onto the sidewalk. I pause once more, take a deep breath, climb the steps to Wyatt's condo, and ring his doorbell.

He opens the door a moment later, a big broad silhouette in the light behind him. He's wearing black sweatpants and a loose gray Condors shirt, his hair tousled. His face registers surprise at seeing me, his head jerking back.

"Hi." I hold his gaze. "Can I come in?"

WYATT

I'M AFRAID TO BELIEVE WHAT I'M SEEING.

Is this really Everly, here at my place?

My gaze wanders over her face. Her eyes are big and dark, her mouth soft and sad. What's going on?

"Uh. Sure." I step aside and she walks in past me.

"We just had our 'family meeting' at Théo and Lacey's place." She drops her purse on a chair and turns to face me, twisting her fingers together. "You know how you always say life is short? So you need to enjoy it?"

"Yeah." The corners of my mouth tick up. "We're here for a good time, not a long time."

"It's true." She swallows. "So true. That's why I'm here."

"For a good time?" I eye her warily. If this is a booty call, I'm not sure I can resist, but I wanted so much more than that with her.

She huffs out a laugh. "Sort of." She shuts her eyes briefly and inhales. "Remember I told you how I was worried about my dad? How he keeps forgetting things and getting confused?"

"Yeah."

"Everyone else has noticed it too. I th-think there's really something wrong with him."

Ah, fuck.

She sucks air into her lungs. "And I was thinking that you're right, we don't have long here, we need to make the most of it, and I decided I should talk to you."

"Okay . . ."

"Can I tell you about Gage?"

Fuck. I clamp my lips tightly together and my stomach lurches. I'm not sure I want to hear this. Except . . . I have to hear it. "Yeah." I gesture to the couch. The TV is still on, but I muted it to answer the door.

She sits, her posture stiff, her fingers still twisting together. "Gage used to play for the Condors."

I sit too, keeping some distance between us, which I hate. "I got that."

"When I was a teenager, about sixteen, my parents had a party one night at our house and he was there. He was . . . interested in me. He kept looking at me and smiling, and talking to me. Flirting. And I . . ."

I keep my mouth shut on the curse words that want to spill out.

"I was interested in him," she admits. "He was older, handsome. He was confident. He was an NHL player. He had a place in the world and people looked up to him, and the way he treated me made me feel . . . grown up. I was always more attracted to older boys—"

"Dan Diaz," I mutter before I can stop myself.

She purses her lips and tilts her head in a mildly reproving gesture. "Since I'm spilling my guts, you might as well know I've been to therapy about this, and I've come to terms with my so-called daddy issues. Part of the attraction with Gage was knowing that my dad would hit the roof if he found out what was going on. Because any attention from Dad was better than being ignored."

"He ignored you?" My jaw slackens.

"Not deliberately. My dad loves me. But he had three sons who all played hockey. He had a big business to run. A hockey team. He was traveling all over the place going to games. Those things got his attention. Not me."

My chest feels like a boa constrictor has wrapped around it. It's hard to breathe.

"Gage told me he was getting a divorce."

"He was fucking *married?*" I stare at her.

"Yes. And he wasn't getting a divorce." She rolls her eyes. "*Then.* They did end up divorced."

"Christ."

"It was stupid," she continues in a low voice. "I know it was, but at the time I was a dumb teenager. I thought it was so exciting. We couldn't be seen together in public, he couldn't tell his friends about me, he couldn't meet my friends, I couldn't tell my parents."

"They found out, I gather."

"Yes. I didn't do it on purpose, but I took a risk of having Gage come over when they were out. I knew they could come home anytime. Probably deep down inside I *wanted* to get caught. I wanted them to know what was going on. Actually, I've realized there was part of me that was scared about what was happening with Gage . . . because I knew it was bad. And they did come home and find us together."

My teeth are clenched so tightly, my molars are in danger of cracking.

"We were on the couch, making out," she adds, reading where my mind has gone. "You can imagine the scene. I thought my dad was going to have a stroke. I was even worried about my mom. She was crying, I was crying . . . Dad broke Gage's nose. There was blood everywhere, Dad was yelling and saying he was going to call the police, Mom was trying to calm him down. They were so horrified. I think when my dad talked about contacting the police and called Gage a pedophile, it suddenly slammed into me what a disaster I'd created."

"You?" My blood pressure rises even more, heat building inside me. "*You* created?"

"That was how I felt," she says. "And I still do, to a certain extent."

"He should have been thrown in jail!"

She grimaces. "Well, he wasn't, and we'll never know if Dad did the right thing or not. After Mom and Dad kicked Gage out and I was sent to my room and grounded for the next two years . . ." She smiles wryly. "Mom and Dad talked about it. They didn't want it all public. It was . . . sleazy, I think was the word they used." She bows her head. "It made me *feel* sleazy. And I was so angry. I thought this was the man I loved and we were going to be together, and they'd ruined everything. I ran away from home."

"Oh Jesus." My hands curl into fists, resisting the urge to pull her into my arms. "Jesus Christ."

Staring at me, she says, "Don't *you* think that?"

"Think what?"

"That I was sleazy."

My jaw drops in horror. "Fuck no."

She draws in a long, shaky breath, her eyes going shiny. "Wyatt . . ."

My eyes sting too, my throat thick. I don't cry very often. I fight the urge back. "You're not sleazy. That was not your fault."

She sucks on her trembling bottom lip, a tear leaking from one corner of her eye. "Thank you."

"Go on. Gage got traded then, didn't he?"

"Yes. Dad did that. He made sure if Gage said anything about it, one word, or ever tried to contact me again, the world would know he was a creep who preyed on underage girls. He got him out of town. I don't actually know what happened between Gage and his wife. I assume he probably did the same thing with another girl . . . s-somewhere else . . ." She chokes to a halt. "I feel horrible about that, if it's what happened. He shouldn't have been able to do that to anyone else."

"Again, not your fault. He was an abuser."

"I know now how ridiculous it was to think that a guy his age would be genuinely interested in a teenager as a girlfriend. I wanted to believe he was really interested in me."

"Yeah." My chest burns. Adrenaline pumps through my veins, making me want to stand up and throw and smash things. I'm so fucking angry on her behalf I can barely think straight.

"I felt so horrible about what I did. How I hurt my parents, and put them into that situation." She swipes fingertips over her cheek. "I've never totally gotten over it."

She has to be perfect.

My heart is hammering against my ribs, a hard pulse in the pit of my stomach. "Fuck, I should have shoved his head in a toilet and drowned him in that bathroom," I growl.

"No. He's not worth it. And it's all in the past."

"Not when he shows up and upsets you like that."

"I'm okay, Wyatt. Yes, it was a painful reminder. I was taken by surprise when he walked in. And he *is* a jerk. I . . ." She tucks some hair behind her ear. "I reacted badly to seeing him. It was a shock. It made me feel like I was making another huge mistake, getting involved with you. Another guy who plays for my dad's team."

My eyes narrow. "That's why you dumped me?"

She sucks briefly on her bottom lip. "Yes. I'm sorry."

I can't breathe. What is she saying? She regrets ending things? She wants to get back together? My heart slams heavily in my chest.

Heather . . . I told Heather I'd think about what she'd said the other night.

I stare at Everly, my eyes burning. I stagger to my feet and take a couple of steps away from her. My gut churns nastily.

"Wyatt?" Her voice is low, tentative. "I'm sorry. I know it's a sordid story. I regret—"

"It's not sordid!" I keep my back to her. "Stop saying that. You were a kid. It's what *he* did that's sickening."

Silence heavy enough to crush us swells in the room.

"Since we're telling our life stories, I guess I should tell you mine," I say roughly. I tip my head back, then turn to face her. I sit again, this time in an armchair across from her.

"Okay." She blinks those beautiful eyes at me.

"I told you Hank was my best buddy."

"Yes."

"We were friends since we played together in Rimouski. He didn't turn pro; he might've had a shot at getting drafted, but he decided to go to university instead. He got an engineering degree, got a job working for a big petrochemical company, and ended up moving down here."

She's watching me. I think I might puke.

"He met Heather and got married. They had Owen. We stayed in touch. One thing we both loved was skiing and snowboarding."

Her eyes flicker and her forehead furrows briefly.

I keep going. "We went on a trip together, snowboarding in the Rockies, in British Columbia. The hockey season had just ended for me, we were out of the playoffs, so Hank and I took off for a week. It was gorgeous, perfect weather. We started into our first run of the day, on a double black diamond run on the back side of the resort."

I stop, pressing a fist to my stomach, memories crowding my mind. "It was so fast. Hank was ahead of me, and then I saw . . ." I swallow. "I saw the snow in front of me give way. It fell down the hill, so fast, right toward Hank."

"Oh God." She covers her mouth with one hand.

"All I could do was watch as it caught up to him. It pushed him toward the trees on the side of the run. I saw his board, and then the snow pulled him right through the trees." My voice is shaking and I take a few seconds to breathe, the images so clear and horrific to me.

"Wyatt," Everly whispers, eyes now full of pain.

"I unstrapped my board and tried to run to him, through all the dirt and branches from the avalanche. I saw him in the snow, his feet uphill. His head was against a tree." I close my eyes. "He was conscious . . . at first. He called me and I scrambled to try to get him, but . . . Christ." I rub a hand over my face. "He kept saying, 'Wyatt, help me.'" Now my voice breaks and Everly is there, kneeling in front of me, curling her hands around mine. I grip her hands. "There was a hole in his throat and his face was smashed." Tears slide down my face. I don't even care. "I was going to undo his bindings, but his leg was basically wrapped around a tree. I took my toque off and tried to use it to stop the bleeding from his throat. Meanwhile I got my cellphone out and tried to call 911, but I couldn't get a signal."

Everly releases my hands and rises up, cupping my face. Tenderly, she wipes the tears away. Her eyes are full of sympathy, not judgment.

"I started yelling for help. In between I was telling Hank to hold on, we'd get out, he'd be okay. But . . . I couldn't save him. By the time help finally got there, he was dead."

I lean my forehead against hers, setting my hands on her shoulders. She feels so small . . . but so strong. For a few moments, neither of us says a word, emotions swamping me, stealing my voice. I'm remembering how I felt, sitting in the snow with my dead best friend, totally helpless.

Finally I draw back. "It's my fault he's dead," I say flatly.

"No! It's not your fault!" Her eyebrows slope down in distress. "You can't believe that."

"It's true." I set my jaw. "That's why I asked to be traded here. Because Heather and Owen are here."

"You *asked* to be traded here? I didn't know that."

"Yeah. We kept it on the down low. I had a word with our GM one day, told him the situation. I said I'd like to move to California, so either the Condors or the Golden Eagles. I was lucky. He made it happen." I pull in a breath through my nostrils. "So I do what I can for the two of them. I owe them. I took Owen's dad. Heather's husband."

"No," she says again, staring at me. "You didn't."

I meet her eyes. "Heather's in love with me."

She jerks back. Sits onto her heels. "Oh."

"She thinks Owen needs a dad."

Everly's head is shaking, back and forth in tiny, jerky movements.

"And he does. I try to be a dad figure for him."

Everly scoots farther away. "Are you . . . in love with her too?"

"No. But I owe them. I owe them my life."

Her eyes widen. She looks stricken. She scrambles to her feet. "You don't owe them your life. That's crazy, Wyatt."

"I owe it to Hank to look after them." My voice cracks.

"Oh God." She pressed her fingers to her mouth, staring at me. "I'm so, so sorry for what you've been through. That's terrible. I'm sorry you lost your friend." She stands staring at me. "I-I'm sorry." She grabs her purse and heads to the door. "I shouldn't have come here."

Guilt punches through me, bands of metal squeezing my chest. I watch her tear out of my condo.

It's for the best.

24

EVERLY

I shouldn't have gone there. I shouldn't have talked to him. I almost told him I love him and then he gave me that bullshit about having to take care of Heather and Owen and her being in love with him and . . . *shit*.

I'm stalking along the sidewalk in the dark to where I left my car when I arrived at Lacey and Théo's place for the meeting. Except tears are blurring my vision and I don't remember where I parked and I can't see the street signs.

I swipe the back of my hand across my nose and let out a little sob.

Fuck. I turn and make my way back to Lacey's place. I punch the doorbell and lean against the wall, crying.

Théo opens the door. Alarm widens his eyes and tightens his features. "What the . . . Everly. Get in here. What's wrong?" He takes my arm and tugs me into the condo. "Are you okay?"

Oh yeah, nobody's ever seen me cry. This is probably tripping him out.

"I need to talk to Lacey." I sniffle pathetically. I have to get my shit together. "I'm sorry to interrupt."

"Don't apologize, it's fine. Lacey!" he shouts over his shoulder in a panicked tone, then turns back to me. "Are you hurt?"

"No. I mean, yes. I'm . . . sad. Very, very sad."

His lips twitch, but his eyes are kind. "I know."

He thinks this is about Dad.

Lacey appears, concern etched on her face. She flies toward me, seeing my tears. "What? What's happening?" She sets her hands on my shoulders.

I lean into her and she wraps her arms around me. "I'm sad."

"I see that." She hugs me, swaying back and forth for a moment. "Come in. Sit."

Thankfully, Théo disappears. Although I guess it doesn't matter anymore if everyone knows my sordid past. I've tried so hard to be what I'm supposed to be, to make Mom and Dad proud of me, but in the end, it doesn't really matter. I can only be who I am. An anxious, neurotic perfectionist. And if that's not good enough—for Wyatt, or for any of my family—too damn bad.

Lacey sits me on the couch, brings me tequila, and lets me talk. She already knows how I feel about Wyatt. I spill the story of what just happened. How I thought I was being brave and living my life on my own terms, telling the truth about my past and how it's affected me, and being honest about my feelings.

I should have known better. I do something spontaneous and instinctive and what happens? I get kicked in the teeth.

"So you *didn't* tell him you love him?" Lacey's eyebrows elevate.

"Um. No. I guess I didn't. He started going on about Heather."

"Who's Heather?"

"Oh hell. I didn't tell you about Heather. And Owen. Oh my God, it's the saddest story." I start crying again.

Lacey hands me the box of Kleenex.

"I don't know if I should tell you." I pluck a tissue and wipe my eyes then blow my nose. "Nobody knows about Heather and Owen."

Lacey cringes. "You said it wasn't his son."

"No, no." I wave a hand. "Owen's not his son. That's true. Wyatt's best friend, Hank, was Owen's father. He died . . . in a snowboarding accident. He and Wyatt were snowboarding."

"Oh no." I can see Lacey's mind leaping ahead.

"Yes. There was an avalanche. Wyatt tried to save his friend, but he c-couldn't." I draw in a steadying breath. "He was devastated, Lacey. Absolutely broken about it. It's why he asked to be traded here, because Heather and Owen are here, and he can look after them."

"Oh my God."

I tell her the rest, about Heather's feelings for Wyatt, and Wyatt's guilt.

Lacey flops back into the couch cushions and stares at the ceiling. "Holy shark testicles."

My mouth falls open, I gape at her, and then I too fall back into the cushions, laughing helplessly. "Jesus, Lacey!"

We roll our heads on the cushions to look at each other, then laugh more, although mine is taking on a hysterical edge. She reaches for my hand and clasps it. "This is a catastrofuck."

I laugh again. "Yes." Then I sober. "I'm also really worried about my dad."

"I know." She squeezes my hand. "And then this on top of that. No wonder you're a mess."

"I *am* a mess, aren't I?" I sigh. "I've tried not to be. But inside I always have been. Cool as a cucumber on the outside; inside, a squirrel on meth."

She chokes on a laugh. "Oh, Everly. You're a beautiful, kind, generous mess."

I sniff. "Thank you." I pause. "What am I going to do?"

"I don't know, honestly." She sinks her teeth into her bottom lip. "Maybe we need to sleep on it? Want to stay here tonight?"

I nod.

"The guest room's ready."

This reminds me of New Year's Eve when I was supposed to share that room with Taylor and ended up passed out in Wyatt's bed. I squeeze my eyes shut against more burning tears and plod into the bedroom.

Lacey's so sweet, bringing me water, a nightie to sleep in, clean towels. "I love you," I whisper to her, hugging her again.

"Love you too. It'll be okay. You'll be okay."

I nod.

Right now it doesn't feel like it. But I will be okay.

THE CONDORS PLAY THE GOLDEN EAGLES ON SUNDAY HERE in Santa Monica. Mom is going to the game because Harrison has been called up from Pasadena, so I decide to attend also. To watch my brother.

Who am I kidding? I'll be watching Wyatt.

I can't stop thinking about him. I admire him so much for what he's done to help his friend's family. What he's sacrificed for them. Leaving the team that drafted him, in the year they won the cup—the ultimate sacrifice for a hockey player. Moving across the country. Spending his time helping them. I ache for what he went through, now knowing the tragedy he survived. I can't believe he would actually marry Heather out of guilt. I want to try to stop him from doing that. But who am I to tell him it's a mistake?

My heart is crushed, bleeding and throbbing. I love him so much. I trusted him enough to tell him the truth about Gage, knowing Lacey was right. You can't have real love and intimacy unless you're honest. And then he was honest right back and broke my heart. I press a hand between my breasts, the ache there stealing my breath.

We're up in Dad's box. Théo's here, of course, but JP is playing against us, with Mark coaching him. Matthew is just down the hall in the visiting GM box to cheer on his team, and on the other side of us, Asher's in the press box. Damn near a family reunion.

It's been a while since the Condors beat the Eagles, but this is a different team this year and they're giving it their best shot. The score is tied at two after the second period, which should mean an entertaining third period.

Asher pops in during the intermission to say hi.

"Condors are playing great defense," he says to Dad. "Totally responsible in their own end. Bell is really playing strong this year. I don't think anyone else on the team has the same ability to keep track of multiple layers of offense like he does. Smart guy."

My throat aches. Even while I feel proud to hear this about Wyatt, it emphasizes how much I miss him.

"And Harrison is really standing out," Asher adds. "He's playing fantastic tonight."

At that moment, Matthew pokes his head in. "Hey, Wynn family. Are we having a reunion here?"

Dad turns and narrows his eyes at his oldest son. Before he can snarl anything, I impulsively say, "Yes, we are. Come in." I gesture.

He strolls in, dressed in a suit and tie, of course, as are Dad and Théo. Asher's more casually dressed in a button-down shirt and dress pants.

Mom's eyes dart back and forth between Dad and Matthew. Asher looks at me and raises an eyebrow. I smile.

"I'm glad you're here, Matthew," I say. "We don't often get this many of us together unless it's a big holiday. I have something I want to say to you and Dad."

Théo's eyes bulge out behind his glasses.

"I know this wasn't the plan," I say to him and Asher. "I don't really give a shit anymore. This feud is ridiculous." I turn my focus to Dad and Matthew, who are both frowning. "We got a copy of the lawsuit. We know what happened. Dad, you need to pay back that money."

Mom speaks up. "Everly. This isn't the time."

"When *is* the time, then?" I'm getting a little heated. I

need to calm down. "Dad. We're all worried about you. About your health."

"I'm healthy as a horse," he growls.

I scoot my chair closer to him to look him in the eye. "You're forgetting things. You get confused. You know this is happening."

His blue eyes gaze back at me. "That's bullshit."

"It's not. You need to go to the doctor. Mom's been trying to convince you and I'm telling you the rest of us agree. I'll take you myself. I—" My voice breaks. "Dad. I love you. I'm worried about you."

His face suddenly looks tired. He pats my knee. "Evvie. Don't worry."

I smile. "You should know me better than that, Dad. Worry's what I do."

"So true." He sighs. "You've always worried about everything. You used to run to the door when I got home from a road trip because you were worried the plane had crashed."

He remembers that. My bottom lip quivers.

"I'll go to the doctor," he says.

"And what about the money?"

His eyes go distant and he frowns.

"Everly. I told you I'm working on it," Mom says in a gentle but firm voice.

I lift my head to fix a stare on her. "You didn't really, Mom. You were all kinds of vague. This has to end and this family has to heal. Money is the most meaningless thing of all to fight over. Dad could be . . ." I stop, my throat closing up. Now I lift my gaze to Matthew, standing watching this,

his forehead furrowed. "You don't know how long we all have here. Is this how you want things to be?"

He flinches. His eyes slide to Dad. He swallows. "No." He clears his throat. "Dad. We'll talk."

"You'll talk to me as well," Mom speaks up. She reaches for Dad's hand and holds it. "We're a team, and you have to accept that."

Matthew's eyes flicker. I glance at Asher and Théo, both watching openmouthed.

"The only thing tougher than a hockey player is his mom," Asher murmurs.

"Dad," Théo says to Matthew, "she's right. You can trust her."

Matthew shoots Théo a frown. "Whose side are you on?"

Théo stands to face his dad. "There are no sides. We're all Wynns."

Matthew's jaw tightens. Then his expression eases. "You're right." He turns to Chelsea and nods, then walks out.

After a couple of beats of silence, Asher says, "Well, that escalated quickly."

I choke on a laugh. I meet Mom's eyes and hers are dancing with amusement too.

"What the hell, Ev?" Asher shakes his head.

"What is the plan you referred to, Everly?" Mom asks sweetly.

Oops. "It's on a need-to-know basis."

She inclines her head. "Fair," she murmurs.

The third period is starting, so Asher hustles out.

I try to focus on the game. I just did something totally not like me.

And it was good.

2 5

WYATT

The TV is on in Heather's living room, some news show, as Owen and I get home from the dinosaur exhibit at the Convention Center.

"We're home!" I call, helping Owen with his shoes.

"In here!" Heather answers from the kitchen.

Owen runs to her. "Mommy! There were real live dinosaurs! One roared at me." He pauses. "It scared me a little."

He'd burst into tears, but we wouldn't tell his mom that. I didn't make him feel ashamed or embarrassed, though. I just dried his tears and told him it was okay to be scared because those dinosaurs are pretty realistic.

"Oh, tell me about it!" she invites.

I follow him, but pause when I hear the name "Everly Wynn" on the TV. My head whips around and I turn into the living room.

"... daughter of hockey legend Bob Wynn, who is the

executive director of the Condors Community Foundation," the newscaster continues. "We reached out for comment on this article but did not get a response. We did speak to the managing director of Safe Charities America, Joseph Link, who produced this report."

They go to a clip of this Joseph Link dude saying, "While the Condors Foundation does successfully raise a lot of money, they scored poor marks on evaluation metrics, such as financial transparency, hoarding cash, and overspending on fundraising, based on analysis of their financial statements of the past three fiscal years."

Hoarding cash? My jaw damn near hits the floor. I gape at the TV.

"In fact, some might say that the Condors Foundation is a puck hog," he finishes with a smirk. "While professional sports teams may have strong track records in sport, when it comes to their charitable foundations, fans may want to consider donating their money to other organizations."

Heat rushes through my body and my hands curl into fists.

"You have got to be fucking kidding me," I snarl.

"What's that?" Heather calls.

This is a big TV station in Los Angeles, with a huge audience. Jesus Christ.

I drop my ass down onto the ottoman. They've gone to another news story, but fuck, my mind is still racing with what I just heard.

Heather comes into the room. "Are you okay? Did the dinosaurs exhaust you?" she teases.

I shake my head, not looking up at her. I stare at the

floor, thinking about Everly. Obviously, she's heard about this, if news reporters are contacting her to ask for comments.

She must be devastated.

I think about how hard she works, the long hours she puts in, the effort she makes to reach out to other potential partners the Foundation can both give money to and obtain donation money from. She has connections in this city like nobody else, and such a winning way about her that she has no trouble getting donors to write big checks or give their time to participate in fundraising events. I know the banquet raised a ton of money.

There's no way the Foundation is hoarding money.

"Wyatt?" Heather sits too.

Everly tries so hard to be perfect. Now I know why. After hearing the story about that asswipe Gage Gregoire, and how upset her parents were, I get it. She made a teenage mistake and rebelled a little. Who among us hasn't? She regrets what she did and never wants to let her parents down again. She also doesn't want to be the center of any negative attention ever again.

This must be crushing her.

"Wyatt? What's wrong?"

I look up at Heather.

Her face changes, her smile fading.

"Everly," I croak out.

She nods.

"There was just a thing . . . on TV . . ." I wave my hand. "She's kind of in trouble."

Heather's lips tremble. But she lifts her chin and holds my gaze. "You're in love with her, aren't you?"

I can't stop the word. It's physically impossible. "Yes." I pause. "I need to go . . ." I stand.

She stands too. Her eyes glossy, she says, "I'm sorry, Wyatt, if I've wrecked things for us. I'll understand if you don't want to come by anymore."

I don't know what to say. We haven't talked any more about us being a family. In my head, it makes sense. But my goddamn heart is hurting over Everly. It'd be great if I could just forget her, but I can't. I don't think I ever will. And spending the rest of my life with someone who's not her . . . I don't know if I can do that, much as I want to be there for my friend's family. I wanted to be someone who could be relied on, someone honorable and responsible. And I was terrified I could never be that guy. I'm still terrified, but I want to try. Marrying Heather isn't the way to do it, though.

"I don't want to lose contact with Owen."

She flinches a little, but nods again. "I understand."

"I'm sorry, Heather."

She wipes her cheek. "Don't apologize for falling in love. I won't apologize to you for that. You're a good man— honorable and loyal. You've always been there for us. I probably should have just kept how I feel about you to myself." Her shaky smile is rueful. "If you love her . . . if you have a chance at a happy ever after . . . go for it. You deserve it."

I'm in awe of her generosity. I know how much love hurts. I hate it that she's hurting. I never wanted that to happen. But I never wanted to fall in love with Everly either, and it happened.

"Hank would appreciate everything you've done for us,"

she continues. "He really would have, Wyatt. I know you feel guilty about what happened. But I also know Hank doesn't blame you."

My throat closes up.

"*I* don't blame you," she adds quietly. "You don't owe us anything. I wish you would get over that."

Christ. My face tightens, pressure building behind my eyes.

"I also know he wouldn't want you to sacrifice your whole life for us."

I let that sink in. Emotion fills my chest. Hank's not here. But yeah . . . I think she's right.

I move to her, set my hands on her shoulders, and kiss her forehead. "You're a good person," I choke out. "And a great mom." I turn away, clearing my throat. "Hey, Owen, buddy! I have to go. Come say goodbye."

He bounces in, a cracker in his hand. "I thought you were staying to eat."

"I can't after all. But I'll see you soon." I give him a big hug.

I jog out to my vehicle and jump in. It's late Saturday afternoon. Everly should be home.

I don't know if there's a happy ending for us, like Heather said. But I do know I have to go to her. I have be there for her, dealing with something like this.

I imagine her having one of her panic attacks, dizzy and nauseous, all alone. What can I do for her? She liked the back rub. And she likes Slurpees . . .

I choose my route so I drive by the 7-Eleven near Everly's place. I wheel in there and fill up a giant Slurpee cup with lemonade slush.

With my phone in one hand and the Slurpee in the other, I ring Everly's doorbell.

I shift from one foot to the other as I wait for her to answer. Maybe she's not home after all. Maybe she's at the office in some kind of PR meeting, trying to deal with this shit.

The door opens.

She stares at me.

Christ, she's beautiful. Her dark hair is all shiny, her face glowing. She's wearing a pair of cropped leggings and a long, loose sweatshirt, her feet bare.

"Wyatt." She blinks those gorgeous long eyelashes. "What . . . are you doing here?"

"I was worried about you," I blurt out. "I saw the news."

"Oh."

"I brought you this." I hand her the Slurpee.

She drops her gaze to it, reaches out to take it, then looks back at me. The corners of her mouth lift. "In case I'm having a panic attack?"

"Yeah." I chomp down on my bottom lip. "Are you okay?"

"I'm fine. Pissed, but fine. Come in."

I follow her into her living room. Her laptop is open on the coffee table, some papers next to it. She sits on the couch. "So you heard the news."

"Yeah." I sit too. "What's that all about? I only caught part of the story."

"This organization has been doing reviews of all charities associated with professional sports. Audits. They've come up with criteria they're measuring us on." She blows out a breath. "We didn't get a good score."

"Yeah, I got that. But what the hell do they know? You work so hard! You raise a lot of money and the Foundation does good things with it."

She smiles, her eyes soft. "Thank you. Yes. We do. But the truth is . . . we could do better."

"That's bullshit."

She pouts her bottom lip out a little, still smiling. "I appreciate your confidence in me."

"Of course I'm confident in you! I love you."

Everything goes still and silent. Our eyes meet. And hold. The connection stretches out. The moment is charged . . . smoldering.

Everly's eyes widen and she opens her mouth as if to speak. Then shuts it. Tries again. "You do?"

I exhale slowly. "I do." It slipped out, but what the hell. Might as well be honest.

"I love you too," she whispers.

Christ. The frozen puck in my gut disappears, relief flowing through my veins like I just mainlined cocaine. (Not that I know what that's like.) I slide off the seat of the couch onto my knees in front of her and clasp her hands.

"What about Heather?" Her voice tremors. "And Owen?"

"I told you, I don't love Heather. She's a friend. I feel a responsibility toward her."

"But she loves you."

I nod, my face tight. "I never wanted to hurt her. But . . . she understands. She said if there's a chance of a happy ending with you, I should go for it." I pause. "And I'm totally resisting the dirty joke about a happy ending."

Her eyes widen, then she drops her head forward, shoulders shaking. "You're terrible."

"Yes. I am."

She lifts her head and moves it from side to side it, lips twitching. "I want to say Heather's a good person, but I'm still a little . . . bitter. Jealous."

I shake my head vigorously, tightening my grip on her hands. "Don't be jealous. I've been honest with her. She knows how I feel about you. I won't see her ever again if that's what you want." I would hate that and I would feel so fucking guilty, but I'd do it if Everly wanted.

She closes her eyes fleetingly. "No. That's not what I want. You're an amazing man, Wyatt, to look after them like that. I'm just glad you're not giving up your whole life for them. Because your friend Hank wouldn't want that. I didn't know him, but I'm sure of that."

"Heather said that too."

"Damn. I don't want to like her."

I smile and lift her hand to kiss it.

"I was worried about that," she admits. "You said you didn't love her, but I thought you were seriously thinking of marrying her."

"I never really was. I kept telling myself it made sense, and I should do it for Hank. But I knew I couldn't."

"I was also pissed at you." Her tone sharpens, although she's still smiling. "For thinking of doing that." She tips her head. "Were you angry at me about what happened with Gage? You seemed . . . angry. I know you said it wasn't my fault, but I'd understand if it, um, turns your stomach."

"Fuck." I close my eyes and press her hand to my mouth. "If it turns my stomach it's because of him. Not you. Don't *ever* think that, princess. I fucking hate that you went through that. But making mistakes is part of growing up." I pause. "Maybe we never outgrow that, though."

"I hate it that you went through what you did too. That must have been so awful." She touches my face. "I understand why you feel guilty, but you did what you could. It wasn't your fault."

I nod, my eyes stinging in the corners. "I tell myself that all the time. I know it wasn't. But yet, I don't think I'll ever stop feeling responsible."

"I love how you've helped Heather and Owen. You're a good man." She stares into my eyes.

Jesus, I'm going to cry again. The kindness and understanding and love in her eyes is shredding me. I never expected to find love like this, and that was okay; I didn't need it. Didn't deserve it. But Everly does, and if it will make her happy, I'll do whatever I can to be worthy of her.

"You're really okay?" I ask hoarsely.

"Yeah. I have a plan."

"Of course you do."

"That jerk Link insulted us. The audit may say we could do better, but that was absolutely unprofessional to accuse us of hoarding money, and to discourage people from donating to us. This is my worst nightmare!"

"I know. That's why I was so worried about you."

"Aw. I love that so much." And I love her smile. "Our legal counsel is writing to him to ask for a public apology for what he said. And . . . I'll look at the audit and see what I can change and do better at." She grimaces. "So the whole world knows now that I'm not perfect. But yeah . . . I'm really okay."

"You're more than okay." My heart swells with admiration for how she's handling this. "You're a strong, amazing woman. And . . . fuck me." I close my eyes. "You're so much more than the perfect princess I thought you were."

She gazes back at me, eyes full of emotion. Her lips tremble. "And you're so much more than the life-of-the-party guy who doesn't care about anything. Except hockey. After I met Owen . . . and Heather, and I saw what you do for them . . . well, you're a pretty strong, amazing man, Wyatt Bell."

"I need to kiss you." I rise up and sit next to her, pulling her onto my lap, threading my hands into her hair, and finding her mouth with mine. She kisses me back, pouring so much emotion into the kiss, we're soon both shaking and panting. "Okay, now I need more than a kiss."

Her lips curve up, her eyes shiny. "I missed you."

"Oh hell yeah, I missed you too."

Her beautiful blue eyes gaze at me with lust and longing. My chest fills with a fizzy sensation while my dick aches with the need to be inside her. Desire surges through my blood and throbs in my balls.

I rise and take her hand to lead her upstairs to her bed. There, I lay her down, gently, reverently, as if she's fragile and precious. She is precious, but I know she's not fragile. She's strong as hell and I love that.

I strip out of my clothes and join her on the bed to remove hers, tugging the leggings down her smooth legs, along with her panties, helping her sit up to lift the sweatshirt over her head. She reaches behind her to undo her bra and I toss it aside, letting my gaze wander over her. "My gorgeous girl."

She reaches up to push my hair back off my forehead, letting her fingers trail over my cheek and jaw. The tenderness of her gesture makes me feel like a fist is squeezing my heart.

"I love you, Wyatt."

"I love you too."

I hold myself above her on my arms and kiss her, my tongue sliding into her mouth. She tastes so sweet. Fire lights up every nerve ending in my body and I lift my mouth from hers to kiss her bare shoulder, sliding my open mouth over her skin. Her soft moan inflames my senses even more.

I kiss her throat and lick my way down between those gorgeous breasts. Her back arches and I close my mouth over one nipple, loving the sweetness, the feel of it on my tongue, the firm flesh pressed to my lips. Heat pours over my body, liquid pleasure running through my veins.

We roll and twist together, mouths fused in long, deep kisses. I worship her with my mouth, my tongue, my hands, everywhere I can reach. When I slip my hand between her legs, I find her velvety wet center, and I circle my thumb over her clit until she vibrates.

I'm drowning in sensation, in the almost unbearable beauty and erotic pleasure, but also in the emotion of it. Something powerful and huge swells inside me.

I lift her thigh and push into her body, watching her face. Her lips part, her eyes gaze up at me, her hands on my chest. Our gazes hold in that intense connection I've never had with anyone else, as heat builds and shimmers around us. My heart beats in a slow, heavy rhythm against my ribs. The love and devotion in her eyes is my own reflected back at me. "I feel so lucky right now."

Her smile is shaky but so, so lovely. "Me too."

I slowly slide in and out of her slick heat as she squeezes around me, her hands pressed to my chest. Sensation coils inside me, hot and heavy.

"Wyatt."

I gaze down at her, riveted by the sight of her beautiful face as I thrust deeper, harder. She lifts into me, hot little whimpers and soft sighs escape her lips, building as she gets closer, and closer. Her fingernails dig into my pecs. Then her body tightens, her pussy rippling around me, her cries exquisitely beautiful in my ears.

"Watching you come is the most goddam gorgeous thing I've ever seen." I fall over her, bury my face in the side of her neck, and breathe in that rich, sexy scent. My chest clenches at the perfection of it, the overwhelming intensity of it, the rush of emotion inside me so strong.

Yes, it's sex. But it's also love.

My thighs quake and my balls contract, the tension at the base of my spine sizzling painfully. Electricity shoots up my spine, scorching every nerve ending in my body as I come, my cock jerking inside her in almost painful, wrenching spasms.

She wraps her arms around my back and holds on like she never wants to let go. Good. I never want to let her go either. My face buried in her hair, I draw in long, ragged breaths.

"Everly." I lift my head so I can kiss her, a long, tender kiss of devotion and promise. "I love you."

"I talked to Mom and Dad and Matthew about the lawsuit."

My arms hold her, the soft sheets tucked around us, legs twined together, both of us sleepy and lazy. "Whoa. You did?"

"Yeah. We were all together at the game against the Eagles—well, not all of us; Théo was there, and Asher stopped in and then Matthew, and I just thought, fuck it, I'm laying it out there."

I cough out a laugh.

"And I convinced Dad to go to the doctor. I don't think Matthew realized how bad things are getting and how worried we are. Théo helped too."

"That's good." I kiss her temple. "Not *good*, of course, but hopefully you'll get answers and maybe some kind of treatment."

"Yes. And Dad and Matthew agreed to talk. Hopefully they'll follow through on that. And Matthew accepted that Mom has to be there too."

"Wow. You did good, princess." I give her a squeeze. I'm so fucking proud of her I could burst with it. For what she just told me, but also how she's reacting to the news of that audit of the Foundation. She let me see inside her. She's anxious and she worries a lot and needs to be perfect. What happened when she was sixteen was awful, and I know she feels like that makes her weak. But the truth is, she's resilient. Kind and generous. She makes things happen and never quits. She just needs to slow down a bit and really connect with people. And yeah, take time to laugh and experience the joys of life, because it's true that it can end anytime.

"I'm sorry how I reacted that night that Gage showed up." She sighs. "Seeing him reminded me of the biggest mistake I ever made. I've tried so hard to never do something like that again. My parents were ashamed and had to do things they probably shouldn't have to protect me."

"I don't believe they were ashamed of you. I think they were probably worried. Which is understandable."

"Yes. You could be right. But I never wanted to experience their disappointment like that again. And dating you—another player for my dad's team—seemed like a potentially huge mistake. My dad's health put things in perspective, though. Now I understand why you live life in the moment. I want to live life in more moments with you. That was why I came to see you that night. When I realized my dad might not be around . . . or might not be himself much longer . . . I realized how important it is to make the most of the time we do have. I learned that from you." She pauses, and my heart squeezes. "But then, I also saw how much you care about Owen, and Heather. You may talk about life being all fun, but you also care about people in your life. And I realized the mistake I *really* made was letting you go."

My arms tighten around her and I close my eyes on a rush of emotion. Joy. Worship. Gratitude. Love.

Thank you for reading! I hope you enjoyed Everly and Wyatt's hate to love story!

Would you like to read more of Everly and Wyatt? Click here to read their epilogue!

https://kellyjamieson.myflodesk.com/f3th0mfghb

And Wynn Hockey continues! Read on for an excerpt from *For the Win*

ARYA

"Oh my God!" Everly cries.

I grab my paddle board and rest my forearms on it, staring at Harrison. I'm befuddled. And cold.

"Are you okay?" he asks. "I am so sorry."

The class is totally disrupted now. Everyone is murmuring and making shocked noises. I don't even know what to say. This has never happened to me. "I'm fine," I say through clenched teeth. "Wet, obviously."

"I'm really sorry," he says again, and he does look contrite. "You can blame him." He jerks his head at the guy who made the anal joke.

That guy gives me a guilty grimace. "Sorry."

I blow out a breath and turn my glare back on Harrison. I'd like to tear a strip off him, but that's not what yoga is supposed to be about. Peace. Oneness. Harmony. *I am capable of anything.* I take another breath and relax my body, including my face. "Are you able to continue with the class?" I ask him.

"Yeah, yeah," he says quickly. "For sure. Uh, are you?"

I roll onto my paddleboard and strip off the thin zip-front hoodie I'm wearing. I drop it to the board behind me. "Yes." I find my center and stand, now in my wet sports bra and yoga shorts. My hair's in a ponytail, which is good, although it's dripping water down my back. I gaze around at the group. "Sometimes you need yoga. Sometimes you need a beer." I pause. "Sometimes you need both."

Laughter ripples through the morning air.

"Let's resume." I keep my voice calm, a half smile on my face. "One more time . . . exhale, fold forward . . . inhale, reach up." I hold that pose for a few seconds. *I am capable of anything.* "Exhale, fold forward, and bring your hands to the board as we squat down and bring the right knee back."

This time there are no smart-ass comments from the peanut gallery. I survey the group to see how everyone's doing, including Harrison. His face more serious, he seems focused on the pose.

"You want two ninety-degree angles with your legs," I continue, moving my knee and foot into the correct position and watching the others. "Good. Coming up into half warrior . . ." I lift my arms and stretch them out in front of me. "Shoulders back . . . inhale . . . and lift the arms up."

I sense Harrison's gaze on me. Which is weird, because almost everyone in the class watches me to see how I do it, but I *feel* his eyes on me. I say the next words, just waiting for his reaction. "Lift your heart to the sun."

He stretches his arms up and lengthens his torso, not making any jokes. How about that.

Sweet smiling Jesus, he has an amazing body. Although

a bit tight. If we were in the studio, I'd be setting a hand in the small of his back, making adjustments to his pose.

We go through the rest of the class without incident. "Let's finish up with a nice child's pose." I stretch my arms out in front of me on the board. "Let your body melt into the board."

I follow my own advice, shutting out the rest of the class, particularly that one guy with the naughty boy smile and hot body, letting my muscles relax, tension seep out of me. I focus on the gentle movement of the water beneath me, my breathing, the warmth of the sun on my back.

Class is over and we all paddle back to shore. This basin is quiet and calm, perfect for my classes. I'm so lucky that Taj has his paddleboard business here and I get to piggyback on to that.

I have another class in my studio at noon, so I head toward the change room so I can put on dry clothes and dry my hair. As I approach the change room, Harrison steps in front of me.

"I want to apologize again," he says earnestly.

He has amazing blue eyes.

"I didn't intend for that to happen, it was an accident, and I'm really sorry that we disrupted your class."

"It's fine." I don't smile, but I keep my tone courteous. "Forgiveness and letting go are an important part of yoga."

He studies my face. "That's very . . . generous of you. We were assholes." He scrunches up his face. "Sorry."

I have to smile now. "It's okay, I may have thought that myself. But exhalation is the act of letting go."

"Could I take you out for a drink . . . or dinner? To make it up to you?"

I blink. "That's not necessary."

"I know it's not, but I'd like to." His smile is genuine and open.

Getting hit on by customers is not usual, since my classes are made up of mostly women, although it has happened. I don't date *anyone*, never mind customers, and especially not men I don't know. "I'm sorry, but no."

"Oh." His face clouds. "Everly said she thinks you have a boyfriend."

What? "No," I say before I can stop myself.

Shit.

His eyes brighten again. "Okay, then!"

"But I can't go out with you."

Disappointment tugs at his lips again. He opens his mouth to say something more, and I sense he's going to try to persuade me. My fingers and toes tingle as adrenaline surges through my body, my stomach clenching. "I have to go."

I bolt into the ladies' change room and shut the door behind me. Fear has my heart leaping in my chest, and for a moment I wish I could lock the door behind me. There are other women in the room, though.

I am brave.

I lift my chin and smile, making my way to the locker in the back where I keep my things. My insides knotted, my skin clammy, I fake a calm that I don't feel as I change into a pair of cropped yoga pants and a top. Then I head to the counter and mirrors along one wall to dry my hair.

I convinced Taj to let me make some improvements to this change room, so it didn't look like the marina bathroom it once was. I added a couple of hair dryers and a few feminine accessories. It's not the ideal setup, but it works for the couple of classes a week I do here.

Breathe in courage . . . breathe out doubt.

Harrison Whoever is probably harmless, but I don't like to be pushed. I overreacted, I know it. I'm working on it.

When I exit the change room, I find Everly still hanging around. The man with her—the one who made the joke that caused Harrison to fall into the ocean—is with her. She approaches me, and he's a couple steps behind her. Big guy, very handsome.

"Arya," she says. "I'm so sorry about the class."

I smile at her. I like Everly. She's been coming to my class for a while, along with her friend Taylor, and she's always been in to it and respectful of the practice. "No need for you to apologize."

"He's my brother," she says. "Harrison." She rolls her eyes. "I convinced him to come that first time, so I feel responsible for his antics."

"You're not responsible for anyone but yourself."

"You're so sweet. You handled that amazingly well."

"*I* apologize," the guy with her speaks up. "I'm Wyatt." He extends a hand and I shake it. "We shouldn't have been joking around like that."

"I told your . . . Harrison that it's fine. I've let it go." I smile. "Shit happens."

They both let out surprised laughs. "It does," Everly agrees.

"It's healthy to find the humor in things," I add, smiling. "I need to get to my next class."

"Do you have a business card?" Everly asks.

I blink. "Yes." I move over to the counter and pluck one from the holder. "Here you go."

No idea why she wants it, but whatever.

"Thanks. See you next week."

Is she going to bring her brother again? Crap.

It doesn't matter. *I am capable of anything.*

Taj and I are sitting on the patio at The Golden Fish on the Venice Boardwalk later that day. The tables are wooden, the sun is low over the ocean, and we're with some of Taj's friends—Arlo, Indigo, and Janey—who are now my friends too. Taj's boyfriend, Ziggy, owns this place, so we hang out here a lot. It's got that casual beach vibe, cool and laid back, with the scent of ocean and sun-warmed sand mingling with coconut sunscreen and marijuana. Lots of marijuana.

I sip my beer, one of the many interesting choices Ziggy has on tap here. Taj is drinking kombucha with Longboard lager. I've finished off my tuna poke bowl, which was delicious.

I look around as Taj and Arlo talk about the beach cleanup they're organizing for next weekend.

I can't believe I'm living here.

This is so far from home. Back in Fargo, North Dakota, the snow might be melting . . . or they might be having a late season blizzard. I'm letting the sun warm my face, sitting near the Pacific Ocean, listening to Hozier, drinking a delicious beer. I let out a long, slow breath of peace.

It might sound weird, but sometimes I get homesick, no matter how wonderful it is here. We all complained about the snow and cold, but weirdly, there are moments I miss it. And I miss my family. But life is good here. Uncomplicated. Relaxed. Chill.

Maybe a wee bit boring, but that's my own fault. I'm learning to take bigger steps, bigger risks. Not like skydiving or anything, just . . . small risks.

"Tell these guys about your class today," Taj says to me with a grin.

I shake my head, smiling ruefully. "I got dumped in the water."

Arlo, Indigo, and Janey laugh, Janey's eyes going wide. "No!"

"Some guys were joking around, and one of them laughed so hard he fell in." I pause. "Actually, I was having a hard time not laughing myself."

"What did they say?"

I repeat Harrison and Wyatt's comments and everyone cracks up.

"So he's flailing around in the water, knocks into my board, and I go in too." I roll my eyes, still smiling. "Oh my God, I was in shock! I couldn't believe that just happened."

"Why are they coming to your class if they're just going to fuck around?" Indigo frowns and flicks her black hair off her face.

"Yeah, I don't know. This guy's been before. His sister is one of my regulars, I guess she convinced him to come, but clearly he's not really into yoga." I pause. "He wanted to take me out to dinner to make up for it."

"Ah!" They all react with the same knowing nod.

I frown. "What?"

"He's just trying to get your attention," Janey says. "That's why he's acting out."

"That's probably why he came to your class," Indigo adds.

"We're not in grade school," I mutter. "He doesn't need to pull my hair or snap my bra strap to get my attention."

They all laugh.

"You obviously turned him down." Taj nudges me with his elbow.

"Of course I turned him down." Taj knows better than anyone why that is.

"Seriously, though . . ." He regards me with a notch between his eyebrows, and touches my shoulder. "You were okay after falling in?"

"Oh yeah. Fine. Good thing I can swim!" I appreciate his concern. He's a good friend.

"That would be important if you're doing classes on the water," Arlo says with a grin.

"Let me know if you need me to hang around or get rid of him if he shows up again," Taj adds.

I want to deal with life on my own. But it's definitely comforting to know there's someone close by who's got my back if I need it.

We have one more beer. The Edison lights strung around the patio glow as the sun lowers below the horizon and the music gets a little louder. It's Saturday night in Venice and crowds of people are still walking along the boardwalk, taking in the little shops and bars. Arlo and Indigo head out first. I watch them walk, heads close together, Arlo's arm around her shoulders. They're such a sweet couple. Then Janey leaves too. I hug her goodbye.

"Bike ride tomorrow?" she says.

Sundays I have no classes. "Sounds good."

"I'll text you."

Ziggy saunters over and takes a seat at our table, across

from Taj and me. "Hey," he says, with a special smile for Taj.

Another sweet couple. I'm happy for my friend that he's found someone so great here in California. He went through some shitty relationships in college. It gives me a flicker of hope that there's someone for everyone, but after what I went through, I don't know how I'll ever have the guts to take a chance again.

ACKNOWLEDGMENTS

As always, huge thanks to the team that helps me in this crazy business—my agent, Emily Sylvan Kim; my sister and my daughter for working the numbers, which I hate with a passion; Cassie at Weaver Way Author Servies, and Emily Carthum for stepping in to help so capably when I was drowning! Many thanks to my author friends who keep me sane, I am so grateful for such a supportive and understanding community. And, as always, huge thanks to my readers! I am always so grateful for being able to share my stories.

ABOUT THE AUTHOR

Kelly Jamieson is a best-selling author of over sixty romance novels and novellas. Her writing has been described as "emotionally complex," "sweet and satisfying," and "blisteringly sexy." She likes coffee (black), wine (mostly white), shoes (especially high heels) and hockey!

Kelly appreciates your help in spreading the word about her books, including sharing with friends! Please leave a review on your favorite book site! You can also join her Facebook group, Kelly Jamieson's Sweet Heat Reader Lounge, to hang out with her, and for exclusive giveaways and sneak peeks of future books.

Visit her website at www.kellyjamieson.com or contact her at info@kellyjamieson.com

OTHER BOOKS BY KELLY JAMIESON

HELLER BROTHERS HOCKEY

BREAKAWAY

FACEOFF

ONE MAN ADVANTAGE

HAT TRICK

OFFSIDE

POWER SERIES

POWER STRUGGLE

POWER PLAY

POWER SHIFT

RULE OF THREE SERIES

RULE OF THREE

RHYTHM OF THREE

REWARD OF THREE

SAN AMARO SINGLES

WITH STRINGS ATTACHED

HOW TO LOVE

SLAMMED

WINDY CITY KINK

SWEET OBSESSION

ALL MESSED UP

PLAYING DIRTY

BREW CREW

LIMITED TIME OFFER

NO OBLIGATION REQUIRED

ACES HOCKEY

MAJOR MISCONDUCT

OFF LIMITS

ICING

TOP SHELF

BACK CHECK

SLAP SHOT

PLAYING HURT

BIG STICK

GAME ON

LAST SHOT

BODY SHOT

HOT SHOT

LONG SHOT

BAYARD HOCKEY

SHUT OUT

CROSS CHECK

WYNN HOCKEY

PLAY TO WIN

IN IT TO WIN IT

WIN BIG

FOR THE WIN

GAME CHANGER

BEARS HOCKEY

MUST LOVE DOGS…AND HOCKEY

YOU HAD ME AT HOCKEY

TALK HOCKEY TO ME

THE O ZONE

GOOD HANDS

SCORING BIG

MERRY PUCKING CHRISTMAS

LIGHT 'EM UP

STORM HOCKEY

CROSSING THE LINE

STANDALONES

THREE OF HEARTS

LOVING MADDIE FROM A TO Z

DANCING IN THE RAIN

LOVE ME

LOVE ME MORE

2 HOT 2 HANDLE

FRIENDS WITH BENEFITS

LOST AND FOUND

ONE WICKED NIGHT

SWEET DEAL

HOW SWEET IT IS

HOT RIDE

CRAZY EVER AFTER

ALL I WANT FOR CHRISTMAS

SEXPRESSO NIGHT

IRISH SEX FAIRY

CONFERENCE CALL

RIGGER

YOU REALLY GOT ME

SCREWED

FIRECRACKER

BIG WITCH ENERGY

HATE ME UNDER THE MISTLETOE

www.ingramcontent.com/pod-product-compliance
Lightning Source LLC
Chambersburg PA
CBHW020647120726
47906CB00001B/155